FIVE DAY FIANCÉ

MICKEY MILLER

Edited by SUE GRIMSHAW

Edited by ELAINE YORK

Edited by BECCA HENSLEY MYSOOR

CONTENTS

1

ALLIE

I*'m so happy to bend the knee for my future partner.*

I STARE at the caption of my ex-boyfriend Mark's Facebook picture with his brand-new wife-to-be, holding her hands over her face, in happy disbelief at his proposal. I dated Mark for five years, and this scenario never happened. He was the king of 'next year', 'you know I love you', and my personal favorite, 'a piece of paper doesn't define the love we share.' It all turned out to be lies.

Now, five months after he broke up with me, he's already moved on with such ease?

My thoughts wander so far off that I don't even hear my coworker Rhonda's heels clicking on the floor close to my desk until she's right behind me.

"Oh, no. You're *not* looking at those again," she says, looking over my shoulder.

Quickly, I click off the Facebook photos and pull up my work email.

Busted.

"Looking at what?" I feign ignorance, knowing she could see exactly what I was doing.

Rhonda shakes her head and sets down the cappuccino she brought me. She sits in one of the chairs in my cubicle and rolls next to me.

"Open that tab," she says, pointing to my browser.

"Nah, I want to stay concentrated on work," I say, guilt bubbling inside me.

Rhonda gives me her patented eyebrow raise. I sigh and pull up the browser as I take my first sip of coffee, feeling myself starting to come to life on this cold, Detroit winter morning.

"Why do you continue to torture yourself like this? This man should be *dead* to you. Dead!" She taps the screen with a pink nail. "It's been months, you should have deleted and blocked him as your Facebook friend already!"

Rhonda knows the whole backstory of me and Mark. Five long years we were an item and I thought for sure our happily ever after would end in nuptials. We even talked about it...okay, not often, but it was not out of the realm of possibility. Our relationship had reached the stage of comfortable love and then he up and dumped me unexpectedly, last fall. This past winter was a tough one as I adjusted to my new reality as a single twenty-something instead of someone who was seemingly on the brink of marriage and a family. Rhonda has been a supportive friend and we've drunk many a bottle of cabernet at one another's apartments ever since. Me trying to drown my depression, Rhonda because, I don't know, I guess she likes red wine.

"I didn't mean to pull that picture up, specifically," I say.

"I was just investigating who's going to be at our mutual friend Peyton's wedding in April. And, guess what? I'm literally the *only* single one there. Every other person attending is married, has a fiancé, or boyfriend."

"Pssh. You can't be the *only* single one there. There's always like, one single guy at these things."

I shake my head. "I have *thoroughly* gone through the invitation list. Trust me. Every guest name is up on their 'tie the knot' website. I'm the *only* single one."

Rhonda twists her face up and nods. "Seriously?"

"This is going to literally be torture. Peyton is one of our best friends, so I can't *not* go. It's basically going to be a five-day college friends' reunion centered around a wedding. Ever since Mark and I broke up, it feels a little like we've been telling our friends to pick a side or something. It's ridiculous. But it's what's happening and it's my reality."

"Why don't you just bring a date? You know, someone you're not serious with, but could have some fun with, too?"

I frown. "Have you ever been to a destination wedding?"

"No. Why?" The look on Rhonda's face almost gives me the giggles.

"So, it's basically five days in a very limited square footage of real estate with this person. All of the events are within the walls of this all-you-can-eat-and-drink-resort. How am I going to find someone this quickly whom I could stand being with nonstop, or who could stand being with me, for five days?"

She shrugs, and her face curves upward in a wry grin. "I'll go with you. When is it?"

I tell her the date in late April. At least I know we'd have fun, I mean, I don't *have* to bring a guy, although I'd rather. I would love to make Mark jealous, or at least see what he missed out on. Though based on posts on Facebook I'm not sure that will happen. Okay, time to be real, it's really so I can just save face. Let's be honest, this trip is going to hurt.

"Ohh, sorry. My mom's birthday is that weekend. It's a big one and she'd kill me if I missed it. There's got to be *someone* you could take as a date, though. I mean, you don't have *anyone?*"

I shake my head. "While I was dating Mark, I didn't keep in touch with the guys I'd dated before. I didn't want to — I thought Mark and I were it. Though I did follow them on social media and it appears they're no longer single either." My anxiety is ramping up now...damn, I didn't want to talk about this at the office.

"There's got to be *someone* you can take with you as a date."

Just then, we hear a reverberating noise rumble on the other side of our cube. It's a low male voice and I can't quite make out what he's saying.

A few seconds later, Jocko Brewer strides around to my cubicle. Jocko is tall, brown-eyed, and handsome with thick brown hair. He's also somehow in a good mood even this early in the morning. Ugh. I wouldn't be surprised if he got some action before work, hence his glowing smile.

He's the top Midwest sales rep at the company, EdTechX. We help keep K-12 schools up to date when it comes to the technology equipment and resources they need in the classroom. Anything from Wi-Fi routers to desktop computers to anti-virus software updates — that's all us.

As the top rep, Jocko's got this constant, cocky smirk that never leaves his face, and there's not one person in the office who hasn't heard his story about the time when he made it to the final four in the NCAA March Madness basketball tournament and almost beat Steph Curry. Would have won if it weren't for a 'bad' call by the referees.

"Morning, ladies," he says with a giant smile. He leans back on my desk like he owns it. "How is my favorite educational strategist doing today?"

His *favorite educational strategist* would be me. Although I never know if he's joking about me being his favorite.

"Never been better," I say, offering a tight smile and trying to focus on the conversation with him instead of my single-life worries.

"I didn't know you were here already or I would have picked you up something for breakfast, a *honey bun* or something *hot* and caffeinated," Rhonda says, blushing. She always does this when Jocko comes around. I actually think it's embarrassing more than cute, he's too worried about himself to notice her or anyone else's interest.

"Oh, that's alright. I stopped drinking coffee this fall. I thought you knew that." His response is kind but clueless to the vibe she's sending.

"Why did you stop drinking coffee?" I question.

He clenches his jaw, and the smile leaves his face for a brief moment. "Customers were telling me I was too intense, coffee was the trigger."

"Oh." I could see that. He can be overpowering in a lot of ways.

Jocko squints. "Do you think I'm too intense, Allie?"

I try to fake like I don't have a stomach full of nerves when he looks at me like he is right now. The truth is, I've never met anyone else who makes me so nervous just by the pure lifeforce he exudes. I've never seen him go anything less than one-hundred miles per hour. His eyes are so lively and vibrant as he stares at me; it's quite intoxicating.

Jocko slaps his knee and laughs deeply. "I'm just jonesing you! I did switch to tea a while back, though. Anyway, Mackey ISD called me this morning, and that deal is closed! Add another two million to my pipeline, Rhonda." He winks at her, then brings his gaze back to me. "I wanted to thank you for your help, Allie. You nailed that presentation with their technology director, and that's what sealed the deal. So, when can I buy you a drink to celebrate? I owe you. Oh, you're invited, too, Rhonda."

"Well, thanks," she says. "You're in luck, we're planning a team happy hour for tonight."

Jocko nods, "Sounds perfect. It's so damn cold here in February. God, I'd do just about anything to get out of this weather. But I guess a few Jack and Cokes at the bar will have to do."

"A happy hour tonight sounds amazing," I say. Jocko really is a good-looking guy. I saw him without a shirt once, at a mutual friend's summer rooftop pool party. Let's just say those are abs that a girl doesn't forget. Now, every time I see him, I can't help but imagine them under his suit.

Of course, Mark had a nice physique, too, but even with all of the workouts he did, he never had that six-pack guys get...not that it mattered to me. Most guys don't ever get that gym-rat build unless they're...well, gym rats, and I'd rather they spent more time with me than they do at the gym.

"Alright, well, I need to get back to work," Rhonda announces. She backs away, and makes a gesture pointing between me and Jocko, and then gives a *maybe?* shrug as she heads back to her desk.

Is she out of her mind?

"What just happened there?" Jocko asks, standing up straighter.

Shoot. Literally nothing makes it past this man.

Well, except for Rhonda's flirtation's apparently.

I purse my lips. "No idea what you're talking about."

He looks between Rhonda and me, waving his pointer

finger between us. "You two just did a little womanly nonverbal communication thing. I saw that."

Called out and royally busted.

"Maybe you're seeing things," I lie, because no — five days with Jocko would not work. *No*.

"Alright," he says, after a long pause. "I need to get back to work, too. But I've got my eye on you two." He points at his eyes, and then at me and Rhonda's cubicles, like Robert De Niro in *Meet the Parents*.

As soon as he's gone, a message from Rhonda pops up on the company chat:

Rhonda: Jocko. He's the perfect date for the destination wedding.

Allie: In what universe?

Rhonda: Well, you want to make Mark jealous, right? Jocko's hot, he's sexy, and he'd fit right in with a crew of athletes like the ones that Peyton rolls with since Jocko played Division I basketball in college. His brother Everett even plays professional football, for goodness sake.

Allie: Uh, no, I'm not trying to make Mark jealous. This is the year of better angels of my nature. I'm not stooping to Mark's level. I'm rising above the wreckage.

Rhonda: Oh, okay. My bad...well, either way, you would be guaranteed a fun time. Plus, I hear he's quite a devil in bed. If you two decide to, you know...

Allie: Oh my gosh! No! We're coworkers, on the same team! That is not a good idea. As the boss's assistant, aren't you supposed to not encourage interoffice romance? Isn't that an H.R. nightmare just waiting to happen?

Rhonda: I'm just trying to look out for my girl. You've been so unhappy this past winter. (You still haven't had a rebound, btw. Yes, I've noticed.). And seriously, Becky in marketing said that about Jocko, so you know it's true. She can't keep her mouth shut. Plus, you'd be in Cancún and you know what they say about what happens in Cancún...

Allie: I'm not looking for a silly rebound. Just because I got burned once doesn't mean I'm going to drop my standards. And that's Vegas...what happens in V-E-G-A-S!

Rhonda: Really? I thought it was Cancún, too. And drop your standards? This is Jocko we're talking about. He's like the singlest of the single guys who has ever singled. Do you know why? Because he's a millionaire with options. That's right. MILLIONS! I see his paychecks since I'm the boss's assistant. Anyway, that's not the point. The point is, he'd be fun to hang with. He's hot. Plus, he's an avowed bachelor so you wouldn't have to worry about him getting needy or weird. You two have always gotten along so well. He'd also be fun to look at on the beach in Cancún...

Allie: Fun to look at?

Rhonda: Oh, come on, don't pretend like you haven't stalked his beach volleyball pics. from last year. You expert Facebook stalker you.

Allie: Okay, fine. Even if I did want to bring him, why would he say yes? To be a part of five days of lost productivity surrounded by strangers and little ole me? That man is a machine. I don't think he's ever taken a vacation of more than two days in all the time I've been working here.

Rhonda: He'd go with 'little ole you' because he likes you.

When I read those words, I won't lie — my heart does the *tiniest* of tumbles. It's nothing crazy, but it's definitely a little something. Even noticing the sensation makes me feel silly, like I'm in sixth grade again and I just found out a cute boy *might* have a crush on me.

Although I'm flattered, if true, part of me is skeptical that Rhonda is right.

Allie: He likes me like a little sister. And because I help him close deals.

Rhonda: You sure about that?

I take a deep breath, and click off the chat box as the emails of the day start to come in from the Instructional Technologists and IT Directors whom I work with from across the country.

The truth is, I'm not sure what to make of Jocko and my connection. I've been at EdTechX for almost three years, and Jocko and I have always gotten along so naturally. Working with him directly has always been sort of special, if I'm being honest with myself.

We've shared many a drunken coworker conversation at our team happy hours and events, and I've even traveled with him to wine and dine clients and we have a blast. But there always seems to be a very clear line between us when it comes to coworker friends and nothing more. And having been with Mark until recently, I've not really even thought about anything more between the two of us.

I flip back to Facebook for one moment, and look at the picture of all of our friends, together with their partners. Hell, even Peyton freaking O'Rourke, whom we all thought would be single until his thirties, is settling down.

I refuse to be the one single girl at the wedding, and for five straight days. Desperate times call for desperate measures.

One thing I am sure of, though, is that this proposal might just require some liquid courage.

2

ALLIE

Speaking of courage, on the way out of work, I get an email from my boss at four forty-three reminding me of my three-year review at five p.m. today, which I swear was supposed to be next week.

I've already got my coat on, ready to head out to tonight's happy hour. My stomach drops with anxiety because I feel completely unprepared for this chat. I only get one review per year, and I was planning on doing a practice run-through this weekend with Rhonda so I could have the best shot at a big raise.

I shoot Matt a message asking if I'd be able to reschedule and he tells me *no* and that I really need to do a better job of keeping an eye on my calendar. Ugh.

Even though I swear I checked my calendar this morning and didn't see this invite, I decide to cut Matt some slack. Admittedly, I've been more anxious than usual this winter, in no small part due to my ruminating thoughts about the state of my unrelationship status. And lately about this darn destination wedding. Damn. I can't exactly blow off a meeting with my boss, so I go.

"Miss Allison, come on in and have a seat," Matt says when I arrive, pointing to a chair in his giant office. He's in his mid-fifties, and to say that he is going bald would be an understatement. He pushes a few strands of gray hair back on his head, attempting to cover a bald area and making an entirely new one with the motion.

"Please, call me Allison," I say, wondering if he calls my colleague Gregory *Mr. Greg* when he comes in for his review. It's also curious that he still doesn't know what to call me after he's been my boss for a year and a half, when he took over the educational strategy division of our company.

He winks. "Habit, Miss Allison. It's hard to break free. Know what I mean? Let's see here..."

I have a hard time getting comfortable in the wooden chair he directs me to sit in a few feet from his desk, and it bugs me that he ignores my request to go by Allison. But I don't press the issue. After all, I'm hoping to get a big pay raise.

"As per my email, it's time for your annual review," he says, clearing his throat. "I assume you're fine with the standard raise again this year? One-point-seven-five percent based on last year's salary?"

I exhale loudly and try to settle in. I wish I were more prepared for this, but now's not the time to panic. "Well, actually, I would like to negotiate up to a five-percent raise for this year. I was doing some research on comparable salaries at other companies, and as a matter of fact, some educational strategists make almost two times what I made last year. And considering the touch-to-close ratio of deals I work on, and the fact that I'm pushing three years here, I believe that's reasonable."

Matt takes a break from looking at his computer, then squints at me, his jaw lowering. "Five...percent? Like a full five?" He raises an eyebrow. "Not one point five...or something? No one asks for that much."

I squint. "Why would I negotiate for something lower than the standard raise?"

"Miss Allison, let's keep this calm, no need to get snippy. I'm just making sure I heard you right."

My colleague Greg told me — off the record, of course — that he negotiated up for a seven percent raise his first year, and another seven when he had his two-year review a couple of months ago. Matt has one thing right, no one negotiates that much, they negotiate more. But it's against policy for me to use his salary and pay increase as my starting ground. And it's quite annoying that a guy in my exact same position is making a good deal more than me. Greg does have the gift of gab, everybody likes him, but I've been working here longer *and* taught him everything he knows. My bad, I guess, for not being aggressive from the start, so this year I'm making up for it. I just wish I had been able to practice my spiel and run over the exact numbers, like I was planning this weekend.

Matt purses his lips together and puts his fingers together on the table menacingly, like Mr. Burns from *The Simpsons*.

"Look, Miss Allison — I mean, Allison. I would love to give you a five-percent raise. Or a ten percent. But it's just not in the budget this year. I'm sure you know we're angling to go public soon. The big bosses upstairs are cutting corners all over the place. This is just not the time to ask for a big raise, unfortunately. We've already allocated the one point seven five, which I assumed you'd be happy with. I'm sorry."

"Are you really sorry?" I know I'm getting 'snippy' as

Matt pointed out, but really, he knows this is BS. He's trying to put one over me and hoping I won't raise a stink.

"Pardon me?" he says, raising an eyebrow again. Yeah, I think I'm pissing him off.

The language he uses sounds eerily similar to what I was told when I vied for a raise last year, albeit not with the same vigor as this year. That negotiation did not go well then either.

With firm resolve, I sit up straight and smile — a negotiation trick I learned from watching Jocko. Never appear flustered. Always be in control. A smile is key. Even works over the phone, according to him.

Of course, he's a guy, I'm a girl — obviously, and the guys seem to get away with more in this company, but it's worth a try.

Unfortunately for me, it's an act. For Jocko, I'm pretty sure he is *always* in control.

"Matt, with due respect, I don't have the exact numbers on hand, but I helped bring in a lot of revenue this year to EdTechX. I know I don't get paid as a salesperson because that's not my role, and I don't expect to make the hundreds of thousands some of them are making. But I think at this point I've shown clear value to the team, and I'd like to be compensated fairly for that value. I think a five-percent raise is minimal comparably."

Matt's jaw stiffens. I get the feeling he wasn't expecting me to put up this much of a fight. "You don't think you're being compensated fairly?"

"Correct."

"Well, how much extra revenue have you brought to the team?"

"As I said, I don't know exactly, but it is a lot. I recently helped Jocko close a multi-million-dollar deal with the addition of my services to the Request For Proposal for Mackey ISD, for example. And there are many more like that. The guys like bringing me in on the closure because I can help them get it done, I'm just good at that."

"Right. Of course. But exactly *how much* did you figure in that decision? And exactly how much money have you brought into the company?"

"Well, uh, as I stated, I don't know exactly. That is something I can't estimate as I assisted in those accounts, uh, unofficially, I guess. As you know, strength of relationships is sort of hard to quantify. But there are quite a few big deals we wouldn't have closed without my relationships with instructional technologists, and that's a fact."

He wrinkles his big forehead. "So you don't know how much? I really need specifics here, Miss Allison."

Pangs of nervousness flow through me and I freeze up. I think I'm losing this argument. "Not exactly. No."

He leans in, squints, and then throws his head back and laughs.

He fucking *laughs*. I should get angry, but honestly, it hurts my feelings. What the fuck is so damn funny?

"Yeah, I mean numbers. They're tough to follow. Am I right?" comes Matt's shit-eating grin reply.

That pisses me off and my body finally warms with an anger from deep inside me. I fantasize about lifting him up, chair and all, and throwing Matt right out the window.

I grind my teeth instead, and don't say a word. I'll probably have an ulcer to go along with my enamel-less teeth when all is said and done.

I'm definitely not smiling anymore. There's no doubt I'm agitated.

"Just kidding, Miss Allison." Heavy accent on the *Miss Allison*. "But seriously. We'll just stick with the one-point-seven-five percent. I'll make a note for your review next year, though. It also wouldn't hurt if you came prepared with actual data and, you know, were on time for your own meeting." Bam. Cut me down just like that. I'm beyond upset.

"Are you serious? I was one minute late. And I swear this was on my calendar for next week." I pull up my calendar on my phone to look for the duplicate invite on next week's agenda, but of course it's mysteriously gone now. Not that it even matters any more, but I just want to know if I'm crazy or not.

I clench my fists at my sides, nails digging so hard into my skin that my palms begin to hurt. I feel like I'm backtracking.

After a long pause, he says, "I'll take that as a yes, your salary is good for now. Thanks so much for getting this out of the way tonight. Now, I've got to run. Big night at the casino. Thanks for coming by."

He stands up with a big fake smile and ushers me out.

My expression is blank, my blood boiling. What a waste of my freaking time. Feeling like you're being pushed around by your boss is one of the worst feelings there is. When push comes to shove, it's like I'm powerless to convey the work I've been doing. But Matt's being a spineless twat who doesn't go to bat for me with upper management is another story. Sometimes I think I would have already left this company if not for Rhonda, Jocko and some of the other people I love working with. I remind myself that not all men are selfish, chauvinistic bullies. Although it's unfortunate one of them has to be my boss.

I might have been caught off guard by this meeting, but I vow that this isn't over.

An expression that my grandfather used to tell me goes through my head...

Don't get mad. Get even.

I just need to figure out how to do that and keep my job.

Matt's words about *making a note for next year* ring in my ear, and they're eerily similar to what I used to hear from Mark.

Suddenly I get the feeling that for my entire life I've been waiting for some ineffable moment to just *happen*. Some strike of lightning that changes my life for the better. But it never does. And I'm left here with a said raise and no boyfriend.

Enough about *next year*, I decide.

This is the year of the 'here and the now'. I will get even. I will take back control. I will no longer be single. I *will* ask Jocko to be my date to the wedding.

Besides, if I keep getting treated like this, Jocko and I won't be coworkers much longer.

What's the worst that could happen if I ask him to join me in Cancún?

My lips curve up in a silly grin, and I remember something Jocko once told me about his strategy on sales calls when I asked him how he's so aggressive all the time.

If you don't ever ask, the answer is always no.

And with those words of wisdom, here we go.

3

ALLIE

"Matt is a dick. You should definitely be making more," Rhonda says, speaking loudly to cut through the noise in the bar and taking a pull on her beer. "How are you ever going to take your trip to Scotland if you don't get a raise?!"

My great-grandmother is from Scotland, and for some reason the country has been calling my name. The problem? I'm dropping a year's worth of travel budget on this destination wedding. Which I don't *mind*, but if I had gotten my raise, I would have had the money to do both without putting anything on a credit card. Now, I wonder if Scotland will ever happen.

"The thing that pisses me off the most is that I *swear* the meeting wasn't even on my calendar for this week! I religiously check my agenda to start my day. So I got called in all last second and I felt totally unprepared." I wonder to myself if my Facebook investigation of the destination wedding this morning could have got me off-kilter.

Rhonda twists her face up and stirs her drink. "I've had other people tell me that there's a way in Microsoft Office someone could change the date of an invite without you noticing. In any case, I'm sorry. I'm going to have a talk with him myself."

Rhonda works in sales operation support — which we call in the biz an S.O.S. She's basically the right-hand woman of our boss, who would be totally unable to function without her. In her role, Rhonda relates to the other bosses a little differently than I do, and the upside? She has more pull. They give her more respect than the rest of us because they have to rely on her. And because she's the type of person who's been at the company forever and knows how to pull strings to get favors done when you need them. Even the higher-ups definitely don't want to get on her bad side.

"Thanks. But, Rhonda, I really don't want you to do it unless you think it'll make a difference. I don't want you to get into any hot water over this. It is what it is, I guess."

"Nonsense, I would do this for anyone. Matt can be an asshat sometimes. Consider it done."

"You're the best."

"Well, have a free beer? We really do need to figure out how to pay you more money. It's just that your position is so unique at the company. It's not like sales, where your salary is a mathematical percentage of what you sell. And we haven't quite figured out a proper compensation model for you." What Rhonda says is true. They haven't even established the position on the org chart, so I'm not sure what that means in the long run. Like my position could be dispensable...

The sales reps know how important we are, though. Schools will buy millions of dollars of equipment from us solely for the reason that I train them in Google Apps for Education, and can teach them how students and teachers can use the new equipment in the classroom so their expensive new technology doesn't just end up collecting dust.

I order another beer, and while I'm happy I don't have to pay, a free beer isn't the same as a raise. The team event tonight is sponsored by a new laptop cart manufacturer. Due to the free drinks, Jocko doesn't have to even buy me the one he owes me. This bums me out because I was looking forward to chatting casually with him. He's been charming the out-of-town sales reps though, who have all been laughing at whatever stories he's been regaling them with tonight. Just run-of-the-mill charm-boy Jocko for you. To put my plan into action, I need to catch him alone. I'm hoping he'll have downed those Jack and Cokes and it'll loosen up his inhibitions so he'll be agreeable to my plan.

Later in the night after things have died down a little, I run into him on the way back from the bathroom. Liquid courage runs through me, and I press my hand to his shoulder.

"Hey, Jocko," I say with a head nod that is probably less smooth in real life than it feels in my slightly buzzed state.

Even when I just *touch* his *shoulder*, a rush of warmth flows through me. I can feel how dense the muscles are underneath. I consider how Rhonda may be right, that I need to lay off my Facebook stalking. But what can I say, it's a learned skill. Or a bad habit.

Maybe both.

"Allie," he smiles, and tips his head to the side a little, his eyes show concern as they meet mine. "You doing okay?" He asks, probably noticing my flummoxed expression.

"Yeah, it's just...could I talk to you for a moment?" Ugh, I'm not slurring, am I? My inner me says maybe, my outer me thinks I'm being cool.

"Uh, okay."

"In private."

"Private?"

He looks suspicious — well, in reality he should be.

"Yes." I can't help but smile, though it's probably more of a goofy grin.

"Well, alrighty then. Is there a top secret deal you're working on?" he asks.

"Something like that."

Pizza Palace is a giant bar and restaurant. So we find an open table in the corner, away from our other coworkers, and sit down across from each other.

"So what are you doing in April? Anything fun?" I ask.

"Let's see, April...well, the schools have spring break sporadically that month, so there will be a light month of work for once. I don't know. It's usually still annoyingly cold then, I was thinking about getting out of Detroit. You?"

"Oh, you know. Just the usual stuff."

"Why do you ask about April?"

"Well...I have a proposal for you." I take a good long swig of my IPA. Jocko's forehead wrinkles, his expression full of intense curiosity.

"I'm all ears, Allie."

"How would you like to be my date for a destination wedding in Cancún?"

His eyes widen and he takes another sip of his drink. "You're asking me on a...date? A travel date, out of the country? Just the two of us?"

I put my hand on his forearm and nod.

His thick, very sexy forearm.

"Oh, I mean, just like a *friends* thing," I say, shrugging my shoulders and trying to seem nonchalant, like I *hadn't* been mulling this over all day long. "I need a date since, you know, I don't have one."

"Ah. Since you and Mark moved on, you haven't found someone you thought you could ask?"

"Oh, Mark? Barely a factor," I lie, waiving a hand in the air. I don't want him to get the idea that I'm some desperate rebound. "I just figured I would ask because you even said you wouldn't mind escaping the cold."

"Allie, this is sort of coming out of left field. You know my rule about dating coworkers."

"Right. Well, it wouldn't be like a *date* date exactly. We'd just be...friends. Like I said." Gah! First my salary negotiation goes to shit and now this looks like it'll follow suit. I'm oh for two today.

"Friends," he nods, sipping his drink, eyeing me in the strangest way, and a sliver of hope appears. Hot damn. Maybe I'm not oh for two. When I look in his eyes, I swear I see a flicker of interest.

"Besides, what about Becky?" I spit out, maybe a little too quickly. "You weren't just friends with her when you guys were, you know, 'together'." Yeah, I actually do the finger quote thing.

He squints. "How'd you know about that?"

"Oh...doesn't everyone?" Hate to tell him, come to find out from Rhonda the whole department was betting on the outcome.

"She swore she would keep that a secret. Well, whatever. Anyway, Becky worked in marketing. That was interdepartmental dating. This would be different. You and I see each other every day."

"Are you *sure*?" I say, giving the best, seductive wiggle of my eyebrows that I can, which might be making it worse at this point. I always think how adorable I look trying to be seductive, but in reality, I'm pretty sure I'm anything but that.

"So you're saying, you want me to come with you to a destination wedding. And be your...companion?"

"My friend — Jocko. I just need someone cool to come with me because everyone else is going to have a date, except me."

He takes a long pull of his drink. "Why is this so important to you?"

I twirl a lock of my hair. "I mean, it's not the end of the world if I don't have someone to go with. But I just thought of what you said once about how you're a total workaholic and haven't taken more than a long weekend vacation in years."

I can see his body rippling underneath his blue collar and tie, and I want to tell him I wouldn't mind being *more* than friends. But he's right, that would complicate our work relationship substantially.

"I'm not too worried about that," I say, trying to assuage his fears. "Don't you want to get out of this polar vortex winter? We're talking about *Cancún,* Jocko! It's a Caribbean paradise!"

He takes a deep breath and flashes me a smile, and I feel the hope rising inside me.

Jocko leans in and says, "Sorry, Allie. No can do."

Pangs of nerves creep up inside me. "Why not? It'll be fun. Please?" Ugh, now I sound desperate — maybe that's because I am?

For a moment, he hesitates. But then he says, "As fun as that sounds...I just can't."

Getting up, he walks back over to where our team is enjoying their happy hour. Rhonda spots me alone and zooms over.

"Hey. Did you ask him? How did it go?"

I shake my head. "Looks like I'm destined to be drinking

margaritas at the bar with the single crew of Aunt Martha and the divorcée crowd," I frown. Gotta admit, his refusal stings a bit. Not a good day for me at all.

I swig the rest of my beer down in one big gulp and it becomes like a weight in my stomach. Well, at least I know the answer. I asked the question and the answer was a resounding no.

But I've got some time to salvage this situation and I'm not going to give up — not yet. I guess it's back to the drawing board.

Having to see Mark again with his fiancé for five straight days is at the bottom of all this. I can't stand the thought of having to be there all by myself, the sad loser whose long-term boyfriend dumped her. The pathetic woman who can't find a date, much less get a decent *raise.*

Geez, maybe I *am* a loser. I make a note to replay that audiobook I recently got about positive self-talk and motivation. Obviously I didn't pay close enough attention on the first run-through.

I glance over at Jocko, who is across the room. He must have just finished telling a story that has the other reps in tears laughing.

He fixes his gaze on me for a few moments, and I swear I see the slightest smile pull at the corner of his lips as he looks at me. A glimmer of hope tugs at my soul.

Maybe I'm just imagining it, and he's eyeing the beer taps behind me, instead.

Wouldn't be the first time I've misread a situation, obviously.

4

JOCKO

My little brother Travis and I agree to meet up for a Friday night beer after my work happy hour to take the edge off. It's been a hell of a work week, what with closing three separate multi-million-dollar deals. To be honest, over the past year that's become fairly ubiquitous for me. Long hours and big deals.

What's not ubiquitous, however, is a coworker asking me to be her date to a five-day destination wedding out of the country. If I'm being honest with myself, that's probably the main cause for this hella-intense work week. All I know is that I need to wind down with my bro.

It's rare that I get to see Travis, as he doesn't usually get to swing through Detroit. He lives quite an interesting life these days, working as a paid male, uhm, *companion.*

"You're an escort, dude," I raz him. "Just admit it. A male prostitute."

He shakes his head. "That is untrue. I just dance and they watch me, and *occasionally* they throw me a few bucks because they want an intelligent, conversational companion to keep them company for an event afterwards. Or a bodyguard to keep the creepy guys away from them. Or I teach them how to gamble. I know it's not a normal job. But it suits me and I like it."

My eyebrows raise. It's true, Travis never could do the nine-to-five thing like I do. "A 'conversational companion'?" I echo, making big bunny ear quote marks with my fingers. "Come on. I'm your brother, and I wasn't fucking born yesterday. If you're sleeping with these women, just own up to it."

Travis has the 'Brewer combination' of rugged good-looks and high intellect. After he graduated from Yale with a degree in Philosophy and Data Science, he worked for years as a data analyst making bank for one of the biggest companies in the U.S. After making more money than he could ever spend, he had an existential crisis, quit, moved to Vegas, got a host of tattoos, and started his current job. Claims he feels better about his life now than when he was working on faceless algorithms behind the scenes to make *the capitalists* more money.

Now he's twenty-eight, part poker player, part philosopher, and part dancer, doing a little bit of making fantasies come true on the side for extra cash.

Conversational fantasies, apparently. Not that I believe one word of that.

I'm his own brother and I don't know what to make of him, sometimes. I suppose Renaissance man is an apt word to describe him. Travis doesn't exactly follow the rules of normal society, just makes up his own rules as he goes along.

"Swear to God, dude," he says, then raises his right hand. "I do *not* sleep with these women. I enjoy spending time with them, too. I get a lot out of it."

"So you've never even *wanted* to sleep with a client?"

"I've been attracted to them, sure. But we both know it's just got to stay at the flirting level and go no further."

I'm skeptical, but I give it to him since he isn't a bullshitter — perhaps he *is* telling the truth about not sleeping with his clients. Wanting to see how much of his conversational companion skills I can put to the test, I give Travis the rundown of Allie and me, wanting his advice and input.

Well, mostly I tell him about Allie. How she's cute. Sweet. So cute and sweet, in fact, I had to turn down her offer because I don't want to be trapped in the same hotel with her for five days, I don't think I could pull that off platonically. She says we'll go just as *friends,* but that's because she doesn't know about all the inappropriate thoughts and visuals that find their way into my brain where she's cast in the leading role. Sleeping in the same hotel room for five days as *friends* would be the worst form of torture.

But I can't get her offer out of my head. I can't go — of course not — but I could use some perspective on what to do now that this elephant is in the room between us, especially come Monday morning when we are back at work. His brotherly perspective and insight hopefully will shine some light on the subject.

"So, this Allie girl," Travis says. "She breaks up with her boyfriend last fall. Now she's still got a plus-one on the invite and she wants to bring you."

"Right."

"So what's the issue?" He heaves his shoulders in a shrug and takes another sip of his beer. "Sounds fun. I don't know how you stand these winters. I heard the temperature hit negative twenty last week? I mean, what the hell!"

There's a reason Travis has always lived in hot climates,

aside from his time on the east coast. He can't stand anything below seventy degrees Fahrenheit.

"I know all that. I mean, the wedding is in April and it'll still be balls cold here."

"April's definitely not a fun month. It's always disappointingly cold and rainy. So what's the hold up?" He leans in and squints, then nods as if I've just told him a secret. "Ohh, I get it."

"Get what?" Maybe Trav will have some insight after all.

"I get why you don't want to go. The girl's annoying! Who wants to spend five straight days in a resort with someone they can't stand, am I right?"

"She's *not* annoying," I correct. "Not even close. I've worked with her for three years and I still enjoy talking to her. She's funny, smart, great voice..." Damn. I'm basically losing my own argument here. It's not like I haven't noticed these things for the past three years. I just put Allie in the category of "has a boyfriend, you may be friends only," and now the fact she's single is still a little hard to process.

Travis's eyes widen with every word I say. "So what's the fucking problem, man? You go to Cancún with her for a few days, give her a ride on the Jocko express, and when you come back, bam! Just pretend like it never happened. And because you were in Cancún, technically, it didn't. What happens in Cancún..." He breaks out into laughter, but I don't. "Oh, okay. I get it. She's not your type. Ah, I see. I mean if you don't find her *pretty,* then that's a problem, too."

"I find her incredibly sexy, as a matter of fact...and it's Vegas, you ass. What happens in Vegas," I blurt out, even surprising myself with how quick my reaction is.

Travis furrows his brow. "I'm running thin with my advice for you, man. What's the hold up? I still don't get it."

"You know how I feel about dipping my pen in the

company ink, in general. It's not something I do." Well that, and there's more to it I'm not going to share with this asshole, regardless of our shared DNA.

"What about Becky in marketing? You didn't seem to have a problem with dipping your pen in her ink."

I slam my hand down on the hardwood table, making a thud so loud a few different people glance over. "How the fuck does everyone know about Becky in marketing?" I'm half-chuckling, but also slightly annoyed because Becky guaranteed me our hookup would stay between us. Apparently keeping her mouth closed is not one of her top skills. I should've known that considering she didn't keep her mouth closed much when we hooked up.

"You invited me to that happy hour when I was in town last year, remember? You know me. I'm like the CIA. I can get anyone to tell me the information I want to know. In this case, it was your drunk boss telling me all of the EdTechX gossip."

I shake my head and sigh. So my boss knows about that, too? Damn. Though, knowing Matt, he's probably living vicariously through that knowledge, he just seems kind of different that way.

"It's not like that with Allie," I continue. "She's an amazing Ed Tech Strategist. She's helped me close like five deals this year already. Big deals. Multimillion-dollar deals. I can't endanger that relationship." And, I'm not sure she's all that into me anyway, not that *that* matters but I wouldn't really want that awkwardness in paradise.

"I see," he says, shoveling a carrot with hummus into his mouth. "Is this keto?"

I shake my head. "Carrots are not keto. Too much sugar."

"Damn! I don't know how you do it, man."

"What do you mean? I get to eat all the good stuff with keto. Bacon, butter, olives."

He squints. "Our Paleolithic ancestors definitely loved fruit. So I don't see why we need to deprive ourselves of it."

"Our ancestors also clubbed dinosaurs over the head and dragged them back to roast over a fire, what's your point? What do you think I should do about the girl, T?" I ask, getting back on topic. I might as well go deep with this and get Travis's full insight.

He shrugs. "Well, you're a deal maker. I'm surprised you didn't just ask yourself 'what's in it for you' and then be done with it."

"Oh, come on. I'm not *always* a deal maker."

"Dude, in third grade you used to trade Jack Stedman your Lunchables for his hot lunch. Please. I've known you too long for you to put one over me."

"Hey, that was a fair deal. Lunchables were *in* back then."

"Alright, man, from where I'm sitting, the way you describe this Allie girl, she seems nice. You could just go to make her happy. And, you know, *not* sleep with her. Like I do with my clients, ya goddamn heathen. Sounds like the girl has had a rough year. Have a little sympathy. Have a little heart."

A pit forms in my stomach at the thought of that. Not the helping her out part, it's more about the other. "I'd be staying in a room with her for a full five days. It's a destination wedding at an all-inclusive resort, so obviously the alcohol is included and in abundance. What if we have a random, booze-fueled hookup? How awkward would that be once we get back to reality?"

Travis laughs. "You'll have a laugh about the whole thing when you get back to work, and she'll keep helping you with your deals. What does an Educational Strategist do, anyway?"

"She helps IT Directors implement their technology curriculum. Meanwhile, we sell them the computers and the wireless infrastructure. She follows up and does the tough stuff. I make the sale, she provides the details and follow-through. She's incredible at what she does."

The bastard chuckles and calls for another martini. "Well, if she's so incredible, tough guy, why don't you marry her?"

I call for another tequila soda lime and raise my eyebrows. "Well, maybe I fucking will. And thanks for all the serious advice. Trav-Trav." I smirk as I bring out my brother's old high school nickname.

"Real mature, Jock-itch. Real goddamn mature. This coming from a guy who doesn't think he could go five full days with a girl — to do something nice for her — without sleeping with her. What kind of cocky bastard are you to think she would automatically want to get with you anyway? Sounds like you'd just be a warm body to keep her from flying solo."

"I didn't *say* she would want to hookup. I said *what if* something happened."

"Maybe *I* should be her date, that's sort of my thing, after all," he jokes. "I don't even know this girl, but the way you talk about her, she must be awesome. You don't usually sing women's praises."

"Watch it," I smirk. Nothing like a good, brotherly rivalry to get your blood pumping.

I sometimes got a vibe that Allie notices me. In that way.

Maybe.

It's that flirty tension that rings in the air when it's six thirty p.m., I'm still at work, and she stops by my desk to say goodnight with a smile that's genuine. Or vice versa, like that one time I caught her staying late and watching show tunes and giggling at her desk. Even the time I caught her singing along because she thought no one was around at work, and her cheeks turned as red as a tomato when she realized she was most definitely not alone. No one should be that smiley when you are staying late at work on a Tuesday. And she doesn't smile that way with other guys.

Although, it's possible I'm imagining it.

And I swear, since she broke up with what's-his-face, there's been a couple of times where I noticed her lingering, watching my eye movement. Maybe seeing if I'm interested?

Damn, I think this tequila is getting to me. I better slow the hell down.

"Stop overthinking it," he says as our server brings us two more drinks. "She's nice, you want to do something nice for her, then do it. You don't, don't. It's Cancún, anyhow. It's impossible not to have a good time in Cancún." Someone opens the door, and a cold gust of air comes rushing into the bar. A collective sound of temperature shock reverberates throughout the bar.

"How'd your last date go with that hot brunette, anyhow?" he asks.

I shrug. "It went."

"Not into her?"

I shake my head. "She was cute but there was zero chemistry."

"Have you...*ever* had a serious relationship?"

"Please," I scoff. "Does anyone do serious relationships anymore? Anyway, you see that Pistons game the other night?"

"Whoa, whoa, whoa," Travis puts a hand up. "You can't

just say *anyway* and totally change the subject to basketball. Why you skirting my question?"

I shrug my shoulders defensively. "I'm not skirting your question."

"You said, 'please', which did not answer my question, and then you changed the subject to sports. That is literally the definition of skirting a question."

"Because it was a dumb question. One which you know the answer to."

"I'm just thinking back. You're twenty-nine now, and you've never had a real relationship."

"Whatever, dude. I dated Melissa Woodstock for like two years."

His jaw drops. "That was literally in fifth grade! You two didn't even kiss!"

"Did, too."

"Yeah, and then you broke up with her because you said the kiss was making things 'too' serious," he chides mockingly.

"We were going to separate middle schools! How was I supposed to do long distance?" Weak, I know, but I've got to keep my bro off the relationship topic.

Travis throws his head back he's laughing so hard. "Have you dated anyone seriously?"

"Will you shut up about fucking dating? I like my life. Jesus, you're starting to sound like Mom. She's like '*Jocky, when are you going to get a fiancée? I'm so worried about you. I knew your four brothers weren't going to settle down, but I had so much hope for you.*'"

"Wow. Sensitive issue, geez," Travis says, finally signaling that he'll stop giving me the third degree.

"Like I said, did you see the Pistons' game last night?" I ask again.

He nods reluctantly. "Fine. We can talk about the damn Pistons."

Travis has always been a good Irish twin. He's less than a year younger than me, so we were both in the same grade together. But my mom, for some reason, is way more concerned about my settling down than him or any of her other sons.

He's an oddball himself, and would much rather talk about 'real things' than sports things.

But he relents because he knows Mom is all over me lately to get married, and her tunnel-vision focus is unfair. I can't even sit down to a conversation with her without a passive-aggressive verbal maneuver asking if I'm seeing anyone seriously.

Almost at the same instance, I get a text from my mom and hold my phone up for T to see.

Mom: Hey, honey, did you hear? Your old friend Tate got engaged. Such a nice boy, that Tate! Be sure to congratulate him! Did you see the ring he bought his fiancée?

Let me translate that into Momma Jocko speak for you:

Mom (translated): Hey, honey, are you still single and breaking hearts? Your friend Tate, who is younger than you, got engaged. I think twenty-eight is a great age to get engaged. Or twenty-nine, like you. Don't you think?

Okay, okay. Maybe I'm going a bit overboard. But the gist is true. My mother, bless her heart, misses no chance to throw my unmarried status in my face. Plus, Travis is right, I haven't even given her hope that I *might be* in a relationship of any kind yet.

I think since Travis spent his early twenties with the same girl — even though it didn't work out between them — our mother has spared him her ire.

Travis bursts into laughter at the irony of that text coming in at the same time we were talking about my single life. I just roll my eyes and say, "Let's get out of here, man."

The fact is, though, the hints are getting a little out of hand. As I ride in the Uber home that night, my mind mulls over a new plan.

Maybe it's completely crazy.

Or maybe it's so crazy it just might work.

Hell, if anyone can pull off crazy, it's me.

If Allie wants me to be her date for five days to this destination wedding — I'll one-up her.

And get my mom off my back at the same time. In sales, we like to call that a win-win.

WHEN I GET to work on Monday, I textchat Allie and invite her down to join me for coffee at the café in our building.

Well, tea for me. Because as I mentioned, the world can't handle caffeinated Jocko.

We meet and then I guide her to the back of the room where we find a vacant booth.

Allie's a very pretty girl. I don't know what *it* is, but she's got it, and plenty of it. Blond hair, dark green eyes, a fair complexion with a few freckles. I lean back and watch her as she sips her coffee, leaving a red lipstick stain on the mug.

"So? What did you want to chat about?" she asks, glancing at her watch, obviously uncomfortable, probably because our last conversation was sort of awkward when I turned her down.

I decide to just bite the bullet, so I say, "I thought about your invite to the destination wedding. And I'm ready to accept. If it's still on the table, of course. I think it would be a very fun time, in a lot of ways."

Her eyes soften and she smiles. "Seriously? Oh my gosh! Jocko! Thank you, thank you, thank you! We're going to have so much fun!"

She licks her lips as if she's about to jump across the table and kiss me. Damn, seeing her this happy warms my heart. But I'm not done with my offer.

"Whoa now, hold on, just a minute. I've got to give you my stipulation."

"Oh boy. Here we go," she says, pulling back her excitement.

"I'll go with you on one condition," I smirk.

"Which is...?"

I look around to make sure no one from work is nearby. Then, I reach into my suit pocket, pull out a ring box, and get down on one knee next to her.

"Allie Jenkins, will you marry me?" I ask.

Her face goes pale.

"Um, what?" she croaks, wide-eyed.

5

ALLIE

My jaw drops to the floor, and I try to pick it up but I can't.

"I think I'm fainting," I say, and Jocko rushes around to my side of the booth to stop me from tipping over.

"Allie, you okay?"

He holds a ring box in one hand, my shoulders with the other and I can see him laughing at me.

"What the hell are you doing?" I bite out in a hushed tone, my shock wearing off.

Thank the Lords of Monday no one saw us.

When I've recovered, he sits back in the booth across from me, grinning from ear to year, ring still in hand. My blood pressure rises and I don't know if it's from ire or from the fact that even on a Monday morning, Jocko looks sexy in a suit, as usual.

"This is our special coffee shop," he winks. "I always knew I'd do it here."

My stomach clenches, what's with the charade, is he trying to embarrass me? Some sick way of getting me back for asking him to Cancún? "I don't know *what* you're doing. But you've got a minute to explain yourself."

"You drunkenly asked me to be your wedding date the other day. Anyway, like I said, I'm accepting. But on one condition: I want to go...as your fiancé."

I blink a few times. "I'm not sure I understand." His stupid smile aggravates the hell out of me.

"Hear me out. My mom is all on me to 'get married' and 'grow up' when I think everyone who knows me, knows that's just not going to happen. At least until I'm forty or so. So, here's what we do. We stage an engagement, I go to this wedding with you and snap some pics for my mom. When we get back, you'll 'break up' with me. Ipso facto, she'll be so sympathetic for her son with the broken heart, and every single time I visit her in Nebraska, which is several times a year, the main conversation can stop being about me and my bachelor lifestyle. Our work friends won't even have to be any the wiser."

I run a hand through my hair. "I need to process this. So after we snap some of those ring pics, you want me to break up with you?"

"Right. After I'm your fake boyfriend for the trip."

"You mean fiancé."

"Boom. See, Allie? You're so damn smart. That's why we're going to make the best short-term engaged couple."

"You mean *fake* engaged couple."

"You just did it again. We're off to the races with this fake relationship. We cover for each other so well."

I sigh and take a long pull of my hot coffee, letting the liquid slowly make its way down my throat. Outside, it's cold and drifts of snow blow around as pedestrians with scarves and winter coats walk through downtown Detroit.

The fact that I'm actually considering this incredibly

unorthodox proposal is a testament to how off-the-rails my life has become lately.

"I just...Jocko...I have so many questions. Like, where did you get that ring? How exactly will we *'fake'* being in a relationship? What's the airspeed velocity of an unladen swallow? And *where on Earth did you get that ring?*"

"Let's just say, our engagement might be fake. But the diamond isn't." He winks, and the way he looks intensely at me makes my skin tingle. "If we're gonna do this, we're going full throttle and having some fun. Also, I appreciate the Monty Python *Quest for the Holy Grail* and the unladen swallow reference. God, we're going to get along great for these five days. Aren't we?"

I glance at my watch, not wanting to acknowledge him asking about how great we are going to get along because part of me sort of thinks the same thing, and that could be dangerous. "So my fifteen minutes of coffee time are up. I need to get back to my desk. Can we continue this conversation later?"

"Good idea. How about my place at eight?"

"*Sure*, honeybuns. Should I wear something sexy?" I say, my voice dripping with sarcasm.

I stand up, and he gives me an up-and-down. "Honestly, you already look sexy," he winks.

I'm speechless at hearing Jocko call me 'sexy.' And he seems earnest. Not exactly how I was expecting to start my Monday morning, with coffee and a proposal.

I head back up to my desk, flabbergasted at what just went down, and my mind overloaded with a hundred different emotions.

On Friday I was so sad he had turned down my proposal. I spent the whole weekend feeling lousy about myself, about my life, about pretty much everything. I tried to climb out of my dark mood but nothing seemed to help. After this, though, I feel as if I've been jolted hard from my routine and hit with a dizzy spell.

The rest of the day, I can barely concentrate on work as my head spins with thoughts of Jocko and me at the destination wedding, not only as dates but as *fake fiancés?*

I find that the more I think about it, the more the idea seems, well, not as crazy as it first sounded.

Mark's engaged to his new girl five months after breaking up with me.

Why not me?

Even if the engagement is just for five days.

And that ring. That *ring*.

THAT NIGHT, after having a glass of wine at my place, I call up Jocko.

After one ring, he answers in a low, gravelly voice.

"Hey, future wife."

Tingles ratchet through me.

"Hey, future ex-husband," I joke, upping the ante.

"Oh, please," he says back, sounding serious. "We both know that would never happen. So when are you getting here?" he adds. "It's eight fifteen."

"I don't need to come," I say. "I'm in."

"Fuck yes. Why the change of mind? Why didn't you come to celebrate anyway?"

I don't tell Jocko that I don't exactly trust myself in a room alone with him...drinking champagne or any other type of adult beverage. I don't know what we'd do.

"Just tell me where you got the ring," I say.

"It's a heritage ring, was my great grandmother's."

"What? Why would you give that to me for just a fake engagement?"

"I trust you, Allie. You've never dropped the ball on a project. You're the most responsible person I know. If we're going to do this thing, we're going all in. I mean, we'll keep it confined to the five days we're there, of course. No one needs to know anything more, right? What happens in Cancún, stays in Cancún. Don't you think?"

Jesus, there's that phrase again...it's Vegas, people — VEGAS! But at this point, I'll take Cancún and allow it to keep all of our deception within its borders.

As I focus on the word *confined*, though, my mind flashes to being pushed down on a bed by Jocko's strong arms. I'm pretty sure my body temperature rises at the visual. The more I try to force the feeling down, the more it bubbles up.

I take a big gulp of my second glass of wine. "Sounds like a plan."

"So when's this trip? I can't wait to get the fuck out of Detroit."

"It's the week after Easter. We'd leave on a Wednesday."

"Perfect. I'll break the news about you to my mom as we are getting on the plane that morning."

"The news?"

"About our engagement."

Pangs of guilt rise inside me. It's the one hang-up I have about this arrangement. "Are you really sure that's the right thing to do? Play with your family's emotions like that?"

"Don't worry about me. If I'm going to be your hired man for five days, I'm getting something out of it. And trust me, I will do one hell of a job as your hired man. Who is getting married, anyhow?"

"My friend from college...Peyton O'Rourke."

I hear expletives on the other side of the phone. "Peyton

fucking O'Rourke? AKA the Super Bowl champion quarterback?"

"That's him! We used to party together in the dorms freshmen year."

"Jesus fuck, Allie. You've got to tell a guy these things. I met him once last summer at a party for my brother who plays for the Grizzlies. Cool guy. And Maddy, too."

"Oh. You'll fit right in, then," I say, and roll my eyes.

How could I forget Jocko's brother Everett plays professional football? Of freaking *course* Jocko would be acquainted with last year's Super Bowl champion, somehow. He's just that kind of guy. If he meets you once, he makes an impression on you.

"Yeah, even though he and my brother are sworn enemies on the football field, they know each other off of it. That's so cool you're friends with him. Why do you get cooler every other fun fact I learn about you, Allie?" he adds.

My body warms again.

Why does even a little compliment like that from Jocko make me feel like a million bucks?

"Oh, I've got much more up my sleeve. You just wait," I say.

"I know you do. I'm starting a 'vacation with Allie countdown.' Just...hey, do me one favor. Let's keep this between us, okay? Let's not talk about this at the office. This is just for my family. Probably best our clients don't think we're, you know, engaged. Remember, *confined.*"

I take another sip of my wine. "Confined. Right. Only for those five days."

"I can't wait for this. We're going to crush it so hard. So much fun."

We pause for a few beats, and yes — I admit — I'm

looking at Jocko's Instagram pictures from college spring break right now. Maybe I do have a problem. Or maybe the problem is that he's just so damn unfairly muscular. And no one who looks as good as he does in a suit should be allowed to have a tattoo like the arrow he has, nearly hidden on his upper left arm. It's such an unfair — and sexy — surprise. A question pops into my mind.

"One more thing."

"Anything, wifey."

"Please don't call me wifey," I say, though he can't see my smile through the phone.

"Sorry. What is it, hon-...Allie-face?"

"Allie-face, really?"

"I feel like I need a nickname for you for the wedding. I'm trying it out, Smoopy-pie. What do you need?"

"Just stop now, please." I can't stop the laugh that bubbles out of me when I try to make him stop with the cheesiest terms of endearment. But back to the question I had to ask. "Can you tell me a little more about this keto diet?" I ask.

"Sure, I can. You looking to get toned for this wedding or something?"

"You know, I just want us to take good 'engagement' pics. This is me winking through the phone. I'm winking. Can you tell?"

"So you want to look hot as fuck in a bikini, is what you're telling me?"

"Yes."

"I know it's winter, but if you still look anything like you did during that roofdeck party, this won't be hard. I still remember how hot you looked that day. Everyone was checking you out."

"Were they?" I croak. "I don't remember that." My body

washes over in tingles from head to toe that Jocko took note of me. I thought I was the one staring at *him* that day.

"Anyway, yes, I can give you a friendly rundown of keto and take you through some workouts since I used to be a trainer on the side to pay my way through college."

The word *friendly* isn't lost on me, and I'm reminded that my crush isn't reciprocated. His observation about me being 'hot' isn't a come-on, it's just Jocko being Jocko. He's not a bullshitter.

"Meet me in the gym tomorrow afternoon. I will train the fuck out of you. On one condition."

"What's that?"

"You let me call you wifey when we're alone."

"You're ridiculous."

"Smoopy-pie?"

"Not a chance."

"See you tomorrow, Allie."

And revenge plan is kicking into gear.

I saw the hashtag #revengebody trending on Twitter the other day, and it motivated me. Maybe it's not the healthiest motivation to work on my booty, but I sure do feel motivated all of a sudden. Plus, I'm excitedly anxious about getting to hang out with Jocko more in a non-office context.

Holding the phone in my hand without hanging up, a strange tingle tumbles through me. It's been a long winter — the longest of my life — and for the first time I feel like there could be some excitement on the horizon.

Jocko doesn't hang up, and neither do I. We both linger for a moment listening to each other's breathing.

"And, Jocko — thanks. I'm really happy we're doing this. The whole destination wedding thing."

"Oh, please. I'm going for entirely selfish reasons."

"What are those?"

"I like spending time with you."

And just like that, I melt into my bed. When I don't say anything for too long of a period, he says goodbye and hangs up.

Two months can't come soon enough.

But for now, I'm certain I'll have interesting dreams tonight.

DAY 1: THE WEDDING TRIP BEGINS

Detroit, Michigan

Two Months Later

6

JOCKO

On a dreary Wednesday morning in late April, Allie and I are in the Detroit Metropolitan Airport before the sun is up waiting for our flight to leave, and what's on my mind?

Cojones.

What some people don't get is that closing deals and getting the girl requires a similar skill set: you just have to have brass balls. You've got to tell a client how damn expensive your new product will be without toning yourself down. They can *feel* your lack of confidence through the phone.

Same thing with women. There comes a point — usually after a date goes really well, perhaps a couple of cocktails in as you are walking on the sidewalk hand in hand — where you just need to give her the *look*, roll your hands down her hips onto her skirt or dress, press her into the nearest wall surface and kiss the fuck out of her before she knows what hit her.

When you hear her breathing hard, maybe you press her hands gently into the brick wall above her head and just stare into her eyes and lick your lips like you're the big bad wolf about to devour your next meal. With an option to gently wrap one hand around close to her neck and feel her pulse, observe that it's racing. Then flit your eyes down her neck, picking your next point of entry.

Running a hand up her thigh, cupping her ass and exploring right where the smooth leg flesh turns into her ass, that's my favorite when it happens.

From there, you just use your instincts. Best to be spontaneous.

I'll be honest. Some guys don't have *los cojones* to pull this one off. They wait too long, until the moment is passed, and live a life filled with regret and missed opportunities. Personally, I revel in these types of moments. I live to sink into that world where I become an instinctual, dominant man who responds to a woman's every subtle vocal intonation, every slight upturn of the hips, every pleasureful moan.

Yet when it comes to Allie Jenkins, I freeze up like a high school freshmen on his first date. Even just sitting in an airport with her like I am right now makes my blood pressure rise. It makes no goddamn sense to me.

So you can imagine how hard my heart is beating as I pull the ring box out of my pocket and hand it to her. Maybe part of it is the fact that it's five a.m. in the morning and she's casually sipping on a latte, looking out the window into the pink glowing sky as she sits next to me. To all onlookers, she undoubtedly looks like my fiancée. Hot girl in a baseball cap and glasses and a handsome young man, rings on their fingers, laughing together.

"Glasses today, eh?" I say, making small talk.

She nods. "I usually wear contacts, but I figure we might try to get some sleep on the flight, and I don't like sleeping in them, especially with the dry air on airplanes."

She usually doesn't wear her glasses at work, although I vividly remember her wearing them the first day and how sexy she looked in them. She probably doesn't realize how hot she looks with them. Something about seeing her out of work in casualwear makes her all the more gorgeous to me. I feel like I'm seeing a piece of her other guys we work with won't get to see.

I sit back and rest my arm on the back of the seat. Thing is, if you looked a little closer, maybe you could see the façade of it all. In our shyness, our gestures. We're not like the other couple a few seats down, snuggling and taking selfies. We're a little more awkward. Tentative. We don't know each other's habits.

Yet.

"So we're really doing this fake engagement thing, eh?" she says, lifting up her hand to look at the ring on her finger.

I nod, my heart rocking. "Crazy, I know. But let's fucking do it."

"I still can't believe you seriously are trusting me with your great grandmother's ring."

"I do. I think we both know you're the organized, responsible one in this partnership."

"Oh, yeah? And what are you?"

"I'm the fire," I wink. I take a selfie of us in the airport. Part of me feels a smidge guilty for pulling the wool over my mom's eyes, so to speak. Well, more than a smidge. But in the end, I think this little idea will buy me some more time where my mom isn't worried about her favorite son.

Shit, it worked for Travis, although I don't think his break-up was meant to happen. Regardless, I need this to work for me.

God, I'm so smart.

I send the pic to my mom with a short but sweet

message about my "engagement" so I can set the wheels of my plan in motion. I then switch my phone into airplane mode.

Allie is about to slip the ring off her hand again when I stop her.

"What are you doing?"

"Putting the ring in my pocket," she says.

"Why would you do that?"

She shrugs. "I mean, we'll only need it when we're at the resort, right? We're not 'engaged' right now."

"Wrong. What if we see someone from the wedding party on the plane?"

Reluctantly, she crosses her arms and puts the ring back on her finger. "Which other poor saps would be taking this early-as-hell flight?"

"This is the best way to travel. We'll get to the resort by ten, check-in, take a nap, and be ready to hit the swim-up bar by noon."

Just then, we're called to board our flight. Her long blond hair falls to her shoulders, and she's wearing a hoodie that God willing, we won't need when we arrive to Cancún.

Not going to lie, I check out my fiancée's ass as she walks in front of me in the boarding line in her skinny jeans.

For the past seven weeks or so, I've been training her in the gym. I've never seen someone quite so motivated to whip herself into shape. And it shows. I was very attracted to her *before* she started working out. And with our seven weeks of training, she's only gotten hotter and more toned.

I shake my head out and remind myself that this is *Allie-face*. My coworker. My good friend. Rhonda even called me her *work husband*.

Also, Allie's ass is just one of many amazing facets of this girl who has been a bright spot in my life over the past few years. Yes, she's boner-inducing hot. But that's not why I've chosen to be her date for this trip. We've had hour-long work-chat conversations debating the best Adam Sandler movie. We're like Jim and Pam from *The Office*. And she just broke up with Roy.

Allie and I will have five days of fun. Five days together on a resort, where what we do has no real-life consequences.

I'm not planning on hooking up with her. But if we *were* to hook up, that would be totally off-the-record...

Right?

As we wait in our seats for the other passengers to file in — we're in one of the first rows — she nudges me. "Hey, so don't you think it's about time we come up with a game plan?"

"What do you mean?"

"Well, we should have a story ready for how everything went down. How did we fall in love, and all that."

"Why don't we just wing it?" I suggest.

"Are you good at improv?"

I smile. "You kidding me? I'm a born bullshitter."

"Winging it, then," she agrees. "Sounds like a good plan."

I lean back in my seat and stare out the window onto the cold, dark tarmac.

She leans back and puts her arm on my shoulder. "Don't worry, Jay. The pain will all be over soon."

I close my eyes. I like it when she calls me Jay. "I can already picture the swim-up bar. I've been having vivid dreams about it."

"Oh?"

"Yes. And the occasional nightmare where we arrive and there is no swim-up bar to swim up to."

"The horror!"

The plane takes off, and we laugh and chat and debate about the first drink we're going to have at the swim-up bar that most definitely is there.

I also make sure I've got all my Allie facts up to date. Working with someone for three years, you find out a plethora of information about them. Plus, our daily workouts this winter have acted as a fun way for us to casually develop a better connection. But it's always good to review.

Allie Jenkins, twenty-six years old. She was born in a far northern suburb of Detroit, then relocated to Kansas City when her dad's job got moved in grade school. Her mom met her dad in a bar their sophomore year of college and the two never looked back. After high school, she headed to the University of Texas, where she studied marketing. After school, she did Teach For America and taught in the inner city of Detroit for three years. Then she found the position at EdTechX. Now she coaches technology directors and teachers on how to integrate technology into the curriculum. She's the oldest in her family, and has a strong nurturing side but also a drive for organization. Five siblings in their family: two sisters and two brothers. Her two sisters are married and living in the Kansas City suburbs. Her two brothers have moved to LA and New York, respectively.

"You've got everything right on point," she says, and then recites back everything about me.

I'm born in a small town in Nebraska. Fair, brownish blond hair from my very Irish dad and darker skin and shady brown eyes from my very Italian mother. Dad worked in a meatpacking plant, Mom was a homemaker and a part-time assistant in the local schools for students with special needs. I've got five siblings, all brothers except for one, none married as of yet, although my little brother is close, and

Everett might not be far behind either, though he hasn't announced it to the family.

For some reason though, my mom picked me as her pride and joy of the family to get married and produce offspring. I went to University of Michigan to play college ball. Almost beat Steph Curry my senior year in the March Madness tournament. Got the job in sales at EdTechX straight out of college, and have crushed it there throughout my twenties, making great money although I'm a borderline workaholic.

"Good. Now, what about the *important* questions?" I ask, and I feel my heart hammering a little harder. Seven a.m. on a flight to Cancún might not be the best time to ask some of these things. But I've been wondering about Allie ever since we set up this whole vacation. Well, even before that, if I'm being honest.

She squints. "I mean, I think we've got it covered. We know each other pretty well."

I glance at the seats around us in the airplane. Luckily, just about everyone seems to be still passed out, and not paying attention to our conversation. I don't want what I'm about to say to be overheard.

I give Allie a serious look. "If we're faking a relationship, I think I need to know some other things about you. Like in the bed stuff."

"Bed stuff?"

"Yeah. What are your turn-ons? Turn-offs?"

Her face flushes red. "Why would that come up in conversation?"

"I don't know. What if we play like, the newlywed game or something?"

Allie rolls her eyes, resistant. "That game is like twenty years old. We'll be fine."

"Well, what if I just want to know for my own curiosity?"

She laughs awkwardly, and is saved from having to respond when the flight attendant appears at the end of our row asking if we'd like anything to drink.

The guy at the end of our row wakes up, and so do the people behind us.

Allie changes the subject, and the moment has passed.

After another hour, I stare out the window at the bright sun as we make our way to Cancún, and a smile plasters itself onto my face.

My theory is, there's only one reason she would dodge my question about her turn-ons so hard: she's thought about it before. And she's trying to keep that wall up between us, too. I can't say I blame her. God knows it could be awkward as hell if we hook up on this trip, and then get back to work and are in meetings together.

On the other hand. We're in fucking *Cancún*.

And as I look out the window of the airplane and watch the water whiz by below, I get a funny feeling that these next five days in a tropical paradise with Allie are going to be magical.

7

ALLIE

After we get our bags, Jocko and I find our driver and wait in the back of the shuttle bus that will be taking us to Temptation Isle, the resort where the wedding will be held.

An interesting name for a place to make a lifelong commitment if you ask me.

I'm slightly tired and cranky due to the fact that I only got about two hours of sleep last night, but I remind myself that as soon as we get to the resort I'll be able to crash.

Jocko, on the other hand, stares out the window of the bus with fresh eyes. Then, he absent-mindedly puts his hand on my knee.

A rush of heat runs through my whole body and I tense up. God, his hands are big. Is he doing this purposely to mess with me? No. Jocko can be a dick sometimes, but he wouldn't just straight up mess with me. He's probably spacing out, getting in *fiancé* mode. But what was with that *what turns you on* question he asked me on the plane?

My mind definitely does not work as well when I'm sleep deprived as I am now. I return to my default setting.

Obviously, when he asked me what my turn-ons are, a few things came right to mind.

Guys in suits.

Guys with ridged abs.

Guys with nice sized...equipment.

Okay, there, I said it. What can I say? I appreciate style, a man who takes care of his body, and a nice package. Just being honest here.

But as these thoughts crept into my brain when he asked the question, I realized if I said them out loud, I would basically just be describing Jocko. In my mind's eye, I could already see the lordly smirk forming on his face if I were to list all of my turn-ons. So I resisted, and thankfully, was saved by the flight attendant asking for our drink orders. That was a godsend.

And how do I know about Jocko's, ahem, wonder down under? We can thank Becky in marketing for that, sort of...

Her comments piqued my interest. So when Jocko and I worked out together at the gym, I noted that weightlifting clothes for guys with marvelous thighs accentuate a certain area, and well — you take it from there.

Anyway, now I'm getting all hot and bothered as Jocko nonchalantly digs his fingers lightly into my thighs over the denim of my jeans. Physical contact is one thing we haven't discussed yet as a part of our arrangement. But it's only natural that if we're together for five days as a couple we'll be doing some touching in public. Handholding, leg touching, maybe a foot massage at some point.

God, I would kill for a foot massage.

And then it happens.

We hear our driver speaking in accented English, telling another couple to get in the shuttle. My eyes lock on Mark's, and he's as surprised to see me as I am to see him. I realize it would be inevitable, but this soon? On two hours of sleep?

Ugh. *Kill me now.*

I feel my anxiety rocket through the roof, slap my hand over Jocko's and hold onto it tightly. He notices instantly, and flashes me a soft smile.

"You okay?" he asks.

I nod and take a deep breath. "Just tired."

"I feel you. Can't wait to get to the room and rest."

Mark and his girl sit in the front row, which is mercifully out of earshot for us in the back.

I have to hand it to Jocko — he does have a way of putting me at ease. He's rarely fazed by anything. I've seen him get yelled at by our customers for technology gone very wrong — usually totally out of his control — and he's able to calmly apologize and talk million-dollar clients out of going to another company.

I'm confident I couldn't have chosen a better ally for this five-day adventure.

A HALF-HOUR LATER, we pull through the resort gates, and I linger in the shuttle while Jocko gets out and grabs our luggage. He pops his head back in.

"You coming?" he asks.

I nod. "Yes. Coming."

"We're here!" he smiles. "Fuck yes. This place is gorgeous. God, I can't believe we're here. Vacation, Allie! This is going to be awesome!"

I can't help but grin a little at Jocko's enthusiasm. It's contagious. Summoning some inner strength, I get out of the shuttle and we walk up the ornate, white-tiled stairs where we're greeted by servers with a welcome glass of champagne.

"Don't mind if I do," Jocko says as he takes two glasses from the tray. "Let's get this party started."

"No, thanks," I wave him off. "It's just too early to get started," I say.

He gives me a funny look, but shrugs as we walk to the check-in counter.

"Where are our bags?" I ask.

"The porters get them for us. They'll bring them straight up to our room."

When we're called over to a desk, our attendant tells us with a smile that our room is unfortunately still being cleaned and will not be available until approximately three p.m.

"But I'm really tired, is there any way it could be sooner?" I ask.

He shakes his head. "I'm quite sorry. You are welcome to use all of the facilities we have available until that time. We have a pool, a spa, restaurants, the beach, a bar..."

"Thank you. We'll check back soon," Jocko says. He senses my distress and wraps his arm around me as we walk away from the desk. I have my head down. "Don't worry, Allie. It'll be O-"

I collide with someone so hard, it knocks the wind out of me, and when I look up, to my horror, I realize it's *Mark*.

We lock eyes, and both of us freeze up.

"Oh, excuse us," Jocko says politely, and his eyes smolder when he recognizes Mark, whom he's seen at work events over the past few years.

"Hey," Mark says, quietly.

"Hey," I manage to squeak out in reply.

The brunette next to him looks confused, sensing the tension between Mark and me.

I clear my throat. "Uh, Jocko, you know my ex, Mark. Mark, this is my *fiancé*, Jocko."

Mark's forehead wrinkles in surprise, and his eyes flit to the giant-ass ring on my finger. Well done, Great Grandmother Brewer.

Or whatever your maiden name was.

"Oh. I didn't know you got engaged," Mark comments.

I shrug, acting like it's no big deal. "We're not really trying to brag about it on social media, you know?" The words come out, a clear dig. I didn't mean for them to be so passive aggressive, but hey. I turn to the brunette. "Allie," I say, doing my best not to breathe fire.

"I'm Barbara," she smiles. "Nice to meet you. I've heard lots of good things."

I fumble for words. It's not exactly what I was expecting to hear from her.

Mark is good-looking, tall and thin. Barbara is of slight build, I hate to admit it, but she's definitely cute. Her bangs frame a symmetrical, smiling face.

"Nice to meet you, too," I manage to say.

"So how long have you been engaged?" she asks.

"Oh, a month," I blurt out. And even though it's a lie, I have to admit it feels kind of good to say it for some messed-up reason.

Jocko grins and interjects, wrapping his arm around me. "Yep. One month. And it's been a fun month, hasn't it, honey?" He wiggles his eyebrows, then winks — so slapstick it's almost like Will Ferrell in *Wedding Crashers.*

Mark and Barbara don't know what to make of Jocko's behavior. If anyone else acted so ridiculously you might suspect he was being a dick, but he pulls it off so naturally.

"Well, hun, we should probably get moved into our room. What do you say?" Mark says, pulling away from the conversation.

"You guys got checked into your room?"

"Yep! Everyone's so nice here," Barb says.

Jocko squeezes my shoulder, and we wave goodbye as they head to the elevator, keycards in hand.

"Let's get something to eat," Jocko takes my hand and guides me to the seafood restaurant outside.

I'm left stammering for an explanation as to why the two of them are being so cordial when all I want is to watch them get into a fight and one of them storm off down the beach.

LUCKILY, some delicious seafood stir fry, a margarita and a salty ocean breeze are able to calm my nerves while we wait for our room to become available. The resort is gigantic. There are a few different pools for swimming and relaxing, a hot tub, and at least three different bars outside, not even counting the swim-up bar. Then there is the picturesque sandy beach that touches the ocean, where the waves crash into the shore from the Caribbean coast. The resort employees move about with smiles in white button-down uniforms that make them look somehow both futuristic and anachronistic at the same time.

It's still before three when we finish lunch, so we get a couple of cocktails and lounge at one of the outdoor bars. The temperature is in the upper seventies and perfect shorts weather, but I've annoyingly still got my jeans on since my swimwear is in my suitcase. Jocko sports aviator sunglasses and a blue tank top, and there's no denying he looks as hot as any Instagram model right now.

"Yo, so, we need to talk about something," he says, leaning in.

My heart skips a quick beat. "Oh. About the fake engagement, you mean? I liked how you jumped right on the detail about us being engaged for a month. You're good at improv."

"I'm not worried about our backstory," Jocko says. "We've got great chemistry and I don't miss a word you say, so that won't be a problem."

"So what is it?"

He clenches his jaw and his eyes flicker in the radiating sun. "Why didn't you tell me your ex was going to be here, Allie?"

I shrug. "Oh, I didn't realize that was an important detail."

He snorts. "Bullshit. I saw how hard you froze up back there."

My body shivers a little, even though there's a warm breeze hitting me. "I didn't want to make a big deal out of him being here. I'm not trying to make him jealous or anything...if that's what you're thinking. But I just thought it would be awkward if I were the *only* single one here." I put my hand on his shoulder. "And I'm being serious when I say I *do* really appreciate you coming to this thing with me."

He scrubs a hand across his jaw. "Look, Allie. I like you, as a friend, if you don't know that by now. I've heard about your break-up, obviously, and it sucks to get your heart broken. But I don't appreciate you keeping that big detail from me. If we're doing this five-day deal, you've got to be open with me about everything. As your good friend, I'm a little disappointed you kept that from me."

"Good friends who'll be sleeping in the same bed," I mutter under my breath.

"Right," he says, leaning back. I take my hand off his shoulder. "You made sure we got a king-sized bed, right?"

"Double king. That's what I ordered."

"Perfect. I like to spread out. That way, we won't have to bump each other in the night."

My eyes drift out to the ocean, then come back to Jocko. "Are we crazy for doing this? Are we bad people?"

He shakes his head. "Why would we be bad people?"

"For faking it."

"Absolutely not. As long as we're honest with each other, that's what counts."

I lean forward, the breeze hitting me just right, my margarita buzz sets in, and a sense of belonging takes over. "Even before my relationship with Mark ended, we had some rocky years. I had this ball of tension in my stomach all the time. It never seemed to go away."

"And *that* is why I don't do relationships."

I scoff. "Because you're afraid of having a ball of tension in your stomach?"

"Yes. It's too much work to keep another person happy."

"If it's a good relationship, you're not worried about keeping them happy. You're happy apart, and you're even more happy together. That's all. It's natural, almost organic."

"I just don't want to worry about a family until I'm set, work-wise. I don't want to run into these situations like you and Mark had. I want to enjoy my life. And for me, that means being free to date who I want and do what I want."

"I see. Well, that's an interesting point of view you've got. I'm glad we have the sort of relationship where we can talk about these kinds of things. Actually, I was thinking about how the fact that we're *not* hooking up kind of makes these conversations less awkward. Like since we *know* nothing is going to happen between us on this trip, we can talk objectively about relationships. This will be therapeutic, I think."

He nods, and licks his lips before swigging down the last of his champagne. "Therapeutic. Right."

My heart flutters just a tad, though, thinking about his hand on my thigh earlier. That wasn't into hookup territory. But it was definitely into ambiguous attraction territory.

That was *something* he did. And it wasn't *nothing* I felt.

Yet neither of us seems to want to acknowledge that *something* verbally.

"Question though," he says. "What if we have to kiss? We'll have to. At least once."

"We could kiss. Sure. No problem."

One of his eyebrows lifts. "Oh? So you don't have a problem if I kiss you right now?"

I can't tell if he's baiting me, or messing with me, or what is going on.

When he leans forward to kiss me, I'm not ready for it. I'm scared, and I have only kissed one man since Mark and I broke up. And I was very drunk on New Year's Eve, so that didn't even really count.

When he leans forward, I pull back like I'm a nun, opting instead to turn my cheek.

Something coils in my stomach instantly, and I regret having shut him down. My whole heart wants to kiss him. But my mind blocks me from thinking this is a good idea. Maybe it's some silly H.R. video I watched about the *consequences of hooking up with a colleague* that is lodged in the back of my subconscious. Perhaps I don't want to be the next *Becky from Marketing* — who Jocko seems to intentionally avoid at company parties now. We've got a great working relationship. And as odd as this faux arrangement is, with a ring on my finger and sleeping in the same room, we can't cross this line.

"Sorry," I whisper softly, but to my horror, the sound of my voice is drowned out by another, much deeper voice.

"Well, holy shit, if it isn't the goddamn queen of Fleeker dorm! Allie fucking Jenkins, how the hell are ya!"

Peyton O'Rourke has always had this deep, booming voice. I'm instantly brought back to freshmen year where I had the luck of rooming in the women's hall adjacent to him. My freshmen year roommate was one of his girlfriends. After he found out his lady was cheating on him, he went on a bit of a sex binge.

However, the smile on his face as he strolls up to me with his wife-to-be Maddy is nothing like I've ever seen.

I get off my bar stool and give him a hug. "Peyton! So good to see you! And Maddy, nice to meet you again!"

I hug Maddy, too. Maddy and I have met in passing this past year at a couple of reunion meetups between our friends in Detroit, and once when I had to swing though Texas for a work trip. Peyton, despite his superstardom as an NFL quarterback, retains his down-to-Earth demeanor. It's why he's a good friend, and it's why I couldn't miss his wedding. She's got the bride-glow that happy women seem to get before their wedding. And hell, if I were her, I'd be pretty happy, too, to be marrying one of the (former) most sought after bachelors in America.

I introduce Jocko to them as my *date*, feeling weird all of a sudden for some reason using the word *fiancé* in front of my friends. It feels more fake than I'm comfortable with. And I hate telling a lie to the bride and groom.

Peyton recognizes Jocko from a party they met at last summer, and they exchange a few pleasantries about the event. Then Maddy and Jocko hit it off chatting about something, and Peyton waves me to the side of the bar a few seats down, out of their earshot. He calls for another couple of drinks for us.

"You alright?"

"Fine," I smile. "I mean, the breakup was a little rough. But I'll be fine."

He eyes my ring finger. "Since when did you get *engaged*? I didn't hear anything about this."

"Oh, it was quick. Just happened recently. I'm stoked, though." The words come out, but even I have to admit they sound less convincing with Peyton than they did with Mark. I'm a horrible liar, and I feel bad about having to voice these untruths to Peyton.

"Really?" Peyton says, and then turns to me with those piercing grey eyes. "Because I just saw you pull away from your *fiancé* when he tried to kiss you. What's up with that?"

"You saw that? Oh, well, he just...said a weird joke I didn't like."

"A joke." Peyton purses his lips. Chills run down my spine. "Look, if things aren't going well with this guy, you just let me know. You really jumped into something quickly after the breakup."

"Well, so did Mark."

Peyton nods. "The tragedies of life. I had some long chats with Mark about you."

"You did?"

"Yeah. If you want me to tell you all about it, we can talk about them at some point."

"That sounds good. And for real, Peyton, don't worry about me. Jocko is great. He is. No need for you to get all protective of me like you were freshmen year."

He smirks and sips his cocktail. Peyton is like an overly

protective brother. Freshmen year, he made it his personal mission to vet all the guys who wanted to date me.

Lightly, he pushes his knuckles into my shoulder. "Just know, I've got your back."

"Stop worrying about me. This week is about you and Maddy. That's it. We're all here for you."

"Aw, stop. It's a celebration for all of our friends. I just want everyone to have a good time."

Before we can continue the conversation, Maddy and Jocko walk over to us, and Maddy lightly touches Peyton's chin to point it toward her, then plants a big kiss on his lips.

"Just because I can," she whispers, looking into his eyes.

They stare at us for a few moments, like they're waiting for us to do the same.

"Well, we better get going up to our room!" I say. "Almost three o'clock. And we desperately need a nap."

"Right. A *nap,*" Maddy winks, then giggles. "Great to see you, Allie. And nice to see you again too, Jocko. Maybe we'll hang after your nap. No official events planned tonight, but we'll all be mulling around the resort. But don't forget the cocktail hour tomorrow."

Even though it's a quarter to three, our room is mercifully ready. We head up to the room, and I can practically feel my body relaxing as I look at our bed, perfectly made. The white walls in the room are bright, and I drop my things off to the side and head out on the balcony immediately.

"What a view!" I exclaim. It looks out over the resort next door, which has three adjacent pools. The ocean is a beautiful deep sea blue-green color.

When I spin around. Jocko is staring at the bed. "Yeah, uh, we've got a problem."

"What problem?"

"This is a queen size. I thought you said the room had a double king?"

I approach the bed, and he's right. "But I *ordered* a double king size. This isn't right."

"It's okay," he says. "I'm fine with it if you are."

"I'm so tired right now, I just need to pass out."

"Same. We'll deal with this later. Leave that balcony door open. The breeze feels amazing."

Jocko goes to the bathroom, which leads me to glance in the general direction of the shower and sink area, and I realize something: the shower is clear glass, except for a blue swirly design right where one's lower private parts would appear — depending on one's height. My girls would be on full display in that shower.

A rock forms in my stomach. That is *not* a variable I was planning on. I have enough trouble as it is covering up my attraction to Jocko. I don't know what thoughts would enter my head if I'm in the room and he's naked on the other side of the glass.

Then, to make matters worse, I hear the water in the shower start. Jocko throws on some music with his cell phone, and nonchalantly starts singing in the shower. And I can see *everything.*

Well, by *everything,* I mean the lower V of his abs, and all the way up to his upper thighs. The rest of his body is blurred by the little strip of non-see-through glass.

As he spins around and lets out a loud groan, it's notable that he's clearly enjoying the hot water running over his sudsy body. Tingles run along my spine, finally landing in between my legs.

Fuck this guy. Seriously.

I pretend like I'm slowly disrobing for my nap, which I guess I am. But I'm also caught in a trance, my eyes drawn toward him like a magnet. There is no denying that Jocko is visually sexy as hell. The deep ridges of his abs are still etched into my imagination from the pool party. I seem to have forgotten how perfectly his obliques pop out against his hips, though. The glass steams up, but I can still spot the tattoo on his arm as he threads his hands through his hair. With his arms lifted, he reveals the subtle arrow on his left tricep.

I lick my lips, then turn around.

Must not get caught staring.

I stare out the window like I care about something out there as I take my tank top off. I'm lucky I turn around when I do because as I'm shimmying out of my skinny jeans, the shower shuts off.

The jeans give me a little trouble as I try to slide out of them, and I pause for a moment, my waistband not quite over the curve of my butt yet.

Did my ass get bigger or something? I wiggle some more, glance in the mirror on the side of the room, and get them down to my thighs so I'm finally able to slide them off.

"Doing okay there?" Jocko's voice booms behind me, and my stomach churns.

Oh, boy. That means Jocko just saw me...checking out my own ass in the mirror with just my lace panties on.

"Yeah, fine. Just wanted to get into my shorts to take a nap," I play it off, then turn to him as I pull on Texas U short shorts over my panties.

"Hey, It's okay. I check out my ass, too," he winks. He removes his towel, and for a split second, I brace myself.

Holy shit. He's about to get naked. This is the big reveal.

But then, the white towel comes off his hips to reveal that he's wearing grey briefs underneath.

Not what I was expecting, but I still do my damndest not to stare.

"And for the record, I think yours *has* gotten bigger," he adds, toweling off his hair almost like a dog, then jumping into bed, on top of the covers.

"Why are you commenting on my ass?" I ask, surprising my own self at the slightly bitchy tone my question takes.

With his arms behind his head, he laughs, the comment seeming to brush off him. "Oh, come on, Allie. We've been working out together for the past seven weeks. How am I *not* supposed to notice? I'm a man, after all. I saw you struggling to get out of those jeans. Your ass looks terrific in them, by the way."

"Does it?" I say, and I have to admit the physical compliment gives me a bump of confidence. I slide an oversized t-shirt on, and slip off my bra. "I can't believe you saw that. *And* I can't believe these showers are see-through. Well, except for the crotch area."

"I think it's kind of hot, actually," he says in a deep, gravelly voice.

I sink into the bed next to him, and my leg accidentally touches his because he's right — a queen mattress is too small for a guy like Jocko and a girl like me. I'm not as tall as him — at six feet and some inches — but I'm not so tiny either.

We both recoil a little at the touch of our flesh. I think we both know it's wrong. But I wish it was right.

My body heats again from even that slight brush of our flesh. I steal another glance at his torso. He's all arched backward on the bed with his arms behind him and his ribs out and that goddamn sexy *V* that leads to the bulge hiding — not very well, mind you — underneath his grey cotton briefs.

With the way his arm wraps around his head, I see his tattoo again on his muscular upper arm.

"Hey, what's the meaning of your tattoo?" I ask.

Jocko shrugs. "Just something silly I got with a few of my basketball teammates in college. It's an arrow, signifying forward motion. I don't believe in dwelling on the past."

"Oh."

Jocko's eyes linger on mine for a moment before he closes them. I'm so used to Jocko joking about everything, it catches me by surprise that he gives me a straightforward answer about his tattoo. Maybe his sleepiness is bringing out his serious side.

Even though it's sort of a corny reason to get a tattoo, it strikes a chord with me. I've been dwelling on my failed relationship for how long now?

Butterflies flutter in my stomach, and I wonder if Jocko has more depth than most people give him credit for. Maybe, even though it seems totally natural, he actually does put thought into maintaining the effortlessly happy-go-lucky aura of charm that surrounds him everywhere he goes.

I decide that if he's going to sleep on top of the covers, I'll do the sensible thing and get under, at least the top sheet, to keep some separation between us. Because even though I've always considered him attractive, now I feel myself drawn to him in on an even deeper level.

There's a palpable tension in the air as we lie next to each other, less than six inches away and separated only by cloth.

"How long do you think you'll sleep for?" he asks with his eyes still closed, his voice low and groggy.

"Not sure. I'm pretty fried though. At least three hours," I say.

"Sounds like a plan. And then we can get up and have dinner tonight."

"I like it. Sleep tight, Jay."

"Thanks. You, too."

I close my eyes and feign sleep for about fifteen minutes.

No, actually, I *try* to sleep, but I can't because my heart is beating a mile a minute. As he's trying to fade into dream state, he involuntarily breathes these incredibly sexy, deep throaty growls.

I use all my power not to slide my hand down my stomach and between my legs.

Until I hear him fast asleep, breathing deeply.

I can't deny myself all week, can I?

I slide two fingers down onto my clit, and I'm as wet as the Caribbean Sea. Jocko lets out a low moan and I flinch, opening my eyes. I swear I see his cock twitch. Huh. Never saw that when I was living with Mark.

Ugh. With all of my resolve, I put my hand firmly at my side, then slide a pillow between my knees and turn over on my side.

I have a pretty good feeling what I'll be dreaming about during this nap.

8

JOCKO

In the late afternoon, I flutter my eyes open from a deep, pleasing slumber. Golden light from the sunset seeps into our room, illuminating Allie as she sleeps so peacefully.

I take a deep breath, look down, and realize I have a full boner.

"Jesus Christ," I mutter quietly, coming out of my deep sleep stupor. I was having one of those intense dreams where you know it was crazy as hell, but you don't remember a damn thing about it. Judging by the rocket ship I'm currently sporting between my legs, I wonder if the dream was of a sexual nature.

As I fully come to consciousness, I stare over at Allie. The sheet fell off her in her sleep. Her little shorts that say U Texas on the ass ride up her legs, giving me a full view of the limbs I saw earlier.

Yes, I stole a glance when I got out of the shower earlier as she was trying to wiggle out of her jeans. So sue me. If you were staying with a girl you had had a crush on for three years, but whom you told yourself was off limits, and suddenly you got the chance to sneak a peek at her...what would you do?

Plus, she was taking her *time* getting out of those jeans. I have my suspicions that she timed her disrobing session just so she would flash me as I was coming out of the shower. She heard it turn off. She knew what she was doing...right?

I sit up in bed and collect myself. Allie is confusing to me. First, she puts her hand on top of mine when I touch her leg — and that was an *accidental* touch on my part. For a moment, I actually thought we were a couple. Clear acceptance of my advance.

But when I go to kiss her — *bam* — she pulls away like I'm infected with the measles.

What is this girl's deal, turning me down like that?

I wanted to kiss her so badly. But I get it, the deal was platonic so if and when we get to that point could take time. I'm not mad, just ready because it's like the elephant in the room.

I stand up and look down again. She breathes softly with her cheek against the pillow. She's gorgeous. *Fuck me,* she's *beyond* gorgeous.

The fact that I know her so well, and have an idea of what's behind those eyes makes her even sexier to me.

At the same time, seeing her in this new light...in bed, taking her clothes off...I'll be damned if I don't want to put *work friend* Allie in a box, and let *sex kitten* Allie out to play during this trip.

I swear I saw her checking me out when I was toweling myself off post-shower. But *the kiss pull away*...that doesn't make sense at all.

When I stand up, I'm still at full mast and I realize this is not the way I want to go to dinner tonight. I've got my stylish white Tommy Bahama pants all picked out, and yes, they make me look good but they're shit when it comes to hiding a full-fledged Woodrow Wilson between my legs.

This calls for action. Stat. The sun is setting, and judging by the clock, we've been sleeping for almost four hours. Which means she'll probably wake up soon.

Pulling off my briefs, I steal into the shower and turn on the water. With hot water this time, unlike the cold shower I tried to take earlier to douse my desire.

I let the warm water splay down my back, and that's when I realize: I can *watch* her while I work on my masters degree right now.

My cock could *not* get any harder as I fist it with my right hand, holding the base with my left. I close my eyes for a few moments, because this feels too wrong, like I'm taking advantage of Allie if I look at her while I'm pumping my cock.

So I close my eyes and think about a girl I used to date months ago. But as quickly as she comes into the fantasy, Allie appears and pushes her out.

I'm serious. She literally *pushes* the other girl out.

"Hey, Jocko, what are you doing?"

"You caught me," I groan, fisting my cock in the shower.

Of course, I don't do this *out loud*. No way I'm taking a chance on waking her up.

"I did," she says. "Now what are you going to do about it?"

"Allie...we can't do this. I like you. I like like you."

"Oh, how sweet. You like like me." She giggles. "Are we in sixth grade?"

I grab her and spin her around. "You know what I mean. I'm bad with words when I'm really into someone."

She grins, then runs her hand down my abs until it reaches my cock. "Mmm. I've thought about this since the first day I started working here. I've always wanted to do this."

Yes, you have, Allie. Yes, you have.

I pump my cock back and forth with both hands now. Fuck, I'm close.

I open my eyes and stare at her. Fuck it. She's so damn hot and she's what I want. I want to do her in all the ways. I want to fuck her mouth then spin her around, press her up against this glass window like we're in our own version of the movie *Titanic,* and fuck her silly until she understands just how into her I am. Just how *in her* I am.

I close my eyes again and return to fantasy land. Her name even escapes me in a low growl. "Fuck yes, Allie," I mutter, then shut my mouth quickly.

The dual fantasy and reality of it all is too much to handle. She's eight feet away from me, sleeping and letting out those cute little moan-breaths, and here I am, pumping my thick, hard length to the thought of pressing my cock deep and up and inside her as she clenches around me.

Then, a ball of anxiety whirls inside me when I hear her voice.

Her *actual* voice. "Jocko? You showering again?"

I open my eyes and she's not in the bed anymore, where I was staring. Instead, she is near the sink just outside the glass shower door, which *thank God* is all steamed up.

I lose myself at hearing her voice. The first time I met her, of all things, it was her damn *voice* I found the sexiest. Great because we have a ton of work conference calls together. Not great because right now, hearing those vibrations pushes me over the edge.

My lower abs tense and my balls tingle and I throw my head back as the feeling of my orgasm rocks through me, and I ejaculate all over the glass wall.

Luckily, she's standing on the other side of the shower, so there's no way she can see what I just did.

I direct the shower head toward my juices and clean them off my body and the wall.

I'm still a little lightheaded as I yank the shower door open.

"Yeah," I mumble. "Showered again. Just felt a little grimy after that nap. Had the nap sweats."

She's wearing a robe, looking hot as hell, and I realize she's *naked* under that cotton cloth.

My dick, which is post-orgasm and not totally soft yet, twitches.

I realize her jaw is wide open and she shoots me a dazed look.

"How'd you sleep?" I ask as I step out of the shower. I'm pretty sure my blood flow is still being taken over by my penis.

"Pants," she murmurs.

"Pants? What's that got to do with how you slept?" I put my hands on my hips. "Oh, you wish you slept in pants? Huh. I thought it was pretty hot in here even just in briefs and sleeping on top of the covers."

She clears her throat. "You don't have any pants on, Jocko," she says loudly, and a little awkwardly.

I glance down, and go cross-eyed. Instantly, I throw a hand in front of my junk. But it does little to cover up the fact that she just got a full-on Magic Mike with Benefits show for a solid fifteen seconds.

"Oh. *Those* pants. I'm so sorry. I didn't even realize," I say. "My bad."

"Fine, it's fine," she says, not making eye contact with me. "It was bound to happen at some point. You saw my butt. I saw your business. Quid pro quo."

I grab a white towel and wrap it around my waist. "It wasn't an even trade, though. I didn't see your naked butt. I only saw your ass under your black lace panties. You just got the full Monty from me."

"And you've got an eye for detail." She shrugs. "Or maybe since you've been my trainer in the gym this spring, you sort of have a stake in my ass."

As soon as she completes her sentence, she throws her hand over her mouth. "Oh my gosh. Well, that came out a little wrong-sounding."

I throw my head back in laughter. "Ah, Allie-face. You kill me. So, uh, how about you get ready and then we'll head out to dinner?"

"That's the plan," she says, red-faced.

She slips into the shower, then sticks a hand out to put her robe on the nearest hook. I head over to the other side of the room and put my clothes on.

As I do, I can see a steamy version of Allie Jenkins through the glass. She's totally naked, and she's totally hot as she suds herself up.

I steal a surreptitious glance at the shower. How can I not? The way the glass blurs in the middle, I can see her smooth, wet thighs almost up to her butt. Then, her middle blurs for a little while. But through the foggy glass I can make out the outline of her breasts as she runs her hands over them.

Jesus, that's hot.

My cock twitches again, and I realize my plan to relieve the tension has failed miserably.

In fact, I might be even more tense than before.

When she steps out of the shower in a robe with her hair all wet, I realize this may end up being the hardest five days of my life. In more ways than just one.

~

"So how do I look?" Allie says cheerfully, doing a spin for me in the room just before we head out. She's got a white and blue wrap dress on and she looks so hot in it that all I can think about is how she would look *out* of it.

"You look, uh, pretty, pretty, pretty good," I say, sounding like Larry David from *Curb Your Enthusiasm.*

She lights up. "You think so?"

I clench a hand behind my back. I have to fight not to *stare* at her the whole time I'm with her. Mark must have been an asshat if she's this insecure about her appearance when it's totally unwarranted.

If we weren't coworkers, I would be pressing her up against the nearest wall — which right now happens to be the outside of the shower glass — kissing her, stripping that thing off her, and calling room service so we can have dinner in bed and I can give her a night of pleasure she'll never forget.

Instead, I reciprocate, doing a little spin myself. I've got on white pants, white shoes, and a fancy white short-sleeve button down.

"You look like a villain from a James Bond movie," she giggles.

"You've seen those movies? Jesus. This is why you're the coolest chick ever."

She nods and opens the door for us to head to dinner. "Peyton used to make me watch them freshmen year. And I went as a 'Bond Girl' for Halloween that year."

I don't even comment on that, because what am I going to say to her?

Tell her how every other little detail I'm learning about her makes me wish we could be much more than friends?

I've thought about it, and I decide to take the sincere route. I'm not trying to put one over on her.

"Hey, wait one second," I say, and push the door closed. "We still need to talk about something."

Her face flushes. "What's that?"

"The kiss earlier. The way you gave me your cheek."

"Sorry. I just wasn't ready. And I was tired."

"I get that. And you don't have to be sorry to preserve my self-esteem or anything."

"Well, I'm glad I didn't shatter your confidence," she jokes.

"Oh, I think we both know that's impossible," I grin. "But look, I'm your date. Logically, everyone thinks you're my fiancée. I'm not saying we have to make out hardcore or something. But we should be able to give each other a peck on the cheek. Or maybe the lips."

"But, Jay, I'm worried..."

"Worried about what?"

She shakes her head. "I mean, nothing. It's just, we're friends...who are kissing. That's all. And I've only kissed one guy since Mark. I'm nervous, I guess."

"It makes total sense that you would be nervous. It's my fault. I shouldn't have kissed you without making sure you were ready."

"Yeah. The timing was a little awkward. But you're right — we'll have to kiss a couple times in public."

"Right," I nod. "I think we should practice."

"Right now?"

"Your friends are going to be around tonight, right? So if there's a wedding toast or whatever, we'll be ready."

She blows out a loud exhale. "Okay. Fine. You're right. Let's do it." She closes her eyes and braces herself. I laugh.

"I'm not kissing you like that."

"Oh, come on. I'm ready."

I take her hand and lead her over to the balcony. It's

beautiful out here. The sun has just set, and the afterglow colors are setting in: what's left of the blue sky plus a mix of violet, pink, orange, and red.

I lean her against the balcony, and put her hands on my shoulders. "Why are you so nervous around me?"

I can practically feel her body shaking. "It's not just you. I honestly haven't ever had to get out and *date* or whatever it is that people do. I was with Mark since college. For better or worse I got comfortable with him, and I just assumed we would get married. I'm not good at meeting guys. And it's even worse when we have to cross that line of becoming physical. The one guy I kissed since Mark was at a New Year's Eve concert at midnight, and as soon as we kissed I ran out of the bar, called a cab, and went home without saying a word."

I burst out laughing. "You did not do that! Poor guy. You probably broke his heart."

"I just didn't want him expecting something if we kissed."

"Expecting what?"

She pauses, then further clarifies, "Expecting that I would go down on him or have sex with him or something? I don't know."

"I see." I put my hands on her hips. *Fuck, her hips.* Our bodies hover an inch from each other. "Allie, not sure if you know this, but I'll say it out loud just to make sure. You're a good friend. We've known each other three years. You're not some throwaway girl I'm trying to bring home for a one-night stand from the bar. If we kiss, that doesn't mean anything but what it means — we're kissing. I'm serious when I say we shouldn't hook up this trip. A kiss is one thing, but I know that more than that could come with baggage. And as for my expectations — I have zero. I'm just looking forward to having an amazing time with you while we're here."

She nods, and I visibly see her body release tension, her shoulders lowering. "Holy shit. It feels so great to hear you reinforce that. I'm just a little confused right now. This queen-size bed, the shower situation, having to kiss you... but knowing that there aren't any expectations makes me so much more comfortable."

"I heard what Peyton said when he pulled you aside," I admit. "He noticed your pull back."

"Yes, he did. And he was suspicious."

"Yeah. So let's just have some fun with this. And, maybe this is the dark side of me speaking, but..." I lean into her ear and whisper. "If we happen to make Mark a little jealous, so be it. Even if we're just playing pretend. Can you do that?"

She nods, smiles faintly, and sniffles a little bit. "Thanks," she whispers, and she wipes a tear that falls onto her cheek before it can mess up her makeup.

I grin, tip her chin up toward me, and stare into her eyes. "By the way, you don't look 'pretty good' tonight. You look sexy as fuck. If you don't mind me saying so."

"I don't mind." Her grin broadens, and I move in.

This time, she eagerly accepts my lips on hers. She even wraps her hand around my head and pulls me in toward her.

I do a countdown in my brain....

One Mississippi. Two Mississippi. Three Mississippi.

How long is a practice kiss supposed to last?

I wouldn't know, because I've never done a practice kiss before. Every kiss I've ever given has been completely intentional.

She moans a little into my mouth, and the next thing I

know, I'm pressing her into the balcony railing with my hips, gripping the small of her back, and we're way past ten Mississippi's.

I wouldn't mind going all the way to one hundred, to be honest.

But with all of my willpower, I somehow managed to pull away, and we're both left staring into each other's eyes, breathless.

"Good...practice," she says seemingly unaffected, but is she? I stare deeper into her eyes, looking for an answer, but I'm left perplexed.

"Yeah. Practice," I echo.

"Time for dinner."

I nod, and she goes around me, back into the room. With her hand on the doorknob, she turns to look at me.

"Jocko? You coming?"

"Yes," I nod. "Coming."

And meanwhile, I know the food here is delicious, but damn if I don't wish there was something else on the menu tonight.

9

ALLIE

After dinner, we have a few cocktails with the group and I feel like I'm slowly coming back to life, finally recovering from the early-morning flight with a little jetlag thrown in and from Jocko. We meet up with everyone at the bar, and everyone is relaxing, catching up on things similar to a class reunion gathering. After a couple of hours or so, all of the couples make plans to head down to the jacuzzi which is open twenty-four hours.

Great, Jocko in all of his glory, like I haven't seen enough of that. Not that I'm complaining, but I am because it's hands off, don't touch. It has to be for a lot of reasons, but good Lord he's so tempting. That 'practice kiss' will be forever etched into my being. Never in my life have I been kissed like that by someone. In my mind, I justify that Jocko probably has a lot of experience kissing girls, and he's just a good kisser, in general. He's flirtatious and a player, so of course he'd kiss like a pro.

It can't be just me, though.

After we run up to the room to change into our suits, we

meet up with Peyton and Maddy, whom I really adore, to walk down to the pool and jacuzzi area. As if I haven't been tortured enough by Jocko today, he nonchalantly walks in front of me, chatting with Peyton. They have to be two of the best-looking guys on the planet. Even in just the dim glimmer of the nighttime lights from the resort as they walk in their swim trunks, it's evident that both of them have rippling muscles in all the right places.

As Maddy rolls behind me, chatting with another NFL football player's wife, I wonder how I'm going to get through these five days now, even more so after that practice kiss on the balcony.

The funny thing is, it wasn't necessarily the kiss itself that warmed me up hotter than I'd ever been. It was the things Jocko said, about how he's just looking forward to spending some time with me with zero expectations. His words were heartfelt and sincere. And as corny as it was, I needed to hear them. From him. Since he's so hard to read most of the time, when he gave me that compliment it resonated deep down in me.

Dinner was torture for me. Jocko and I made small talk with the other guests at the table, and I couldn't stop picturing him naked as I'd seen him exiting the shower.

Dear God in heaven, lead me not into temptation.

We keep walking, and I shudder as the sound of the jacuzzi jets near.

No. We will not *be doing* anything *of the sort, Allie.* My inner logic pipes up. Jocko made it clear the kiss was for *practice*, and that he would be *respecting your boundaries.*

But what if just this once, I don't want my boundaries respected? I argue back. *What if I want to be led into temptation...would that be so bad?*

This *is* Temptation Isle, after all.

Jocko cracks a joke and smacks Peyton on the shoulder. The man is not intimidated by anyone. He's not even a little starstruck, hanging out with the top quarterback in the NFL and a bunch of other professional players? He's fitting right in with my friends, almost annoyingly well.

At least a dozen wedding guests are already in the jacuzzi. Drinks flow, music plays and voices buzz loudly. A warm breeze blows up from the ocean, which is just below from where we are.

I dip my legs into the giant jacuzzi and catch a glimpse of Jocko in the moonlight. His tattoo looks extra sexy, and his normal light colored hair looks dark, slicked back and wet from the water.

All I can think about is how fantastic it felt having those big arms wrapped around me, those nimble fingers slipping onto my back, while I grabbed a fistful of his hair and pressed his mouth into mine. If even for just a moment, I felt like we were more than just coworkers, and that we might strip down right there.

Thankfully, his *reason* kicked in and we made it out of there with no scars.

We might be in Cancún, far away from the office, but I think about my amazing job and how far I've come and how I really would like to keep things non-awkward back home.

And really, can people really do that? The whole 'what happens-somewhere-stays-there' attitude is just something silly people say to comfort themselves. Just because you change the name of the location, I'm not so sure feelings don't get hurt and things *do* change. For me they would, anyway.

"Heyyy!" someone says loudly, a little too nicely.

Speaking of awkward.

Mark's fiancée Barbara appears next to me with a drink in one hand and a big smile on her face. Tipsy much?

"Oh, hi, Barbara," I say, forcing a grin. "How's it going?"

"Oh, you can call me Barb. And it's great! Beautiful night. How about you?"

"I can't complain." Suddenly I feel the need to touch my neck with my left hand, because the ring Jocko has let me use challenges *Barb's* bauble. Mark did well, but Jocko's great-grandma — even better.

"You're empty-handed," she says. "Here, take a beer. I grabbed extra from our fridge."

Gah, she's aloof, totally missing my ring flash. "Thanks," I say, taking the *Cerveza Sol* from her hand and unscrewing the top. I take a nice healthy swig.

"So, I just wanted to say..." she begins, and I brace myself.

"I know you're Mark's ex and all. He told me about you. He had good things to say about you. I just wanted to reach out and talk and make sure things weren't, you know, awkward for the week."

"Pssh," I wave an arm in the air. The left one, with the sparkling reminder, for her and me. "Why would they be awkward? We're all adults. We can be mature."

Just then, Jocko gets up and lets out a big *WOOOOO* and a few of the guys around him chuckle, totally disproving my point about maturity. I guess I'll never fully get why guys do some things.

I purse my lips. "Well, most of us."

"I've had hard breakups, too. It sucks. But obviously something good can come of it. And I'm so happy you've moved on, too. I know it's probably weird, but Mark and I just connected on another level, and it happened so fast.

Nice ring, by the way," she says, touching my hand. "Is that a legacy?"

Finally — I wasn't sure what other 'subtle' moves I could have made. I nod, saying, "Jocko's great grandmother's. It means a lot to their family, and me — I was just stunned when he gave it to me..." Ha! If she only knew. "I mean, not that I didn't think, you know, that, well...that he'd give me something so special." Oh my. Way to go and slay that conversation. Jeez.

"Wow. You two must really be in love."

Just then, I see Mark coming down the path to the hot tub. "Oh, there's my man...catch ya later," Barb says, wading over to Mark. She kisses him before he gets in, then once he's in she sits on his lap and they make out some more.

"Disgusting," I mutter, crossing my arms. I hate feeling like a stick in the mud, but I can't help it seeing the two of them. As much as I try to convince myself I'm okay with him moving on...the truth is, I'm not.

I feel a poke on my right side and I jump a little.

"Hey, hun," Jocko grins. "You having a good time?"

"Total ball," I say, finishing off the rest of my *Sol.*

Jocko puts his hand on my cheek gently, then glances over at Barb and Mark. "Don't lie to me. Be straight. I noticed you two talking."

It amazes me how Jocko can go from bro-ing out and yelling like a heathen, to reading my emotions and being sincere with me.

"Honestly? I'm hurting right now. It's so visible. And it doesn't feel good."

He looks at me, takes a swig of his beer, then looks out into the distance. The moonlight reflects off his dark eyes. God, those *eyelashes.*

Putting his hand on the back of my neck, he tips his forehead into me.

"Stop thinking so hard and kiss me."

"But I-"

"Just do it," he says, his words a low and throaty order.

Everything happens so quickly, Jocko knows not to give me a moment to think, and suddenly I do as he says and let myself go. A surge of heat rips through me as I lean into him and kiss him softly in the moonlight, hearing the waves crashing behind us on the shore. My hand has a mind of its own, and it slides into the water and caresses his chest and abs. But I've got enough sense to stop before I get too low.

After a minute, we pull apart. "Thanks," I say softly. I needed that in more ways than one, and I'm wondering how he knew that, how he picked up on that? I guess I've never really seen this side of him... or have I?

He's always been supportive at EdTechX, thinking of me as he maneuvers his deals to make sure I'm available to work with him. Checking on me when I'm working late in the office, even walking me out to the car when it's nighttime to make sure, as he puts it, 'no one gets me.'

Maybe this is part of that — looking out for me in another sort of way?

Ack, quit thinking!

His mouth curves up in that patented troublemaker's smirk. "I'm just grateful I get to be here with you. Your friends are really cool, Allie. Thanks for the invitation. And for going along with my crazy plan."

"You fit in so easily with them. You're having a great time." He does, I mean, if this were real, Jocko would be perfect.

"Are you having a great time?"

I nod. "Oh, yes. Good time down here." In my peripheral

vision, I can see Mark and Barb going at each other like no one's watching.

He laughs. "You're the worst liar ever. C'mon. Let's go to bed."

My eyes widen, and Jocko must see the expression written on my face.

"Like sleep. Obviously. Sleep time."

"Right." Of course. *Sigh.* I'm totally ready to leave. As we climb out of the pool, Jocko reaches for my hands to pull me up and I stumble into his chest. He grins as he steadies me, gathering my hand touching his lips to my wrist — a swoon-worthy move that I feel down to my toes. The whole scene was so natural for him, like we really meant something more to one another.

Glancing back down the jacuzzi, I see the slobberfest is still on, and although it stings a bit to be here to witness it all, I know one thing's for sure, I've had enough of the Mark and Barb show to last me a lifetime.

THE WALK back to the room is uneventful. We chat lightly about the trip, the sites to see and so on. They left us more free time on this trip than I anticipated. Back in the room, we turn our backs to change into our PJs, and of course, he sleeps shirtless, even at night. This time, I sleep in a big shirt with just panties.

I consider going no panties, which is my preferred sleep state, but I figure that will just send a very wrong message to this already precarious friendship which we've built up here.

It's all very *I Love Lucy* when he turns off the lights and hops between the covers, and I don't fall asleep immediately.

I'm still feeling vulnerable. This whole trip has upset me more than I expected and seeing Mark, in love, really hurts. I realize now what we had never looked like what he's sharing with Barb.

"Hey, Jay," I say. "You still awake?"

"Yeah." He spins around to face me on his side.

"Would it be weird if I asked you to hold me?"

He laughs. "It's only weird if we make it weird. I'd say that's fine."

"You are literally the best. Thank you so much." I hate being this needy, I'm not usually that way, but Jocko seems to be more of a comfort than I ever expected.

Don't get me wrong, he's sexy hot and tempting as hell, but I don't think he sees me like that. We've been working together, we've been friends now for a while, and he seems to be able to calm my inner self, who seems to think I'm a loser.

I spin around, and wiggle my body into him. God, he feels amazing. His abs press up against my back. His arm wraps around my side, and his chin touches my shoulder. His...

Dear God in heaven, is that him touching my ass?

So nix that he doesn't think of me that way because the hardness that is nudging me in my rear definitely has interest. Though guys can ramp it up for most anything, so maybe I shouldn't think so highly of myself. Could just be a glitch. Like when he was dozing off for his nap earlier and I saw him twitch.

Ugh, inner Allie can be annoying as heck.

After a few deep breaths, I settle in. I requested him to cuddle me so this is just something I'm going to have to deal with.

He's a man, and men have cocks, Allie!

And Jocko's big kahuna just happens to be sandwiched — through his briefs, thank God — up against my ass, protected only by two thin layers of cotton.

"'Night, Allie," he whispers, apparently not sensing my panic at all. "Sweet dreams."

He kisses my neck, and goosebumps erupt across every inch of my skin. Obviously, he's not having the same conversation in his head that I am.

He's just...kissing me goodnight.

Like a good, fake fiancé should.

All I can think of is, *who is this man lying next to me, and what have they done with Jocko?*

The Jocko I know is overly cocky, crushes deals, crushes dating, and his motto with women is *never be the first or the last.*

Who is this imposter?

And why do I like him even more now?

The guy is not what I expected him to be at all, and I'm finding that I want more. What I have to figure out first is if this Jocko is the real one because if he is, he's been hiding from me. His body warms mine as I drift off to dreamland, and I'm grateful for whatever he's doing with me. Because it's been a long winter spent alone and I need this.

DAY 2

10

ALLIE

"I booked us a couple's massage for today," Jocko says with a big grin when we get back from breakfast. "You're too damn tense, and I think it'll do your body some good."

It's not the first time he's suggested a massage. After our workouts at the gym these last months, he's always been a proponent of having someone work out the kinks — just never as a 'couple'. I smile and run my hand through his hair, playing along with our charade. "Honey! You're such a sweetheart."

"I know. You can thank me later," he says with a wink.

For some reason, I read into what he says with a sexual connotation and lower my voice, not that anyone's around us to overhear, though it pays to be careful. "What's that supposed to mean?"

"Uh, you know, like help me close more of those deals?"

"Oh. Ohhh. Damn, I almost forgot we work together for a minute," I laugh. Back to reality.

"Allie," he laughs. "You kill me. What did you think I

meant?" Though the look on his face is equally as confused as the one I'm feeling.

"Oh. That's what I was thinking, too," I lie.

After an hour of lounging by the pool and reading, stacking up the sun and yes we enjoy a drink or two at the swim-up bar, we head up to the spa. They check us in, and I head through the women's locker room and Jocko in the direction of the men's. We meet on the other side. His massage therapist's name is Lila. Mine is Federico.

They lead us to our 'couples' room and the smell is relaxing, this pineappley scent combined with jasmine.

We don't say too much during the hour session, but I do a lot of grunting. Federico is a little tough on my muscles.

"Um, is this like a deep tissue massage?" I ask him. Because it is not what I expected from a 'couples' massage. Not that I've had one before, but just that relaxation would be the primary focus.

He smiles. "Sí."

"Oh, I'll just do a regular."

"No inglés," he says with a big grin.

"Oof," I say as he presses hard into my back. God, this isn't working for me. I mean, this is painful. "Legs?" I protest. "Would you do the legs? *Cómo se dice* legs?"

"Sí," Federico says, before continuing to do my upper back. He has no idea what I'm saying.

I turn my head and glance over at Jocko to see if he's receiving the same abuse, and I hear, "Oh yeah, that's the spot, Lila! Right there."

I can't be certain because it's dark and I don't have my glasses on because my contacts were bothering me when I tried to put them in today, but I'm pretty sure she's massaging his asscheek. I didn't know that was a thing.

Though judging from Jocko's praise, he's not receiving the same unpleasantness Federico is giving.

In another instant Federico's hands are on me and he's kneading me so hard, I feel like I'll turn to dough and start rising in this Caribbean heat if I don't make him stop.

When we leave the room, Jocko thanks them and tries to tip both therapists but they don't accept. It's an all-inclusive resort, and tips are frowned upon apparently. We take our robes and head into the sauna. I'm barely able to move as not only are my muscles sore, they've been turned into Jell-O and I'm wobbling like a three-year-old.

"Dammit," I say as we walk in. "I think I'm even more tense now than before."

"Damn. I'm sorry. Let's head to the sauna and try to steam away your aches and pains. Federico didn't do it for you?"

I give Jocko the stink-eye and he smirks, followed by a grin like he knew what was happening all along. I'll kill him if this was a pre-planned joke of his.

Jocko is always spoofing the guys in the office, never me up until maybe now...paybacks can be rewarding, I'm thinking.

Once we're in the sauna, the steamy hot feel hits my skin, and so does the sound of a laughing, giggling couple whose faces I can't see through the fog.

But I'd recognize those two voices anywhere.

Seriously? Why God, why?

Do Mark and Barbara plan on making out in their **room** *at any point during this trip?*

We sit silently in the sauna for five or ten minutes, and that does loosen me up a little, at least.

Jocko asks me a question or two, but my mind is off

wandering, and I can't really focus. He gets up, takes my hand, and leads me out of the room.

When we're outside, he puts his hands on my shoulders and turns me to face him. "Allie-face. What's going on? You okay?"

I nod blankly. "I'm fine."

"No, you're *not*. Dammit. Stop lying."

I'm not, he knows it and it's just a lot of things steamrolling through my head right now.

"Fine. I'm just carrying a lot of tension around. That massage sucked, and seriously, are Mark and Barb trying to set the record for the most places a couple has made out in a resort?" I try to bring my hand down to my waist, but my finger glances off the ridges of his hot, sweat-glazed abs. The burning thing happens again to me, down to my core.

"Sorry," I mumble, drawing my hand away from him.

He gives me a strange look. "You're so confusing, you know that, right?"

What is that supposed to mean — "How?" Did that sound annoyed, good.

"You ask me to fucking cuddle last night, and now you're apologizing for accidentally touching my stomach?"

I shake my head, oh well, yeah, "My mind is just all over the place. I need to set myself straight somehow. I just don't know how."

Jocko twists his face around.

Why I expected him to offer some advice was crazy. This is when I need a good friend to help you sort through the weird feelings bombarding you about Mark and Jocko. Maybe Rhonda should have come with me after all? I need my bestie. I'll text or call her soon.

"So your massage truly sucked?"

"It really did. It felt like he was deep elbowing my upper back."

"That sucks. But I've got an idea. Go through the women's locker room and meet me on the other side. We'll head back to our new room."

"Wait…new room?"

Jocko nods. "That tiny bed isn't doing it for me. I checked with the front desk and they had a honeymoon suite available with a double king size. The room is also a little more baller."

A feeling of weightlessness washes over me. "You didn't have to do that. Isn't that expensive?"

"Ha. You're funny, Allie. See, when I'm on a wedding date with my fiancée, nothing is too expensive! Now, come on. I had them move all of our things up to the room." As he walks in the locker room to change, he yells, "See you on the other side."

And I start to think that maybe the other side is more dangerous to my libido than this side is.

"GOOD LORD, NOW *THAT'S* A VIEW!" I giggle wildly as I run to the balcony of the suite. It's on the corner of the floor, so it's got a two-sided walkout with a full view of the ocean on *both* sides of the peninsula. Inside, there's a huge hangout lounge area with a big screen TV, and a separate, giant bedroom area. The bed looks out over the ocean. And it is huge!

"There's even a remote for the blinds," Jocko says, and then demonstrates, moving them up and down in the main room. "Now I truly feel like I'm on vacation."

I run up to him and wrap my arms around his neck. "Thank you, thank you, thank you!"

Without thinking, I stand on my tippy toes and plant a kiss on his lips.

He recoils. "What was that?"

"That was...practice?" I say, nervousness rising in my throat. I want to ask him if he's got a problem with that, then what was with his goodnight kiss on my neck yesterday, but I also feel like it's awkward to bring up at this point.

"That didn't feel like practice," he says in a low voice, hand on my hip.

"I just...got excited. Sorry."

He scoffs. "I told you, stop fucking apologizing."

"You're right. My bad." I reach behind my back and start kneading a spot on my lower spine, going for a quick change in topic. I'm receiving so many mixed messages right now I need to steer clear of any touchy-feely conversation that is bubbling up inside of me. "Seriously, I think that guy might have messed up my back. I feel like I got hit by a truck. At the same time, he missed some spots. I don't get how that's possible."

Jocko heads to a drawer next to the mini fridge and pulls out a tube of something. "Allie, I'm going to be honest. I'm sick and tired of you talking about how bad that massage was. A little complaining is fine, and I know that massage wasn't the best. But I can't listen to this all day."

His face is straight, without a trace of a smile. See, again — mixed messages...am I not the only one seeing them here?

"Oh? Sorry?" Oops, not supposed to say that. Anxiety builds inside me while my muscles have now turned ramrod straight.

He shakes his head and takes a few steps toward me. I back up, my nostrils flaring. Suddenly, I'm on edge, feeling... not frightened exactly, but unsure.

"I *told* you to stop apologizing. Now I'm going to help you relieve this tension and make up for that crappy massage."

"You are?" Eeep, where are we going here.

"Not sure if I ever told you this, but when I was in college, I got injured my sophomore year and for one semester I thought I might become a sports trainer. So I studied a lot about how the body responds to massage among other things. I'm sort of an above-average, amateur massage therapist."

"Seriously? So, what are you saying?" The question comes out in a soft breath.

"I'm saying, strip down and get under the covers right now. And I'm going to finish and fix what Federico couldn't."

My core ripples with excitement. Those nimble hands of his digging into my body is definitely something I could use.

"Yes, sir," I say, then arch an eyebrow. "Do you want me totally naked?"

"Whatever you're comfortable with. I'll give you a moment."

He turns to head out onto the ledge from the common area, bottle of massage oil in hand.

"Where did you get that oil? Was it just laying around the suite?"

"It was an option for the honeymoon suite. I just told them yes to all the deluxe ad-ons. Why not?" He smirks and heads out to the ledge, leaving me alone in the room.

My heart hammers hard as I consider what to take off. First, I take off my Kate Spade black-framed glasses and then consider the more important dilemma:

Do I go naked...or keep the swimsuit on?

These are the questions that try women's souls. *Is there enough time to text Rhonda?*

I stare at my body a moment in the mirror. I'm still glistening with oil from the "massage" from earlier and my body is slippery with sweat from the sauna. I suppose that will be good for the massage he's about to give me. That will make it easier.

But the question remains: what should I take off?

The responsible voice pops up inside me again and bounces around a bit. *Leave the swimsuit on. You're a classy girl. This is a* ***work*** *colleague.*

But as I look out over the water, different colors depending on the angle you are at, I remember what Jocko said as we got off the plane...

What happens in Cancún stays in Cancún.

And right now, conference calls, a cold spring in Detroit, and being in the same office as Jocko seems a world away. My hippie side wants to come out and play. Plus, Jocko is so respectful of my space, and I trust him more than just about any man I know. So why not live a little?

Fuck it.

I strip down totally naked, and jump under the white sheet, pulling it around to the small of my back so it covers me from the waist down.

"Ready!" I shout.

A few moments later, Jocko walks in wearing just his white pineapple swimsuit and a serious look on his face like he's ready to get down to business.

"Excellent," he says. "I'm going to do this right."

Hottest. Massage. Ever.

"Now, the first thing I need you to do is just relax, Allie," he says. "Can you hear the wind blowing outside?"

"Uh-huh," I say. "A little. It sounds relaxing."

"Good. Focus on that. Now you said Federico missed some spots. Where didn't he get?"

The sound of the wind is overwhelmed by the noise of Jocko rubbing his hands together with oil.

"Uh, like my lower back. Thighs. My ass is pretty tight, too," I giggle. "All those workouts we've been doing the past month or two."

Jocko laughs deep and throaty. "Alright. Well, I'll start on your lower back, do the thighs, and if that goes well we can move on. Sound like a plan?"

"Sounds heavenly."

"And hey, you sure you're cool with this?"

A devil's smirk crosses my face, and I crook my finger for Jocko to lean down closer to me. "Come here," I whisper. He leans in. "Massage the shit out of me. Just like your French girls. Don't hold back. I'll tell you if you're doing something I don't want."

He cracks up. "Slightly obscured *Titanic* reference noted. Ah, Allie, this is why you're my favorite."

I grin with my cheek against the mattress, and I want to ask him, *your favorite what?* Co-worker? Fake fiancée? Cuddle buddy?

He peels the blanket back. "Oh, wow. You went with naked," he comments in a tone I'm trying to decipher.

"I did. Is that going to be a problem?"

"Course not," he says, but his voice cracks a little. "I just wasn't expecting that, to be honest."

"Maybe you should have less expectations about me, Jay. I've got a lot of surprises up my sleeve." Ha ha, that's me trying to be sassy and bold.

"I might believe that...except you've got no sleeves on."

I roll my eyes at his silly joke, and his humor loosens me up. He hasn't even touched me yet, and he's doing ten times the job Federico did.

When he leans over me and starts on my lower back

with his hands, a warm sensation starts there and spreads throughout my body.

My problems melt away, and all I feel are his strong hands on me, rubbing back and forth.

"It's good," I say. "Angle could be better, though."

"Hmm. I have an idea."

I feel the material of his swim trunks as he gets on his knees as he mattress straddles my back and massages the oil into my skin. I feel the weight of his boys on my butt, which is still covered by the thin white sheet, and it sends a shot of warmth circulating through my core.

And those *hands*. God, help me. I melt away, and he does what Federico couldn't. Thumbs slide across the muscles of my lower back with ease and dexterity, and I find myself moaning uncontrollably.

"Good God, Jocko," I mutter. "What *can't* you do? Close sales...play basketball...make friends with my friends...give amazing massages... Do you also last forever in bed?" I blurt out, then realize that my last comment is a little direct and more than insinuating.

His hands stop running across my back.

"Joking," I mutter quickly, trying to cover my tracks. "I'm kidding around."

In truth, I am wondering what else those *hands* could do if they were unleashed.

His hands start their pattern again, and my second favorite part is when he reaches to my sides around my hips, threading his hands neatly but firmly up and down.

My favorite part though?

When he reaches lower on my low back, rubbing into my glutes under the sheet.

I want to tell him, *don't stop. Keep going lower. Why not flip me over...?*

Oh, Lordy, Lordy, this feels heavenly. It should be illegal for a man to be this charming, have hands this dexterous, and a body as ripped as Jocko's.

Mark was a good guy, we had great sex, but nothing that took me to the moon and back. Every loyal *Cosmo* reader knows there is sex, and *Sex.* I felt like Mark and I had good sex. Which was fine, I'd marry good sex, thought I was going to, actually. But now I have to wonder. Maybe things do happen for a reason?

I take deeper breaths. I start to hum in rhythm with his hand movements. And fucking *finally*, I do feel the tension leaving my body. It oozes out as I take big breaths, and I thank the heavens for this man whom I'm beginning to think might actually be an angel...or what's the word... archangel — sounds more masculine — sent from above.

"Feel good?" he asks in a deep and throaty tone.

"Feels good," I choke out. Truth is, it feels like I'm high. My whole body feels like warm, cozy happiness. "Would you go a little lower though?"

"Lower? Like this?"

His hands slide down my back and onto my upper glutes. My eyes roll up in the back of my head and I lick my lips. The sensations he's creating in me are relaxing and a bit sexual, too. I'm feeling a little wet and I'm not the least bit ashamed in fact, so I say, "Keep going lower, Jay. I love the way your hands feel. I want to feel them everywhere on me. Maybe even in me."

I hear him inhale a breath through his teeth. Yeah, I said that. Although he doesn't say anything, but his hands move lower. They run across my asscheeks and press back up, and dammit — it does feel heavenly.

But I'm greedy and I want more. I want him to cross the line so bad. I think I need it to happen because maybe then

I'll get Mark out of my head and be able to really relax and enjoy this trip.

Something finally dawns on Jocko as he suddenly says, a little tentatively for such a normally cocky man, "In you? Fuck, Allie. You can't talk like that."

I have to challenge him, "Why not?" Wondering if he'll really go there.

Maybe there's no going back from where we are. He's rubbing his palms up and down my freaking asscheeks and I told him point blank how I'd like to feel him. But if we stop now, they'll be some semblance of *line* we didn't cross when we go back to work.

His big hand touches me especially well, strong and smooth, and I accidentally let out a loud moan. He growls a low, gravelly tone in response.

And now I think both of our cards are out there, on the table.

"Because if that's what you really want, I'm going to have to give it to you. You're pushing me over the edge, Allie."

I wiggle in between his hands, tempting him, under the weight of his body as he straddles my ass. I push my bottom into him, inviting him, daring Jocko to make a move.

Rhonda always said I needed rebound sex, and although that's what I'm thinking we're doing, I know it might be more, for me, anyway. But I can't take it any longer.

We've played this game for too long. I want to know if this attraction is all in my head, or not. I want to know if he's as turned on as I am right now, and if he is? I want him to make me his.

"Jocko," I whisper. "Give it to me. Please. It's been a long winter. And I need you now."

"What about the consequences?" His voice is strained, he's ready, I don't think he'll deny me. And it's now or never for me because I don't think I could ever be this bold again in my life.

I smirk, pressing my cheek against the bedsheet. I think I'm drunk on his hands because I couldn't care less right now about the consequences of us being coworkers.

"I remember someone saying something like what happens in Cancún," I whisper, "Stays in Cancún."

I hear his breaths get louder.

"Fuck, Allie. Fuck, I want you right now."

He leans down and presses his lips to my ear. "And the funny thing is, I don't just want you because of how incredibly hot you look and feel right now."

A soft smile runs over my face, though not knowing what he's going to say it kind of makes me melt a bit inside, taking away some of the hurt of the past knowing that someone wants *me*.

"Why do you want me?"

His hands keep doing their thing, running along my back. I can feel the weight of his muscled chest pressing against my back, too.

"You really want to know?"

"Stop teasing me. Yes. I haven't felt wanted in what seems like ages. Spare me no details."

"I've wanted you since the moment you came into EdTechX for your interview. You had your hair up in a *fuck me bun*. You were wearing your nerdy black glasses and a black skirt that was just long enough to be appropriate for work. I was supposed to give you a quick tour of the cubicle and I could barely think. All I knew was that I wanted to take you into the nearest conference room and rip everything right off of you. Maybe leave the glasses on because I think you look hot in them."

"Oh God," I murmur. How in the heck does he

remember those details? He can't be serious that he was thinking those things about me all this time? "That can't be true. Wait, did you say a 'fuck me bun?' What *is* that?"

His moan is low and throaty, and this time I can *feel* the vibrations of his low voice.

"Mmm-hmm. It *is* true. To me it was a *fuck me bun.* I didn't tell a soul about what I thought about you, though. I couldn't. But because you're not supposed to be attracted to your work colleagues. Especially the ones with boyfriends who work in close quarters to you. So I kept my distance as best as I could."

"I remember that day, too," I say. I'm stunned, but sensitized, so while my brain wants to focus on what he just said, my body wants him in me right now.

Jocko lifts his chest away from my body and keeps lightly kneading my lower back, down my ass to my thighs, and back up again. Sometimes he slips his hands around my stomach, too. My whole body is firing on all cylinders. I decide to confess the rest of my thoughts. "I walked in and I was so nervous while you took me around. I was like who is this tall, hot man in a suit with the deep voice? And *I* could work here alongside him? I was worried because I had a boyfriend and I was so attracted to you. It took all of my strength to act normal and come up with questions for you. All I could think about was what you were hiding under that suit."

He chuckles. "Had no idea you felt that way, babe. But I've still got a suit on right now, you know."

I giggle. "Yeah, a swim suit. And you should take it off," I mewl, because this is going to happen. "I want to feel you before I see you."

"Jeez, Allie. You want to feel my dick against your body?"

"I do."

"I love it when you're forward like that."

I giggle. "You do?"

"I love it when you know what you want. Your strength is a huge turn-on."

I'm so worked up right now, I can barely have this conversation, but I continue because it means something. "That's the problem with being a slightly nerdy looking girl with glasses who works at a tech company. People underestimate me."

"I don't underestimate you."

I feel him lifting his knees off the bed and slipping his swim trunks off. My heart races.

Now I begin rambling, "Remember that time when we had to do a late conference call in January, and we had to stay in the office until like nine p.m. to close the Miami ISD deal?"

"Yes." His bare thighs fall against my skin now. I can feel the flesh of his cock and balls on my ass now.

Holy shit, this is happening.

"Well, I have to say it was hot seeing you manage that deal," I snort. "See? I'm a nerd and I find things like that hot. But as we sat there in the eleventh-floor conference room, you had your tie half undone. And you didn't notice it but your zipper was half down. And you kept thanking me for my hard work and saying how you wished you could do me a favor someday to repay me. But what I really was thinking about doing was unzipping the rest of your zipper, pulling that bulge out of your pants, and making you come."

"I remember that night. You kept talking about the Asian food you were going to eat when you got home."

"Yes! Because I needed to distract myself from...this." I can't stop myself. I reach back and run my hand along

Jocko's penis. Maybe it's that I'm just feeling it, not seeing it from this awkward angle, laying on my stomach.

But it is big.

It is thick.

And it is *hard*. The glimpse from the shower didn't give me the whole perspective.

"Oh. My. God." I murmur. "Do you always get this hard?"

Jocko's voice is low gravel. "When I'm sitting naked on the ass of the woman I've been fantasizing about fucking for over three years? Yeah. I get this hard, Allie. For you. I get this hard."

Whoa, *thinking of me for over three years?* "What are you thinking about right now?" I have to ask.

"I'm thinking how good my cock is going to feel when it's inside your pussy. I'm thinking how I don't have any condoms. I'm wondering how tight you'll be. I'm wondering if your voice will sound as sweet when I'm inside you as it does when we're crushing conference calls. What are you thinking?"

I tell him. "I'm wondering how far we're going to go right now. I'm wondering how your fingers will feel inside me."

He stands up on the bed, and I feel the imprints of his body on the mattress.

"Flip over," he instructs.

I do as he says, onto my back, and he lays down on his side, next to me. I love how huge this bed is. I love that we're looking out on the ocean.

Most of all, I love that this is finally happening. Consequences be damned.

Jocko pulls my lips to him and kisses me deeply. This is a new type of kiss. This isn't a fake, in-front-of-everyone kiss for show. Nor is it a *maybe we're practicing* kiss.

There is no ambiguity in the way his tongue shoots into

my mouth, or in the way my body melts into his, his leg wrapped on top of mine, and his penis resting on my stomach.

Yes, that's right. I can feel the weight of his cock on my stomach, and God, does it turn me on.

But when he slides a hand slowly down my stomach, pausing just before my opening to flick his tongue across both of my nipples, one at a time, I lose it. My hips arch upward and I look into his eyes and his eyelashes are gorgeous. He's my fantasy man, and *holy fuck, his hand is on my clit*.

He presses into my clit lightly, with the same firm but delicate touch he used to massage the tension out of my body. And he just stays there, putting perfect pressure on my clit.

For so long. He doesn't seem bored in the slightest, rubbing his hand in my hair. Meanwhile, the other is exploring parts of my body while I wiggle my hips up and into his dexterous fingers. Good God, I'm so wet.

As if reading my mind, all of a sudden I feel two fingers slide inside me, and curl right up into the best spot of all time.

My first orgasm crescendos, and I scream as it ripples through me.

I expect Jocko to stop, but he doesn't.

"I came," I mutter, sweaty and breathless. "I came."

He smirks, and slaps his cock on my stomach with his free hand, just for fun, apparently. Damn, that is hot.

"I know," he says in a barely audible growl. "And you sounded so sweet, I'd like to do that again."

He's got total control over me now, and his long, thick fingers reach so perfectly inside me. My inner muscles grip tightly around them, and by the time I've come down from my first orgasm, he's already building me up to a second one.

This time, he straddles my stomach and reaches back as he fingers me. I enjoy the weight of him on me, and I love the close-up view of his abs, his V, his broad shoulders as he sits on me. He is an amazing man, amazing friend, and great in bed.

I'm feeling so much right now both physically and emotionally, I refuse to analyze any of it. For once I'm going to enjoy this, him, and let go.

I lick my lips, my eyes fluttering. There's so much stimulation going on right now, I can barely focus. He moves his fingers so slightly, so perfectly, so effortlessly, responding to the way my body thrashes.

My eyes roll up in the back of my head and I cry out. I've never come quite like this.

From the position he's maneuvered us into, I'm able to lean forward, reach and grab hold of his cock, and take him in my mouth.

In my conference room fantasy, I gave him the best, sexiest BJ of his life. I pulled my hair back and performed, licked his penis slowly, tantalizingly, teasing him for ten minutes before he finally begged me to take him in my mouth.

But right now, this is *reality*, and I'm so heated, so turned on, I take him in far as I can in from the start.

Jocko lets go of a huge moan, and now *his* eyes are the ones rolling up in the back of his head for a change.

His noises of pleasure motivate me. Not to mention his fingers inside me which don't miss a beat. No, they move faster now. Deeper. Stronger. I reach an arm around him and grab his ass, forcing him farther down my throat. I want him as deep as I can take him. I want to show him that I'm not *Allie the coworker.* I'm Allie the woman he traveled with to Cancún.

"Fuck yeah, Allie. That's the deepest anyone's ever taken me," he mutters, still doing all of those wonderfully awesome things to me with his hand. I come *again* and twist my hips up, meanwhile moaning onto his dick, almost gagging.

I have to pull my mouth off of him for a moment, and take a few giant lungfuls of air.

A strand of saliva mixed with Jocko's juices strings from my lips to his tip.

"Your mascara is running," he informs me. His lungs are also rising and falling deeply now. "And it's hot as fuck."

I smile faintly, and reach my free hand up to touch his arm. "Hey. Relax. I came three times. Your turn now. Here, maybe you should get on your back."

"Okay," he says, and slides his fingers gently out from inside me. Then, in the hottest move a man has *ever* done involving little ole *me*, he rubs his fingers covered in my juices against his lips, then *licks them*. "Christ, I've been waiting forever to do that. I can't wait to taste you with my tongue."

"On your back, don't distract me," I murmur again, thinking about that visual he just put into my mind.

And wondering to myself that if he can make me come like that with just his fingers, what on Earth would he do with his mouth?

"Yes, boss," he winks, and slides off the bed so he can reposition himself.

But once he's got his feet on the floor, I get another idea. On my back, I slide the back of my head just off the side of the bed. He stands to the side behind my head, and I reach behind him and grab his cock with my head upside down.

"Let's do it this way," I say, licking my lips.

"I'm so turned on right now I can barely stand," he growls, rubbing my tits with his hands.

"Try," I say as I take him into my mouth.

I've never done this before. I don't even know what I would call this position. Spiderman kisses since I'm upside down?

But we're not kissing, so...a Spiderman BJ?

I'm enjoying him so much, his dick is so hard and thick I never want to stop. Why does this man have the ability to turn me into a pile of orgasmic mush?

I use both hands now, because from this position I need them for his length, and that's when I feel him begin to twitch.

"Holy fuck, Allie," he growls. "I'm going to come *a lot.* Where should I..."

His words turn into Charlie Brown babbles. I can't even hear him as I reach one hand behind him and grab his terrifically muscular ass and force him as deeply down my throat as I can. I don't pull back this time ...and I feel his whole body surge with vibration as he unleashes himself into my mouth.

I swallow what I can, and the rest overflows onto my lips and down my neck, the warm feeling oddly comforting. When he's done, I lick the top side of his flesh as he pulls out slowly.

He collapses on the bed next to me, turns me around so we're horizontal on top of the sheets and pulls me into him from behind, kissing my neck.

We lay in a sweaty, sticky, post-orgasmic heap of arms and legs and torsos and nipples pressed up against each other.

He's the big spoon, *obviously,* and I reach back and run my hand along the side of his thigh.

"Mmm. Allie-face," he says in a low whisper. "Where the hell did that come from?"

"Honestly, Jay. I have no fucking clue," I whisper back, as we drift off together. And that's the truth.

But I know after what we just did, my body feels utterly, completely relaxed. My mind is on pause for the first time on this trip, and the shadows of the past are nowhere to be found.

Nice.

"Thanks for relieving my tension," I add, but I can tell by the rhythm of Jocko's breathing that he's fast asleep.

11

JOCKO

I think I've been transported to heaven...or maybe hell.

Heaven because I'm with an angel.

Hell because I was just put through the biggest temptation of my life...and I failed miserably.

I told myself going into this weekend I would keep it locked up. I *promised* myself I wouldn't cross the line with Allie.

And now, it's mid-afternoon in the honeymoon suite, and I'm blinking my eyes open to a new reality.

Allie Jenkins sleeps next to me, *naked.*

Her lovely, voluptuous ass presses up against me. The same ass that she barely squeezed out of her jeans yesterday. And the same one I cuddled against all last night, and tried in vain not to pitch a tent against.

But hold up. This is *also* my cute, bubbly work colleague Allie. My favorite person to do conference calls with. The person whom I see when I'm having a bad day who can light me back up with just her smile.

And now?

We've just had some of the dirtiest sex I've *ever* had in my life. And that's really saying something. Well, okay, we didn't technically have actual sex yet. By my standards, anyway.

I get up and go to the bathroom, and when I come back, I'm bowled over by what I see. Allie is still sleeping softly, her mouth gently twitching. Maybe she's dreaming.

Maybe *I'm* dreaming. This doesn't feel real. Can't be real. Did I get transported to the Matrix somehow?

Slowly, over the past few years at work, Allie started to become one of my best friends and brightest lights in my day, whether she knew it or not. I know she's had a tough winter, and I know she thinks I'm some super-human sales guy who is never in a bad mood. She's told me as much many times.

But the truth is, I was thinking about leaving the company a few years ago, and when she got there, something shifted in me. It's not like I stayed on at EdTechX just to be around her, but I realized that every day, work had become a little more fun when I saw her. Smart, fun, and attractive, she was a pleasure to work with.

I had written off my dreams of having this type of *pleasure* with her.

And now I know that not only does Allie have the personality of my dreams, she also *fucks* like the woman of my dreams.

Or at least, moans, orgasms, and gives head like the woman of my dreams. The *fucks* part is to be determined.

Jesus. My head spins as I look at her, the light streaming from the panoramic window. I just keep staring at her, in disbelief. She's got a few birthmarks on her back. One on her hip. I love getting to know the contours of her body. I love everything about this girl that I find out. I love how her face looked as her eye makeup smeared a little bit, and I love that she didn't care. I love how she can sleep deeply in a room invaded by the light streaming inside.

All of a sudden, my skin tingles and my adrenaline spikes as I watch her. I need to remember this moment. I have to.

So I grab my phone and I snap a picture of her sleeping. For posterity.

This image enters my head and I can't stop it — Allie and I are boarding another plane, going somewhere else, continuing onto some other adventure. She's still got the ring on her finger. We're fucking like that in every country we can get to. We're exploring together. We're learning new things together. We're...

I shake my head, and set my phone down on the nearest surface.

What the fuck am I thinking?

That was *one* fuck. One.

And, again, we didn't even *fuck*.

But I've never meshed with a woman like that, sexually. So Allie-face...likes to be dirty.

Incredibly dirty.

Just the way I like it. The way I need.

But that's not what has me thinking crazy. It's her softness outside of the bedroom. It's the fact that I know she volunteers at a dog shelter two times a month. How much care, smarts, and follow-up she puts into every relationship with a client, just because she's a damn good person, not because it affects her salary.

Which is another matter entirely. I've been having it out with our company's management telling them how they've got to pay her more. I started a war over this, but there's battles still to be won. I won't give up, though.

Fuck me. Who *is* this girl? And how does she already have an avowed bachelor wondering what it would be like to lean into a relationship with one woman for a while?

I'm getting so very ahead of myself. All I am for her is a rebound. And we're going to keep it at that.

I need a drink, I decide. So I call up room service, and tell them to bring up a bottle of champagne with two glasses.

While I'm waiting for them to arrive, I head over to the balcony to get some air and drink a bottle of water. God knows I'm dehydrated from last night. I need to replenish all the fluid I just unleashed with Allie. I'm just amazed her ex let her go after all I know of her now. That shit makes no sense, none at all. I mean, sexually she's right up there, smart, caring, great personality — *watch it, Jocko, sounds like you're really falling for her.*

I look out over the water below. We're on a small strip of land between two different colors of water. On one side, there's the Caribbean Sea, a deep blue ocean. On the other, there's the bay, a greenish color.

I lean against the railing and sip my bottle of water. Maybe that's Allie. Two sides to her. One is the giggling, nerdy girl with the glasses who has an affinity for show tunes and musicals and dogs. The other is a deep ocean of desire.

I run a hand through my hair and look over my shoulder at her again and smile. I decide right then and there that it's my goal to give Allie the best week of her life. Not because it'll make her happy. Well, that's a plus. But it's more complicated than that. It'll make *me* happy to see *her* happy.

God, how shitty to have to go through a breakup like that. Mark doesn't seem like a horrible guy, but the fact that he's moving on so quickly has got to suck for Allie.

And whatever I'm feeling for her right now, we may as well explore it, in spite of our working relationship. Worst comes to worst, we'll just have to leave everything that happened in Cancún here like we've both alluded to. Would be hard, but not impossible. We're both professionals.

I nudge the thought of the future out of my head. This is only day two here. I'm going to focus on the here and the now. Whatever happens between us happens.

I hear my phone buzz in the room, and I go inside to grab it, then walk back out. Allie breathes hard, in some deep sleep, I assume.

When I get back, I have a text from my mom.

Mom: Jocky you need to call me this instant!! How do I not know anything about this girl!?

Anxiety surges in my stomach, and I bite my lip. Okay, *now* I feel bad for making up the whole fiancée story with my mother. I'd like to be able to look forward to going back home to be with my mom and dad, and not have Jocko's decision to be a lifelong bachelor be front and center.

So really, I'm doing it for her. For my family. Once I tell them Allie and I have "broken up" she'll have no choice but to commend me for at least trying.

I get that it's a little bit of a dick move. But a guy's got to do what a guy's got to do. I walk to the corner of the balcony so I won't wake Allie up, and press my mom's number.

"Hey, Mom!" I say when she picks up.

"Jocko! How could you get engaged and not tell me?"

"Well, it was, um, just kind of sudden."

"So who's the girl? Tell me all about her."

I clear my throat. I probably shouldn't tell her I work with Allie because that'll blow my cover. But on the other hand, it's not like my mom ever talks to anyone from my job. So I'm probably safe. The lie will stay contained to this wedding party — none of who work at our relatively small sales company — and my family.

"She's a girl from work. We're kind of not supposed to be dating, so we had to keep it really quiet for a while. So...surprise!"

She blows out a loud breath. "Wow. Just wow. I'm so happy!" she squeals.

Fuck. Cue Jocko feeling even worse about making his mom feel happy. All of a sudden I'm thinking maybe this wasn't the best idea. But there's no going back now.

"I saw the pictures and I'll be honest, I almost thought it was a joke, Jocky! But then I saw my grandmother's ring and I thought, 'well he'd never joke around with that, would he?'"

"Never," I squeak out, and *holy shit,* here come the *real* pangs of guilt. What was I *thinking* when I came up with this plan?

"She's really great," I add. "We're down in Cancún for a wedding, though, so I'll give you more information when I get back. Probably shouldn't eat up my minutes while I'm international."

And, another total lie. I don't give a shit what long distance or roaming costs. I make too much money for that.

"Of course, Jocky. I know. It's just, you should tell your mother these things! I wish you'd be a little more open sometimes, you know?"

"Yes, Mom. I'll try."

"Okay. Now have a good time in Cancún. Say hello to… my gosh, what's her name?! You haven't told me."

"Allie," I say.

I can practically feel my mom tearfully smiling through the phone. "Allie. That's a lovely name. So happy for you two. Call me as soon as you get back."

"Will do," I squeak out.

As soon as I hang up the phone, a distinct, queasy feeling hits me. I believe this is known as *that shitty feeling when you lie to your mother.*

Just ten minutes ago, I thought this was a good idea. What happened?

"Fuck," I mutter through my teeth as I hang my head, leaning my elbows against the railing.

A voice to my right surprises me. "Everything alright?"

It's a female, and I'd recognize the voice if I weren't so in my own world right now.

I turn, and see her sitting on the Juliet balcony adjacent to ours, reading a book.

It's *Barb.*

"Oh, hey," I say, less than enthusiastic. I get it, she doesn't know anyone at this wedding because she's the new girl. But it does seem like she's being overly nice to Allie, trying to play the 'Mark's not such a bad guy' card from the few instances I've seen them interact, like at the hotel desk when we first got here. I can't tell if it's an act, or if she truly is the type who would wish the best on their fiancé's ex-girlfriend.

As I walk over, she stands up and waves. "Yeah, I guess we're next to you…oh my gosh!" she exclaims, then covers her eyes. "Oh. You're naked. Hello!"

"Oh, shit," I say, my stomach tumbling. I quickly grab a towel that's hanging on the chair and put it on. "My bad."

"So what was that all about?" she asks, leaning her

elbows on the railing of her balcony. "If I'm being too nosy, just stop me."

"You're being nosy, but it's okay. I was just telling my mom we got engaged."

She squints. "Didn't Allie say you guys got engaged a month ago?"

I nod, recalling our conversation in passing at the front desk.

"She did."

"Huh. So you waited a whole month to tell your mom?"

"That's right."

"Wow. Well, that's interesting. We called our parents right away."

My insides curdle a little at the fact that I can see the wheels turning in Barb's brain like she's a regular Sherlock Holmes. She might come off as aloof sometimes, but I get the feeling she's more intelligent than she lets on.

I wave my hand through the air. "Yeah, we sort of kept it under wraps."

"I see. How did you ask her?"

My eyes widen. "Oh, I, uh, asked her at her favorite restaurant in Detroit."

"Which is...?"

"Pizza Palace," I blurt out, saying the first place that comes to mind. I make a note to give Allie this detail in case Barb quizzes her.

"Oh, that's sweet. What's her favorite pizza? I bet you ordered it."

"Pepperoni and sausage with olives," I say, just going off my first instinct again.

Just then, Mark comes out onto the balcony to join her.

"Hey, honey, who are you talking to?" he says, before he sees me. "Oh, hey, Jocko. You guys staying next door, eh?"

"Looks like it."

Barb wraps her arm around Mark and gives him a kiss on the cheek. "Jocko was just telling me how he proposed to Allie. He did it at her favorite restaurant, Pizza Palace, and ordered her favorite sausage, pepperoni, and olives pizza."

Mark squints. "Allie...doesn't like olives."

Uh-oh. I'm not in the business of digging myself into a hole of lies. But if anyone can work his way out, it's me.

"She just started liking them," I bark back, noting that I'll need to tell Allie about this lie at some point in case it comes up.

"Huh. That's just surprising," Mark says, and my suspicions rise that they may be onto my shit.

"What about you two, how did you get engaged?" I say, because we need to be talking about anything other than the story I am improvising right now.

They look at each other and smile. "I was traveling for work in Nashville where we met originally," Barb says. "He came and surprised me, and asked me at the very first bar where we ran into each other."

"Well, that's adorable."

I see Allie rising from the bed, and motion for her to put some clothes on.

Probably still groggy, she sticks her tongue out as she pulls her panties on, then starts to walk on the balcony.

"I put panties on," she says as she walks toward me from the room. She can't see Mark and Barb from where she is. "But I don't really see a reason I should..."

And...she's topless on the balcony in direct view of Mark and Barb, whose jaws drop.

"Oh, um, hey," Barb says, a little awkwardly.

I shrug and figure, why not have some fun with this.

"Hey, not like none of us have seen a pair of tits before, am I right? Come here, baby."

Palming her bubble butt, I pull her into my arms for a deep, long kiss that takes her by surprise.

When we pull away, Barb and Mark are gaping at us. "I was just telling these two about how I proposed to you." I speak loudly and clearly, looking her in the eye. "At Pizza Palace. Remember?"

She rubs the sandman out of her eyes with the back of her hand, and squints. "Oh, yes, the proposal. Such a romantic night that was."

Allie can improv right along with me, and I love it. To cinch how much I want her, and how devilish we are together, I crack her on the ass again and pull her into me for another kiss. Deeper this time. More tongue.

She's breathless when we pull our mouths away from each other, and she turns to Mark and Barb, still topless.

Well, alright, then. Someone's going full out *nudist* today.

"I thought he was talking about the *pre*-proposal for a second there," Allie winks, and at this point I think she's just reveling in this little improvised scene we're making up on the spot in front of Barb and Mark.

"What's a pre-proposal?" Mark asks and is staring right at her tits like he hasn't seen them before. And for some reason that pisses me off.

"You know, it's like where you talk about *if* there *potentially* was a proposal, *hypothetically*, how could we do that and would you say yes."

Barb twists up her face. "I haven't heard of that."

"It's definitely a thing," I insert. "And we really enjoy noting all of the milestones of our relationships, even the little ones. Don't get me started on the pre-pre-proposal!

That's like where you talk about where you would hypothetically talk about-"

"I get it," Mark says, cutting me off, and finally moving his eyes off target to glance at his watch. "I think we're going to catch some late afternoon rays and watch the sunset before the pre-wedding dinner and cocktail hour tonight. And, guys, I'm just so glad this isn't awkward, having our rooms next to each other like this."

"Not awkward at all. Have a good night." I even take my hand off of my towel and wave, trying to be gentlemanly in spite of the fact that he was ogling Allie, which he has no right to do anymore.

I thought it would stay up even without me holding it, but my towel falls down due to the faulty knot I tied.

Everyone steals a glance.

"My bad," I say, picking the towel up.

"Just maybe we should instigate a policy of wearing actual clothes on the balcony?" Mark says.

Barb chuckles, taking in my junk 'cause I think she's enjoying the view. "I mean, I think we're all adults here, to be honest."

"You do?" I have to ask and be a smartass.

"Yes. And it's not like you haven't seen her naked before," Barb says to Mark, then turns to us, looking at me. "Sorry, just being honest. I mean, you love each other and so do we. And we all love our bodies. So I don't think there's any insecurity here. Do you?"

I shake my head. "Can't say that there is. And, we *are* in Cancún after all." I glance over at Allie. "And I think we can all admit Allie has terrific tits."

Okay, that might have been too far. Now an awkward tension hangs in the air, and Mark glances between Barb's and Allie's tits, not sure what to say.

But I think Allie doesn't mind my off-color behavior, because she secretly slips a hand onto my ass and rests it there. She bites her lip and looks up at me, grinning, then gets on her tip toes and brushes her lips against my ear.

"We're going to fuck out here tonight," she whispers.

My cock instantly twitches, and I do my best to keep a smile plastered on my face as I look at Barb and Mark.

"True, this *is* Cancún," Mark says, blatantly ignoring my comment about Allie's tits. "Well, sure, I suppose...when in Cancún, we'll do as the Cancúnians do. Is that a phrase? Anyhow, we're gonna head in. See you at dinner."

After the two of them head inside, and we hear their door slide shut, I swallow and turn to Allie. "Really? Whispering like that, are you trying to give me a full-on erection in front of these two? This white towel doesn't exactly hide much, as you can see."

She makes an exaggerated frowny face. "Oh, poor you. Does it turn you on to think about fucking me out here?"

I palm her ass with both hands and spin her around, pressing her against the balcony railing.

"It does. A lot. And I think that's a great idea for our first time." I kiss her neck. I love the way her hair is blowing in the wind right now.

"I think I better go buy some condoms," I say, thinking out loud.

She tips my chin toward her with her finger. "You can if you want. But I'm also on the pill. And God help me, Jocko, but I trust you. If you haven't been with anyone in a while..."

"Since before you invited me to this crazy thing. I haven't been able to jack off to anyone else. Much less consider *sleeping* with someone else."

"Then forget the condoms," she says. Those four words make me salivate, thinking about feeling her bare. "We should get ready for dinner." She slips out of my grip and heads back into the room. I follow her in, and put my hand on her hip to stop her from behind.

"Oh, and one more thing, Allie."

"What's that?" she says, half turning her head.

"Don't wear any panties tonight."

She giggles. "Why would I bother with those?"

12

ALLIE

When we're finished getting ready — I take an hour, Jocko takes ten minutes — we head down to the main floor of the resort and take a little walk along the beach. Gotta love the fact that at a destination wedding, even a guy can get away with wearing white pants (Jocko's obsessed with his) and sandals, and still look formal. I wear a floral white and pink wrap dress.

It's a sunny day and we didn't even get down to use the pool and get some rays yet. But I'll let that slide for today, since we were quite *occupied.*

Thinking about that, which I haven't given much more thought to until now, I realize how much I've come to enjoy being with Jocko. I mean, sexually we're very compatible, well, so far, anyway. I'm glad I'm not going into my head about it all, that I'm just enjoying what we shared and that we've shifted this trip onto a more physical level. I'm taking a page from something Jocko said and just letting my expectations go. Let's face it, I needed to have a rebound at some point, right? Why not it be with my friend, the guy who helped me get this body into shape so when Mark saw me in my glory on the balcony, he could not take his eyes off this toned version of the Allie he used to know — yeah, I noticed.

The part that I haven't reconciled is the coworker part... how does that work when we're back in the office? I mean, I care for Jocko, enjoy his friendship and all, but we can't continue this way back home, right?

Out of your head, Allie — have fun, you're just having fun.

Oh well, something to ponder another day.

Back to the now. With the official wedding ceremony tomorrow, the bridal party and the immediate family of the bride and groom are rehearsing on the beach. How glorious for a wedding. Let's just hope it doesn't rain tomorrow.

We're down by the water, so we dip our toes in for a bit, though neither of us have much to say, then decide to head up to the bar. I order a margarita, and Jocko gets a rum and Coke. His jaw is clenched and he's a little quieter than usual. Since I've known him for three years, I am especially sensitive to his mental state. And the man is rarely at a loss for words. Though, at the moment, I'm wondering if I've got something to do with it.

"The wedding party should be here in about fifteen minutes," I say as the bartender puts the drinks in front of us. "Cheers!" I say with a smile.

"Cheers," he returns, faintly.

I take a sip of my delicious margarita — no straw because those are bad for the environment — and put my hand on Jocko's forearm.

"You okay, Jay? You seem off."

His expression is strained, and I know I'm right. So I decide to be the first to broach the topic, "Look, if we went too far today-"

"It's got nothing to do with you," he finally says. "I loved everything about this afternoon. This was the best afternoon of my life, in fact."

My heart warms, hearing that. He's so sincere that it makes me feel special, but I still need to know, "So what's the matter?"

"I talked to my mom today. You know how my plan was to show her our pictures, then tell her we broke up once I get back home?"

"Yeah, of course." Crazy but that's all his doing. I take no part in it except for posing.

"Well, now that I actually *talked* to her, I feel horrible. I'm *lying* to her. I'm a bad son."

I put my hand on his shoulder because he's serious, this is really eating at him. "It's a crazy plan, you're kind of right. But that doesn't make you a bad *son*. You love your mom, right?"

He responds with conviction, "Yes. I just can't stand this talk of, *'Jocky, when are you getting a girlfriend? When are you getting married?'* It puts too much pressure on me. But..." he takes a deep breath. "I wonder if I'm not going about it the wrong way."

Ahhhhhhh, his conscience is setting in. "Should we call it off? Come clean?" I say it but it's more like I'm thinking out loud.

"No. We can't do that. Rule number one of weddings is not to steal thunder from the bride. And we would do just that. We've just got to pretend like this is something that's really happening until we get back to Detroit. Then, we can kick in the rest of the plan." He takes a swig of his drink and says, "We'll go through with it. No worries, babe, it's on me, I'll figure it out."

I sip my drink and nod, slowly, turning away from Jocko and toward the ocean for a moment. A rush of emotion comes over me. Something doesn't feel right about those words.

We've just got to pretend like this is something that's really happening.

Something is definitely happening here, and it's not pretend. I think we both know it. There were four total orgasms in that bed this afternoon and that is *something,* not *nothing.*

Those were definitely *not* pretend orgasms. I thought Jocko and I were sailing along, on a high, and maybe we are. But his words are a reminder that really, we're just getting started with whatever this is.

We are still friends, I think to myself and hope this doesn't ruin that. Then his hand threads through mine.

"The ring *does* look good on you, though. I have to say."

I turn back to him and muster a grin because I totally agree. "Thanks."

"You look sexy as hell, too. What is it about you and wrap dresses that slays me?"

He's got that devouring look and I have to giggle. "You tell me. You're the guy. I'm just the girl who wears the dress."

Just then, we see Mark and Barb walking past us from the pool, heading up to their room to change. We give each other obligatory waves.

"So, Jay. Question. Maybe I'm overstepping bounds here, but why *are* you so against getting into a real relationship?" I'm not sure why I ask this question, because it's not about me for sure, but the curiosity is there. Ever since we started working together, that was always the office rumor and the story he tells, too. He's always claimed he wouldn't consider marriage until he was at least forty years old.

He shrugs his shoulders and takes a drink, then goes silent. I wait a few beats before I realize this is clearly one of those Jocko brick wall questions that I am not getting a real answer to.

So time for change of topic, "You still doing keto?" I ask, pointing to his rum and Coke. He laughs. "I'm on a keto break. That ship has sailed. This is a week for pure enjoyment."

His pupils shrink, and I can tell he's thinking hard about something.

"What is it?"

"I'm going to ask you something...don't get mad, though. Okay?"

My core tightens because I think he knows my insecurities, so I'm hoping we don't go there. "I mean, I can try. I can't promise, though."

"So you look sexy as fuck. I think we've acknowledged that."

"Thank you. So do you."

"Like you've put in *work* in the gym this winter for how you look."

"Best trainer ever," I say, nudging him. "So thank you for all the booty workout tips you gave me."

"And now, I'm not saying you weren't gorgeous before. I told you the story of the very first time I saw you. Besides, the hottest thing about you is your voice anyway." He grins. "I've always loved when you presented during conference calls, just so I could listen to your voice during the day."

I nod in acceptance of his voice comment, though I'm surprised. To be honest, I get the feeling that my voice isn't my feature that jumps out at most men.

"Well, thanks for the voice compliment. As for my body, it's obvious that I've improved visibly after our workouts." I take a deep breath fearing what will come out of his mouth.

Jocko doesn't usually hesitate to ask something, so it makes me nervous. "So, what's your question?"

"Why were you so motivated in the gym?" he asks.

I shift on my bar stool, a sense of uneasiness setting into me.

"What's that got to do with anything? And why would that make me mad?"

"I'm just curious. Did you just, you know, decide it was time to work out? Or was there something else?"

I take a large gulp of my margarita and sit up a little straighter. "What are you getting at, Jay?"

"It's just, I see the way Mark has been looking at you. And I'm *not* jealous. Okay, well, maybe I am a tad. But that's not what I'm talking about right now. A part of me wonders if you didn't work so hard because you *wanted* to make him a little jealous."

I swallow harshly, and a quiver rolls across my spine.

"So you're saying I was JUST working out because I wanted to wiggle my beach body in front of my ex?"

"Not exactly."

"Well, that's what it sounds like." And, truth be told, he's right. It was more than a factor in my motivation this winter.

He stammers.

"Look, since we arrived here we've been hanging out like all day, 24/7," I say. "I'm just going to go grab some air for a few minutes by the beach. I'm probably overreacting."

Without saying anything more, I head off. Jocko doesn't follow.

It's true — we've been with each other almost every waking minute for the last day and a half, and that's hard to do with anyone.

Things have been moving so fast, and Jocko's question threw me for a loop. So much so I couldn't answer him, and in some way it made me feel bad, so some air by myself right now will do me good.

What am I supposed to say, yes, I totally get off on being motivated by revenge body hashtag and I might even post some transformation pictures?

Luckily, there's another bar at the end of the beach, by the hot tub, that's about to close down. It's practically empty here, so I order another margarita and sit at the end of the bar, by myself, just me and the bartender.

What on Earth am I doing? I wonder as I look at my ring.

I'm at my friend Peyton's wedding...*faking* an engagement? For *what*, exactly? Because Jocko is the hottest man on the face of the planet who wants to pull a con on his mom?

I sigh and wonder if I've been played. Jocko *is* a player. He's the definition of player. He'll never not be a player, and if I think I'm just going to come along and swoop him out of his ideal bachelor lifestyle, *I'm* the idiot.

At least the sound of the waves crashing onto the shore is soothing as I sit, watching Paco the bartender smile as he puts away clean glasses, organizing the bar for tomorrow.

But the fucked-up thing is more about why I just stormed out ...

He's a little bit right.

I'd never felt more motivated to get in the gym then I had the last almost two months. The fact that Jocko happens to be essentially a personal trainer because of his days playing sports in college made our sessions all the more productive. And *yes*, I *enjoyed* reveling in the fact that I would get my bikini body in full swing for this trip. And that Mark would be here and see me and regret breaking up with me. There, I admitted it, and it sounds stupid and a little shallow.

"This seat taken?"

The voice is Jocko's. The accent is Forrest Gump.

"You can sit here if you want to," I say in Jenny's voice, and I can't help but break a smile.

That's been a running joke with us at work going on three years.

He sits next to me, beer in his hand. "I didn't mean to offend you by what I said. I'm not judging you. Shit, you should know I've got no place to judge you. My mind just went there because I'm a *guy* and I see the way guys look at you. And I saw how hard you worked out. And I-" he stops midsentence, pauses, and takes another sip of his beer.

I wait and realize he's not going to say more, so I prod, "I feel like you were about to say something big right there."

He nods. "You asked me a question back there that I sort of brushed off."

"About why you don't want to get married?"

He nods again. "Let me try and answer, as best as I can. My parents are still together, yes. But when I was in middle school, my dad moved out for a while. I think he fell for this other woman, albeit temporarily. The full memory is still a little hazy to me. You know how it is when you're young."

"Oh. But they got back together?"

"Well, my mom at that point, if I'm being honest...she had sort of let herself go. She had a lot of stress, to be fair, having us kids and the job as a special ed assistant. And I'm not blaming her. But she stopped taking care of herself. And my dad left her. Said he couldn't be with someone who didn't have respect for her well-being and, yes, her body. And, well, that year, I'd never seen someone so motivated to make healthy lifestyle habits. She started meditating, doing yoga, and lost a ton of weight. She turned back into — ugh, I can't believe I'm saying this about my own mom, but — a

MILF. It was wild. All of us kids took notice. And a year later, she and my father made up and they've been much better ever since. But since then, I just assumed it was a sad fact about human nature, and I noticed the same thing sometimes with various friends of mine. It wasn't until the breakup that they decided to get their life in order."

Interesting, but I'm lost, "So what's this got to do with you wanting to be a bachelor forever?"

"I just worry that if I ever really commit to someone, we'll let ourselves go. We'll stop growing as people." He takes a slow sip of his drink. I can see in the depth of his eyes this is something that really troubles him.

Ahhh, now this is making sense. "And you saw that I grew a lot after my breakup in terms of taking care of myself. Thus, confirming your hypothesis."

"This is a tough conversation," he says, nodding. "But I'm glad we're having it."

"Honestly, it wasn't *just* to make him jealous or something. But sure, that was a factor. You offered to train me, and I figured 'Jocko is an amazing trainer and he's offering for free? Why not?' It was a little bit motivation at the right time, and a little bit coincidence."

"I figured. Sorry, I feel like an idiot for asking that question now. Weird question."

I lean in toward him and rub his back. "Not a weird question. Well, maybe a little weird. But regardless, I want you to be able to ask the weird questions with me. It's important if-"

I almost have to cover my mouth, but luckily, I'm able to play it off. "If we're going to make it through this week."

Oh my. I was about to say *if we're going to be long term.* Eee-gads, where is that coming from?

I take another swig of my margarita. Not only am I

talking to the king of the bachelors here, but it has also been less than six hours since we officially crossed the line from 'kinda-sorta flirting doing this fake fiancé destination wedding date thing' to 'friends who give each other orgasms.'

So yeah, it's probably best if I keep thoughts of babies and weddings to myself. Even though we're *at* a wedding and we just did things that quickly progress to baby making.

Jocko and I would *definitely* make beautiful babies.

Okay, *enough.* I'm scaring myself.

Luckily, Jocko distracts me by leaning in and giving me another kiss. Not only is he deft with his fingers, he's also extremely good with his lips.

A shiver runs through me when I remember how vehement he was about *tasting me* with his tongue at some point in the near future.

"You okay?" he asks, pulling away from me.

I nod. "Just caught that chilly breeze," I say.

He squints. "Felt warm to me."

"Weird. Was cold to me."

And there we are, at an impasse, because I'm *not* going to tell him that I'm thinking about how his lips and tongue would feel *you-know-where.* Especially not when we're supposed to be heading to a dinner and talking about normal people things very shortly.

He doesn't need to know all the ridiculously dirty thoughts that keep swimming around in my head.

"So," he says in a low growl. "This afternoon was *very* fun."

"Which part?" I grin. "The part where you massaged me or the part where I came multiple times?"

He puts his hand on my thigh and rubs, turning me on again.

"All of the above," he says, then blinks.

I lean toward him and nibble his ear. "And let's not forget the Spiderman BJ I gave you."

"I will never forget that as long as I live," he says, then wrinkles his nose. "I just didn't see that coming."

"Neither did I. I've never done that before. Wait, what do you mean you didn't see it coming?"

"I never imagined you, Allie-face, being that dirty."

I blush. "Why not?"

"I don't know. I just don't see you like that. I guess I'm too used to seeing you at work."

I smirk, and maybe it's the fact I'm a little buzzed. Or maybe it's how drunk he makes me just being near him, and that Paco has left and there's no one near us at the bar, or for what feels like miles around, and I feel like it.

I slide my hand up his leg until it lands on his cock, which feels thick through just one layer of fabric. Well, hello. I'm not the only one without underwear tonight. "You have no idea who I am, or what I'm capable of, Jay. You think I'm innocent? Just wait for tonight."

"Jesus," he growls. "Were you this dirty with Mark?"

"Whoa! Personal question," I say, and pull back, reaching for my drink.

He shrugs. "Seems appropriate if you ask me."

I tense, and take a deep breath. "The truth is, no."

"How was your sex life with him?"

My torso tenses again. Jocko can sense it, because he says, "Hey, if this is too much for you to talk about..."

"No. It's fine. It's just a sad truth. Honestly, we were having very little sex for the last two years of our relationship. I should have seen the breakup coming, because something wasn't right for a long time. Neither of us really knew what it was, though, so I guess we just tried not to acknowledge it. And no, I never gave Mark a Spiderman BJ. That's the honest truth."

"Well, I'm a lucky fucking guy, then, aren't I?" he bellows, and laughs.

I grin broadly, from the heart. It hits me then that one of the things about Jocko that makes him so warm, so easy to be around is that he's not afraid to express that he's grateful to be in my presence. And his expression is always genuine. It even feels a little as though he's drawing energy from me.

"Right there. *That's* something Mark would never do. He would never just look me in the eye and say, 'Damn, I'm lucky, aren't I?' How are you so...Jocko?"

He spins around on his bar stool to face me.

"I believe we don't know when our time is going to come, Allie Jenkins. So we damn well better enjoy the time we have. And let those people around us know how much we enjoy them. And I enjoy you. If it weren't for you, I'd be sitting in a stuffy office in a city that's still stuck in the throes of winter right now. Do you know this will be the first vacation of five days I've taken for the entire time I've been working at EdTechX? And damn, it feels so good to get away."

I nod and take another sip of my drink. "Yes. I've noticed you're a bit of a workaholic."

Leaning forward, he spreads my legs so they press against the outside of his. My dress rides up dangerously high. If there were other people around this part of the resort right now, I wouldn't be doing this. Too public.

Instead, it's one of the hottest scenes of my life. A warm breeze rolls across our faces, and I feel the tension that was between us just minutes ago replaced by a relaxing, warm feeling in my core.

Damn, is he good at the push-pull thing. And he doesn't even try.

"Well, I'm not afraid to say that. Allie, I'm lucky. Seriously lucky. And not just because we're fucking on the balcony tonight, but because I like being able to sp-"

"Wait-wait. Did you just say 'because we're fucking on the balcony tonight'?"

He chuckles. "I mean, you don't remember what you whispered to me? That's not something a guy forgets."

"Oooh. Right. Sorry. Second margarita."

"I mean, if you want to lose your Jocko virginity tonight, we can do that any way you want."

I roll my eyes. "Did you just say 'Jocko virginity?' Like that's an actual *thing?*"

He puts his hands on the flesh of my thighs, working slowly up to my hips.

"That's right. You've never had sex with me. So if we do, you'd be losing your *Jocko virginity*."

"If that wasn't hilarious, I'd be mad that you're so cocky." I shake my head, smiling. "Are you mad that I'm not a virgin?"

He recoils. "Excuse me?"

"Are you mad. That I'm not a virgin?"

He cocks his head, his expression turning dead serious. "Wait, you're not a virgin? I'm sorry, we can't do this. Virgins only."

"*Excuse me?*" He's like whiplash.

He looks at me like I'm an alien, then throws his head back laughing.

"What? What's so funny?" I ask.

"I'm kidding, Allie. What year do you think this is? 1800? Where women are only good if their hymen is still intact? I'm a little insulted, actually."

My body warms, and I have another swallow of my drink. "Honestly, it was a point of contention with me and Mark. He was always a little jealous that I didn't lose it to him."

"How *did* you lose your virginity?"

"Drunk. Freshmen year of college. Some younger guy was visiting from high school. We got near black-out drunk. I barely remember."

"Damn. That doesn't sound fun. He didn't..."

"Force himself on me? Oh, hell no. If anything, I was the aggressive one that night. I just wanted to lose it, you know? I was tired of being Allie the virgin. And he was hot."

"So you lost your v-card to this guy. Did you give him a Spiderman BJ?"

I giggle. "No. I told you. You were the first."

"Okay. Because if you've done that with any other guy, Allie, I swear to God..." Jocko is looking so cute right now, like he's trying to be mad but totally not, grinning from ear to ear.

"Oh? What are you going to do about it?" I challenge him.

He smirks, and his thumbs finally reach the danger zone between my legs. He licks his lips and tilts his head a little as he flips his right hand around and presses into my clit.

I moan involuntarily, and my torso tenses.

"Oh. Oh. Jocko. Here?"

"I told you I want to taste you."

"You can't go down on me here. We're...in public." Okay, I sound a bit panicked because I am.

"There's no one around."

"But someone could come."

"Oh, someone *will* most definitely come. You." Oh my God, he's serious.

"Jocko, please..."

He glances around, and he's right. There is literally *no one* within earshot or eyesight. We're away from most of the action at this bar, and the bartender is gone. We picked a good place.

But kneeling down while I'm on a bar stool? Really?

The man is creative, though, and he looks around to gauge the scene. I see his eyes light up with an idea. I squeal as he lifts me up by my hips. I wrap my legs around him as he kisses me, then opens the bar counter and slips inside. There's a long coffee table stored in the now-closed bar, and he grabs a towel for comfort and tosses it across the table before laying me down.

Then, kneeling on the ground, he doesn't waste time as he licks my inner thigh in the direction of my core until he reaches my clit. I throb and grip the towel behind me as he gets right down to business.

He laps me up eagerly, sending a hand under my dress to caress my boobs.

Yes, both of them. He's got big hands and he manages to touch one nipple with his pinkie, the other with his thumb.

His hand on my chest serves the dual purpose, keeping me anchored to the table because I want to sit up, but if I do, I might pop above bar level and if someone is walking by, they'll know what's going on.

Jocko growls — *he fucking growls* — into my pussy and I feel like this whole session is challenging me. He's tacitly asking me: *you said you're dirty, Allie. Just how dirty can you be?*

My answer? Very. For some reason with Jocko I want to be.

I grab his head with both hands and steer my clit into his tongue which feels incredible. Little prickles of pleasure pop everywhere on my skin. But when he pulls his hand around and runs his two fingers inside me like he did earlier *with* the combination of his tongue on my clit...*I'm done.*

Or should I say, I come *un*done.

I have to put both hands over my mouth to keep myself from screaming and alerting the entire resort to this mating ritual. I pulsate at his will, my hips thrashing against his tongue. He's so damn good.

For a moment, he stops, and I glance at him almost angrily. "Uh, what are you doing?"

"Just wanted to look at you for a sec." He winks, then smirks. "Allie-face."

I can't help laughing. Who *does* that?

Who calls me Allie-face in the middle of going down on me like a hungry dog?

This *man.*

He starts again and curls his fingers up and into me, and I can't help it. I let out a yelp before I'm able to cover my mouth. Jocko doesn't seem to notice — or maybe he just doesn't care.

I clench around his fingers and come like an ocean wave crashing onto the seashore.

When he's done, he gets on his knees and smirks. "Well, that was fun."

I lay back in the dark light, hands above my head, hair splayed out behind me.

Then we hear a voice that makes my stomach curdle.

"Uh, excuse me? Can I get some service here?"

Putting a finger over his lips in the *hush* gesture, he stands up. I pull down my dress, but don't move from the coffee table. If I sit up, this person will surely see me.

"Can I help you?" I see Jocko smile and say.

"Yeah," the voice that I can't see says. "I'll take a Modelo Negra."

"Coming right up."

Jocko reaches down, just to the left of my ear, and opens the mini fridge to grab a beer.

"Here you are. Have a good one, man."

"Thanks."

I hear the man walking away, and finally Jocko gestures for me to stand up.

"That was a close call," I say.

Jocko shrugs. "Not really. I'm sort of amazing at bartending, too," he winks.

Add it to the list of things that make me attracted to Jocko. I've always had a thing for bartenders. "You ready for dinner?" I ask.

"Definitely," he says. "Especially seeing as I already had my appetizer."

"I owe you one," I say.

He shakes his head. "You don't owe me a thing. Now let's go eat some delicious steak."

We walk arm in arm back over to the restaurant where we're supposed to meet for dinner, and now I'm wondering if there is such a thing as love at first orgasm.

Or *fourth* orgasm. Whatever.

Because damned if I'm not starting to fall for the man.

And this feels like a dangerous fall, one I fear might be all by myself.

13

JOCKO

After I run quickly back to the men's room to wash my face, I join Allie and company at dinner, which is already in session. We've got a table of eight with a gathering of her college friends under the reserved area of the eleventh-floor seafood-themed restaurant. Unfortunately, the only seat left for me is right next to Mark.

It's not that I don't *like* the guy. Relationships go haywire for all sorts of reasons, and he doesn't seem like a bad dude. But we've already had one awkward run-in for the day on our Juliet balconies, and I think that's enough, since I'm trying to just enjoy the night with Allie.

Nevertheless, I sit down with a smile and give Allie a kiss on the lips.

"Hey, babe," she says. "I ordered you a steak already, since the waiter came through."

"You know me so well," I say, gripping her shoulder, and it's not lost on me that she just *hey babe'd* me for the first time.

I nod politely to Mark and Barb on my left, and meet a few of Allie's other friends from college at the table.

"We ordered some appetizers," Mark says, nudging me. "Olive?"

I wave him off, and turn to our somewhat elusive server to order a *cerveza*.

"Allie, how about you? Olive?"

I see it happening before it happens.

"Ewww! Gross. No way," she says, pushing the olive plate away.

Shit. I totally forgot to tell Allie that she now *likes* olives since I told that to Barb and Mark.

"Oh," Mark says, measuredly. "I thought you said you liked olives now?"

Mark and Barb shoot each other that *couples look* which tells me they've been talking about the little miscommunication Allie and I had back up on the balcony.

I squeeze Allie's thigh underneath the table and shoot her a subtle-but-not-so-subtle *look*. Leaning close to her ear, I whisper ever so quietly, so no one else can hear, that she now likes olives on pizza. It might be too obvious, but I don't want some silly detail about a pizza topping being the thing that blows our cover as fake fiancés.

Allie squints back at Mark, then says nonchalantly, "Ohh. Right. Well, you know. I like olives on pizza."

"On thin crust," Mark adds.

"That's right."

"You were always a deep-dish person," he insists.

Allie smiles and bites her lip. I would give one-hundred dollars to know what she is thinking behind the veil of those eyes right now, because whatever it is seems positively devilish.

She shrugs. "People change, don't they?"

"Ain't that the truth!"

Thank the lords above.

Peyton O'Rourke's booming voice swings in from behind us, breaking up the conversation and saving the day so we can move on from this conversation topic. He slaps his hand on my shoulder.

"J-Money. Good to see you again," he says, sticking out a hand for me to shake. He makes the rounds at the table.

"J-Money?" Allie giggles in my ear. "I'm going to have to remember that one."

I shrug. Honestly, if the Superbowl MVP wants to give me a nickname, I'm okay with that. And Peyton just seems like one of those guys who gives everyone and their mother a cool nickname. Must be a football thing.

"Once you all finish eating, come join us for the cocktail hour just on the other side of that stylish divider," he says, pointing with his cocktail. "We just finished our dinner so we're over there hanging out and taking pictures. Join us, will ya?"

He slaps his hand on my shoulder, gives me a wink, and I nod.

Fuck yeah. I love when superstars aren't stuck up douchenozzles. Which Peyton clearly isn't.

Our food arrives not too long after. While we're eating, Mark and Barb seem to be giving us weird looks. I worry that they might "discover" us, but then I realize that with how Allie and I have set up our fake engagement, the only way they can really figure it out is if one of us cracks and tells the truth. And why would either of us do that?

Luckily, dinner passes without any more suspicious *olive* incidents that might throw people off, thank God.

~

WE SNAP a plethora of pictures once we join the wedding party after dinner. I do a lot of the snapping since I'm not necessarily an integral part of their friend group, and I don't mind. It's quite an interesting mix of people, from Maddy's friends and parents from her small town in Pentwater, Michigan, to Peyton's plethora of NFL football player friends from Texas where he plays and around the country.

Maddy looks gorgeous in a white wrap dress, and she takes full advantage of the night to wear a sash that says *bride to be.*

Peyton kisses Maddy, and they seem like such a happy couple. The slightest seed of a thought occurs to me that maybe, someday — not tomorrow, or the day after, but someday — I *might* think about putting an end to my eternal bachelorhood.

Or maybe it's just the fact Allie's scent has completely intoxicated me at this point. Allie plus a cerveza and a mojito = best buzz ever.

From where we're standing in the back of the cocktail area, we watch as Peyton walks over and steps up onto a chair and dings his glass of champagne with a spoon.

"Attention, everyone! Attention," he says, and the place quiets down real fast. Surprising considering how drunk everyone is. He clearly knows how to command a room.

"First, I just want to say thank you to everyone for coming. I know destination weddings aren't easy. You've got to get off work, and buy plane tickets, and planning it all. So thank you again. Here-here." He raises his glass for a toast, and we all drink.

"Second. I want to tell a quick story. Everyone asks me all the time, 'when did I know she was the one?' And I'm going to tell you that story tonight. I need to tell it tonight because tomorrow, it's all on the best man," he nods to a very buff guy below him whom I recognize as a wide receiver on Peyton's team, Gill Westinghouse.

"Say what you gotta say, Peyton," Westinghouse says with a slight twang. "Because tomorrow, your ass is mine."

Everyone laughs, including Peyton.

"I can't wait for tomorrow," Peyton continues. "But the other reason I need to tell this story tonight is because I don't want to get choked up on my wedding day."

Rowdy as some of the guests in the crowd are, the murmurs among us instantly cease. Allie squeezes my hand a little harder and I feel her palm sweating. "So when did I know she was the one? It's a fair question. There are two moments. Well, maybe three. As some of you might know, I didn't have the easiest childhood. When I moved to Maddy's town to start high school and live with my grandmother, I didn't know a soul. Maddy was my neighbor. I wasn't the easiest kid to talk to, or to deal with. But when I saw her as I was unloading my stuff from the truck, she smiled and waved to me. That was the first time I fell in love."

Maddy stands to the side, looking at Peyton with glossy eyes and clutching a drink. She wipes away a tear. One of her bridesmaids wraps an arm around her.

"The second time was when I looked out my window one day and I saw her singing-"

"No, Peyton," Maddy chides, good-naturedly. "We're not talking about my secret singing."

Peyton beams. "Yes, we are, Maddy. Because you have a beautiful voice. I heard her singing Neko Case and my heart just about exploded on the spot."

Maddy embarrassingly shakes her head a little, but she's grinning.

"And the third time. Well, Mr. and Mrs. Cooper, we get along now, but it's no secret that I was a troubled kid growing up, especially in high school. And they would invite me over for dinner because they were good people and I was a hungry kid, and my diet consisted basically of corned beef hash or other canned food dinners — if I was *lucky*. But like I said, I was a troubled kid and I wasn't the most well-behaved. And Mr. Cooper tried to put an end to having me over for dinner. I can definitely understand him not wanting a bad influence like me in contact with his daughter."

Another laugh.

"But one day, I happened to see and hear through my window, Maddy pleading with her parents to have me over. And she said, 'Well, if we can't let this poor boy come over for dinner, would you please explain what we're going to church for on Sunday? Because I think we're losing sight of the whole 'help thy neighbor thing.'"

Peyton's eyes gloss over. I steal a glance at Allie, and she's tearing up, too.

He wipes away a tear. "Onions. Someone cutting an onion out there?" he says, and everyone laughs, gladly breaking the tension.

"Anyway, even though it wasn't until almost a decade after that that we got together, I knew right then and there she was the one I wanted on my team. Maddy, I love you and I can't wait to spend the rest of my life on your team."

Peyton's speech is just the right amount of heartfelt and corny. The crowd breaks out in raucous applause, so much so that a few people walk by and peek in to see what the commotion is.

When Peyton comes down off the chair, he hugs and kisses Maddy, and follows that with Mr. and Mrs. Cooper.

Hell, I'm even welling up with emotions I didn't know I was capable of.

It's almost surreal to see an NFL superstar breaking into tears because of his girl.

All I can think is, *I want that*.

Whatever he's feeling for Maddy, that's what I want when I get married.

If I get married. Some day.

Allie hugs me. "Wow," she says. "Just wow."

"I know," I say. "That's love."

14

JOCKO

Peyton's speech takes the air out of the room, and I gladly use the moment to hit the bar and pick up another round of mojitos for Allie and I.

Peyton appears at the bar next to me as I wait.

"J-Money," he says, patting me on the back. "Good to see you again. How the hell are you tonight?"

"Dude, that was a hell of a speech," I say. "I had no idea you thought that way about her."

"Well, of course, man. What, you think I'm gonna marry a girl without being head over heels for her? Shit."

He orders a gin and tonic, and both of ours arrive at the same time. Then he squeezes my shoulder and leans in a little. "J-Money, take a walk with me. Will ya?"

Peyton's tone is eerie. Almost fatherly. But when the fucking groom asks you to take a walk with him, you do it.

"I've got to take this mojito to Allie."

"Hey, Magpie," he says to Maddy, who's head swivels instantly our way. "Can you take this mojito to Allie for Jocko? We're going to take a little stroll."

Again, something weirds me out about his tone and the

way he says *little stroll.* I'm not intimidated by most people, but the man is a cocky rock of muscle, with attitude to match.

"Where are we heading?" I say, drink in hand.

"Just want to chat, man," he says, and leads me down a pathway to the beach. We take off our sandals and walk barefoot along the shore. "So what's this I hear about you almost beating Steph Curry in college?"

I smirk, and tell the story about how, in my senior year when Curry was a junior at Davidson, we were basically guarding each other and having a three-point shootout. "Curry wasn't the Curry we know now, though," I admit. "Once he reached the NBA and had Steve Kehr as coach, he really elevated his game to superstar level."

"Uh-huh. That's great. So, look, man, what's the deal with you and Allie?"

A host of adrenaline is released inside me. I take a sip of my drink. So *this* is what he wanted to talk about. I knew he didn't care about my old basketball playing days. "What's the deal with me and Allie...in what way?"

Peyton gets that big, dimpled smile, and does his soon-to-be patented shoulder slap-and-squeeze. "I mean, how did you fall in love with her, man? When did you *know*?"

I hesitate, and his smile hardens. "I was just thinking today about some of the stories you told at your brother Everett's party last summer. Didn't seem like you were the type to settle down."

I laugh, a little awkwardly. "Oh. That."

For my entire life I'd looked at having an older brother who plays professional football as a huge blessing. This is the first time it's come back to bite me.

Peyton narrows his eyes, unrelenting on his point when I hesitate again. Truth is, I have no idea what to say right here.

He's sharp as a tack, and I feel like he might go right over to Allie and verify whatever I tell him. So I've got to choose my words carefully.

"I'm sensing some resistance coming from you, in terms of expressing your love. So I gotta ask, are you not in love with her? You're getting engaged. You better be in love with her. Look, I know it's kind of weird, but Allie and I go way back to freshmen year of college. She had my back in a very platonic way while I was going through the worst breakup of my life that year. And since then, I've always felt this need to watch over her like she's my little sister or something."

"Oh, I got ya."

I am the *master bullshitter*. Stretching the truth — or even occasionally lying my teeth off — is something I've always been able to pull off. Yet something tells me Peyton's bullshit detector is off the charts, and that I better pull out my A-game stat.

"You got me? And just what do you 'got'?" That slight Texas twang comes out of his voice. "Look, man, you seem like a good guy and all, but if you play with Allie's heart..."

"I'm not playing with anyone's heart," I cut in. I decide I'll be as honest as I can be — without admitting the part about us not being engaged or in love, of course. Luckily, it's not hard to feign feelings for Allie, because I've got a lot of those. "And to answer your question, I knew I was in love with her the first time I saw her. When she walked into the job. I wanted her. I didn't say anything because I couldn't. She was with Mark at the time. Plus, in a by-the-book tech company like ours, inter-office dating isn't exactly smiled upon in the current climate. But trust me, I want the best for her. I want to see her happy, and she makes me happy. So that's love, right?"

Peyton pauses, ankle deep in the ocean, and crosses his

arms. A big gust of wind makes his button down, short-sleeve t-shirt flap against his skin. I step in next to him. We must both look pretty ridiculous right now. Couple of grown ass men in expensive Tommy Bahama beach wear, Huck Finning our khakis so we can wade in the water.

Peyton sips his drink, then steels his gaze on me with sharp, narrow eyes.

"You didn't say you love her."

"Um, what?"

"You said, 'So that's love, right?' You did not say the words, 'I love Allie.' Why not?"

I purse my lips. "Seems like the same thing. It's just semantics."

"Semantics reveal our subconscious thoughts," he says.

And Jesus, I should have known you don't become a repeating Super Bowl champion quarterback without an eye for detail.

His nostrils flare, and he grabs the back of my neck with his hand, then whispers close into my ear. "All I'm saying, J-Money, is if you are fucking around with Allie, I *will* kill you and have your organs harvested to the black market. That way, you'll at least do some good to someone in this world. Do you understand?"

I freeze, feeling my blood run cold. The sound of the waves is drowned out by the beating of my thumping, tell-tale heart, which I pray to God Peyton can't hear. His face is so serious, he looks like John Wayne in one of those old cowboy movies right before he's about to perform some heinous act.

"Not gonna happen," I swallow. "She's my girl. Great girl. I'm lucky. I know that."

And none of that's a lie.

The love thing? Well, we'll have to see about that.

But all of the above are true.

For a moment, as Peyton sips his cocktail and then turns back to me, I wonder if he knows everything. Somehow, he overheard us talking about how this whole week is a façade. He's going to murder me right now, throw me in the ocean, and...

Well, fuck it. I can fight, too, and I've got a hell of a fighting spirit. One of the benefits of growing up in a small Nebraska town is that you get into your fair share of scuffles, and it hardens you. Not like most of the suburban cream cheese I went to college with.

But instead, Peyton's frown turns to a smile, and he slaps me on the back again, his tone light and cheery.

"That's good to hear, brother. Sorry to be a dick. I just wanted to pull you aside because we didn't get to have a one-on-one yet, you know? Nice night for a chat."

"Very nice night."

We turn and head back, walking toward an almost full moon. His tone changes to serious once more.

"But seriously," he says. "Mark already did enough damage, leading her on. He had his problems, too, though, so I forgave him. If you break her heart, I know how to hire a hit man and have the bank to make it look like an accident." He winks.

I pull his own back-slapping move, giving him some of his own medicine. "Don't worry about us, my man. It's your wedding week."

"Sure, sure," he says, then flashes a tight smile. "What's this I hear about Allie liking olives? She *hated* them in college."

I squint.

How does everyone and their best friend know that Allie

hates olives? And how does that information get around so fast?

I guess she and I still have a long way to go.

I make a mental note to be more observant. Not because of anyone's threats... nah, this time's only because I want to.

15

ALLIE

Twenty or thirty people mull around the cocktail area, drinking and socializing as I wait for Jocko to come back with my drink.

It's not that I'm bad at socializing independently. I love going by myself to a café on a Saturday morning, or even to my local brewery a few blocks from my house in downtown Detroit.

But right now my palms are sweaty and I'm clamming up as I talk to Naomi, a college friend who is now an NFL cheerleader and engaged to one of Peyton's groomsmen. She may have even met her husband through her connection to Peyton.

"I just didn't know he had that in him," Naomi says. "I genuinely thought all Peyton got emotional about was football and that dog he and Maddy got last year."

We make small talk for a few minutes about dogs, and she compliments my dress, which actually catches me off guard. I don't get intimidated easily, but she's just one of those women who clearly hit the genetic lottery.

"Yeah, you look really good," she says, and I realize *she's* checking *me* out, as she runs her eyes over me. "Do you have like a workout plan you follow?"

"My cowork-" I catch myself midsentence and clear my throat, adjusting my glasses as I begin to answer her again. *Dammit. Fiancé mode.* "My fiancé put a routine together for me. Jocko and I work out together most days in the gym."

Her eyes widen, and she gives me another up-and-down. "Seriously? Could I get a copy of that program?"

My stomach tingles. Is a Dallas Cowboy cheerleader seriously asking me about *my* workout program?

Bravo, Jocko.

"I mean, I suppose I could write down a few things for you."

"That'd be great." She turns and speaks loudly in the direction of her man. "And maybe Jocko could have a talk with Gill about how it's okay to work out with your fiancée! Ahem!"

Gill Westinghouse rolls his eyes playfully. "Baby, you know I love doing things with you. But I have to get in the *zone* for my workouts."

She frowns. "But I want to work out with you."

With a smirk, Gill wraps an arm around her and kisses her hard. "Aw, well, we can always get a post-workout in." He wiggles his eyebrows. "Or a pre-workout."

She giggles like a little schoolgirl, and I raise my empty glass in a silent cheers to them as they continue making out.

To true love.

Speaking of true love — I mean, fake fiancés — where is Jocko?

My buzz is basically perfect right now. And I almost — *almost* — want to just escape to our room and carry out our plan.

Although I'm still tingling from the way he went down on me not two hours ago.

Seriously, I have not *ever* felt a man be so ravenous for me.

Just then, Mark appears in my peripheral vision, because *of course* he would when I'm thinking about men being ravenous versus those who were not. He wanted me...*sometimes.*

I can say this, though. Mark never wanted me so bad he tossed me on a coffee table behind a bar, kneeled down and turned me into a panting mess of pleasure, then stood up and pretended like he was an actual *bartender* just so he didn't blow my cover.

As risky as that whole public hookup was, I have to admit it was hot as fuck, if I'm being honest. And the fact that Jocko seems to get pleasure from *giving* me pleasure... well lets just say I get butterflies just thinking about it.

I see Maddy making a line for me with two drinks in her hand. "Here's your mojito," she says.

"Thanks," I say as I take it and take a sip. "Where's Jocko, by the way? He was supposed to be getting me this drink."

"Jocko and Peyton took a walk."

"Oh. They're really getting along swimmingly."

Maddy shrugs. "You know Peyton. He's got this way with everyone. The infamous Peyton mystique. Not sure what he wanted to talk about with Jocko."

"Probably sports."

"Yeah! That's it. I think he wanted to hear Jocko's Steph Curry story. So hey, I just wanted to say something real quick to you," Maddy says, pulling me aside.

My heart hammers a little harder. "Oh?"

She nods. "Peyton told me what a great friend you were to him in college. He says some of those years were the toughest years of his life — he had that horrible breakup — and that you helped him not turn to, you know, bad things. Like drugs and alcohol. So I just wanted to say thank you for that."

"Oh, it's no big deal. What are friends for?"

She smiles. "If everyone thought like that, the world would be a better place. Great ring, by the way."

"Thanks! Can't wait to see yours tomorrow."

Mine and Maddy's moment is interrupted when a couple of Maddy's teacher friends come up to us, and I excuse myself to go to the deck to get some air. My peace is interrupted when Barb appears behind me.

"Hey," she smiles. "How are you?"

I let out a frustrated sigh. "Look, Barb, I don't know why you're being so nice, but it's not necessary. We don't have to — and probably shouldn't be — friends." I don't want to be rude, but I don't really like her and she should know that. It's easier if I'm direct, and she can just cut the charade.

"Oh. Well, okay, then."

She turns to face out toward the ocean, but she stays here, with me. A steady breeze soothes both of our faces. "Mark's not a bad guy," she tells me.

I scoff, wanting the conversation to end, but also curious where she's going with this, so I exasperatedly ask, "What are you talking about?"

"When I met him...we talked all about our exes. We kind of connected over it, actually."

My skin prickles, lovely. "Well, I'm glad I was a topic of conversation."

"You know, I've dated guys who just trash talk their exes. '*Oh my God, Marsha was the worst, she was such a bitch, she sucked at cooking.*' And I always thought that was weird, you know? Like, if you're dating such a bitch, what does that say about you? You're the kind of guy who puts up with dating a bitch."

"What did he say about me?" I manage to croak out, then take a big swill of my drink. I can't deny my curiosity.

Barb takes a deep breath. "He said you were great. He said he wished it had worked out with you two, and he wishes you the best." A single chuckle escapes her mouth. "And you know what the funny thing is? That's when I knew *this is a good guy*. He's not trashing his ex, even though he could, in order to make himself out to be some kind of victim. Mark didn't do any of that. He said he wished he could have been a better man with you, but he just couldn't figure it out."

My shoulders drop, and I pinch the bridge of my nose as a wave of emotion swells in me. Well, there I have it. *He* couldn't figure it out, *it* being me or rather, our relationship. Newsflash, neither could I.

We were good together for a while, but our differences got in the way — little things like where to go for dinner, music preferences, and so on. I got tired of giving in and Mark knew it, but he was very staid in his ways, I guess we grew apart. But shit, it still hurt. Had I faced our slow detachment when it was happening we might have parted on less-painful terms. Gah! Who knows?

"I'm sorry," she says. "I'm probably still speaking out of turn. What I want to say is that Mark isn't ashamed that he dated you or something. I think it's one of the things that makes our relationship strong. We talk about everything. I've got my exes, too. And he was very clear that he wanted me to be nice to you. Sorry if that made it awkward."

"Look, I appreciate you trying to be nice to me, but what I'm up to is none of your business."

A few beats pass, and Barb kind of stares out awkwardly

in the distance, her body twisting around. "So that's the end of this conversation," I add.

Finally, Barb says, "I'm going to head back to where the rest of the people are. I'll try not to be too...awkward, or whatever." She shrugs. "But I *am* just an awkward person. Sorry."

I nod, and take a deep breath, happy to hear her footsteps as she walks away.

Right now, I need to be alone.

In the distance, close to the ocean, I can make out the two figures of Jocko and Peyton wading in the ocean and chatting. I wonder what they're talking about.

I take a few deep breaths, and I'm considering heading back to the party when I turn around and see — *guess who.*

Fuck. My. Life.

"Oh," Mark says, rubbing the back of his neck. "I was just looking for Barb. Someone said they saw her out here."

I shake my head. "She went back to the party."

"Ah. I see." His eyes roam around before they land on me. "Mind if we talk for a minute?"

I clench my non-drink hand at my side.

What is this? *Corner Allie night?*

"Might as well," I grit out. I'm at least several drinks in at this point, so there's never a better time for a little awkward ex conversation.

"You...doing okay?" he asks.

"Oh, do not start with this condescension," I burst out.

He pinches his eyebrows. "How is that a condescending question?"

"You're asking me like you would ask a first grader. *Are you doing okay, honey? I know math can be hard.*"

"That's not what I meant."

"Well, what did you mean?"

He runs a hand through his hair. "I'm just trying to talk to you, Allie. Have a civil conversation for once."

"Did we not before? And why does that even matter? We're broken up, *Mark*. We're not anything now. We *shouldn't* be worried about conversing. Hell, we shouldn't even be in the same zip code or country."

"Why are you getting so defensive? I'm just trying to talk. We're going to be seeing each other in the future when our college friends get together from time to time. So we might as well not avoid each other."

"I'm not avoiding you. But that doesn't mean I want to have a late-night, heart-to-heart conversation with you."

He runs a hand down his chin as if he had a goatee.

"Barb seems great," I say. It comes out as a passive-aggressive comment, so I try to emphasize. "I really mean that."

"Happened so fast," he says, nodding. He takes a few steps toward me, but keeps a distance of a few paces.

"You're telling me."

"You and Jocko seemed to have happened equally as fast."

"Just sorta came outta nowhere," I say. If only he knew.

"That's good. Seems like he gets you." He squints out in the ocean, then looks at me. "Since when did you start liking olives?"

"Seriously? Are we doing the olive thing again?"

He shrugs. "Sorry, I'm just curious. Did your taste buds change? I mean, we *did* go out to eat together for five years. And never once did you eat olives."

"Things change," I say, sighing, and noting that Jocko better come up with a more believable lie next time. Or at least one that doesn't involve me pretending to like something I hate.

He takes a swig of his beer and nods. "Things do change. People change. Just...I hope you're not rushing into something with this guy."

"Are you serious?!" I scoff. "You are *not* allowed to give me relationship advice."

He puts his palms up. "Silly me, I know. I still want you to be *happy* even though we're broken up. Long term. I mean, he seems okay but — Jocko, really? What kind of name is that?"

"So I shouldn't be dating him because he has a weird name?"

"That's not the point. I guess I've just noticed you two acting a little...weird."

"Weird how?"

"Well, like on the balcony. Really? You need to walk out half naked with your boobs completely out? Barb isn't the jealous type. Plus, we are very secure in our relationship. And, I don't know. Just something about the way you two interact...just sets my Spidey sense off."

I finish my drink, cross my arms and step up to him.

"How dare you! You have no right to comment on my relationship," I spurt out. "If Jocko and I are swingers and we want to go into town and find some Cancún strippers to hook up with tonight, that's *our* business."

He shakes his head. "That's just not *you* though. And you know it."

I bite my lip, measuring my next words as carefully as I can when I've got the kind of buzz I do right now. "Maybe the *me* that you knew isn't *me* anymore. You ever consider that? Maybe I'm someone else now. Someone new."

Or, maybe you never knew me at all. At least, you never knew the me I wanted to be.

And I'm a very different *me* now.

Now I'm the girl who gets head behind the closed bar around sundown in a very public place. By the man with the golden tongue.

Though it's a bitter pill to swallow that I was with a man for five years who didn't truly *get me.*

"Sorry. My bad. You're right. I just want to look out for you."

"Please. You lost that privilege when you broke up with me."

He continues. "I just have to wonder, is Jocko the type for you? Come on, I used to go to your work events. I heard the stories from him *firsthand.*"

"What stories?"

"He's a man-whore, b-"

"Stop," I grit out. "And you did *not* almost call me babe."

Mark continues, "Jocko's not the type to settle down. He's made that clear as day himself. That's all."

"What, so I'm not the type of girl a guy would want to settle down for?" I spew.

He stutters, and I squeeze my empty mojito so hard, I'm surprised the glass doesn't break.

He's got no comeback for that.

"I'm going back to the bar," I say through tight lips. "Have a nice night, Mark."

As I walk back to the cocktail area, my skin is hot. My insides are on fire, too, with a combination of anger about my run-ins with Mark and Barb, and wondering how far I'll go with Jocko tonight.

Our reserved cocktail area has closed down, and now everyone is apparently down on the first floor at the bar. I take the elevator down — Mark does, as well, awkward — but we don't say anything.

I burst out after the eleven-floor ride, and speed walk toward the reggaetón music. When I get to the bar I see Naomi, edging in at the corner. It's a public bar, so it's a combination of guests from our party and other guests staying at the resort.

"Hey! I was wondering where you went!" she says, and I note that her accent gets more southern the more she drinks. "You want a tequila shot?"

"Make it two," I say, needing something to quell the anxiety growing within.

"Damn, girl!" she says, and as she waves to the bartender my mind wanders.

I know Mark is trying to be a nice guy and watch out for me...or something. Part of me wonders if he's not just attempting to extend this aura of control over me. He was never overtly *controlling*. He never told me *my way or the highway* directly.

But slowly, with him, I saw my life eroding. He'd ask me passive-aggressive questions that seemed innocent enough, in a way.

Oh, are you getting together with your work friends again tonight? Hm. Well, okay, then.

Really? You want to take a three-week vacation to Colombia to learn Spanish? Do you want to change professions? No, I'm not trying to shoot you down, babe. Sometimes you just have to be realistic.

You want to watch porn? I don't know...that seems like something a man does with a dirty girl, you know?

Yes, I asked him if he wanted to watch porn. To which he said no.

I space back in as Naomi hands me two tequila shots.

"Cheers," she says. "One tequila, two tequila, three tequila, floor!"

I lick the salt and take the first shot, which goes down easy.

The second shot, however, is a little rough. The lime slice saves me as I burp a little in my mouth.

Burp. Not puke.

I'm not a puker. Haven't puked since freshmen year of college, actually. And I remember (well, it was told to me) that Peyton was the one holding back my hair as I expelled the copious alcohol I had drunk.

"I'm going to have one more," I say.

"You sure?" Naomi says. "The wedding's tomorrow, don't forget."

"The wedding's not until the evening," I scoff. "I'll be fine. Plus, I ate a lot of tacos for dinner, so I've got a good base going in. Más tequila, por favor!"

The bartender serves one up, and Naomi shrugs and joins me.

I glance back out at the dance floor, the seductive beat of the reggaetón music opening me up to the night. Without much thought, I head out to the dance floor to tear it up. I think Naomi follows behind me, but I'm not really sure.

And that's the last thing I remember that night.

DAY 3: WEDDING DAY

16

ALLIE

Freshmen year of college, Naomi and my college roommate, Elaine Samulski, were all drinking in my dorm room during fall semester. At this point in my life, I was a good girl who didn't drink a lot. I did not run with the "cool kids" in high school and didn't go to high school parties. I wasn't tempted.

But the three of us were bonding, and Mike Russell had brought us a marked-up bottle of tequila (he was going to the trouble of driving into town for the booze, after all, and risking arrest with a fake ID).

We weren't about to let this special night — and bottle — go to waste. All done up in the types of slinky, skin-tight dresses you can only get away with freshmen year of college, we downed our first two tequila shots, complete with the salt and lime setup. Those we bought at the grocery store ourselves. We were thrifty, at least.

All of us were amateur drinkers, and after we took the first couple of tequila shots, we asked each other if we could feel anything.

Nope, we all agreed.

So we did the logical thing that any eighteen-year old girls would do outside of adult supervision: we took four more shots each.

A half-hour later, when we stood up to get to the frat party, we sat right back down, so drunk we could barely walk.

Naomi and Elaine puked their brains out, but I metabolized the alcohol like a champ.

The next morning I woke up at the crack of dawn in a cold sweat, utterly dehydrated. I spent the whole day in bed, *wishing* I would have vomited up the alcohol. Peyton brought me a six-pack of Gatorade, aspirin, and even a beer (a little hair of the dog will do you good, Al), but even that didn't help me feel better.

It was the worst hangover of my life, and I vowed I would never do such a thing to my body again.

I succeeded.

Until today.

I wake up in a freezing hot sweat. When a sliver of light sneaks through the middle of the curtains and shines on my face, I begin to melt like a vampire.

"Jocko. Shut the curtains," I mutter, closing my eyes hard and nuzzling my head into the pillow. No answer.

"Jay?"

I turn myself over on my side, enjoying the fetal position for a few minutes before I finally gather the strength to push myself up.

I'm rife with soreness. My head. My chest. My stomach. Legs and arms. Everything throbs. An added layer of dread hits me when I realize I'm totally naked. And then, my mind flashes to last night, well, actually, this morning, when I woke up for a split second.

I examine the room in a panic. Clothes flung all over the

room, most of the garments messily strewn on the ground. My panties. My bra. Jocko's pants. His boxers.

What the hell happened last night?

I jump in the shower to try and calm my nerves, but it does little. It's not even nine a.m. Why is Jocko not here? He was up as late as me...*right?*

My heart races with anxiety. Oh God. Jocko and I had planned to do *it* last night. I'd whispered the sweet, sexy nothings into his ear that every man wants to hear. And I meant it. I wanted him to do me in all of the places, in all parts of the room. And especially on the balcony.

And judging by the evidence, that's exactly what we did last night.

By the time I get out of the shower, a second wave of hangover pain sets in and it's all I can do to lie back on a pile of pillows with a towel wrapped around my body.

I curse whoever invented tequila, and Mark and Barb and myself for not being able to deal with my anxiety yesterday, and Peyton for stealing Jocko away from me for a walk.

At that moment, the door bursts open.

"Allie-face!" Jocko's voice booms. "How ya feeling?"

"Like I'm going to die."

He strolls inside and lets the door fall closed.

"I'm not surprised, to be honest."

"You're not?"

"I haven't seen a girl that drunk in years. Do you remember the speech you gave, standing on top of the bar?"

A jolt of cold adrenaline rolls through me. "Dear God. No. I didn't. You're lying."

He's carrying a big tray of something he sets down on the small table closest to the window. "You did."

I cringe in horror. "I didn't upstage the bride, did I?"

He shrugs. "I'd say your little announcement was in

good faith. You told everyone that this was the best wedding of all time, and that Peyton was the best guy, and thank you for coming."

"That doesn't sound so bad."

"Luckily, I think someone got it on camera for you, so you can watch it."

"I think I'll pass."

"In any case, I'm guessing you're a little hungover. So I thought you might like some breakfast in bed."

Slight relief pours through me. I lean over to the nightstand to grab my glasses, and my head throbs at every movement. Ack, I can eat breakfast without them, so I slide back and sit up to enjoy my meal. "That sounds heavenly."

The smell of aftershave intensifies, sexy and clean as he lays on the bed on my right side.

"It's the least I can do, especially after everything that happened last night."

Goosebumps roll across my skin from head to toe, and I open my mouth to speak, but I can't formulate my question in a way that seems appropriate.

Pulling out a table tray from somewhere, he sets the legs on either side of me, then turns and grabs a plate with scrambled eggs, biscuits, a croissant, sausage, fruit, water, OJ, and coffee.

"Breakfast is served, my lady."

"Thank you." I stir the eggs with my fork, and opt to chug the glass of ice water first.

"So what *did* we do yesterday, exactly?" I prod delicately. "From your perspective."

Jocko's eyebrows rise as high on his forehead as they will go. "You don't remember?"

I shrug, and gently shake my head. "The details are a little hazy."

"You don't remember fucking for two straight hours on the balcony?"

I drop the water on my chest, which luckily causes the majority to fall right onto my towel.

"Okay, Jay, I'm gonna be honest. I don't remember anything from last night past me taking tequila shots at the bar and you finding me on the dance floor. We...did it last night?"

He waves a hand in the air. "Naw. I'm just joshing you."

I punch him in the shoulder. "You dick! I'm in quite a state right now."

"Obviously. Here's what we really did."

He pulls out his phone and shows me a selfie he took last night in our bathroom of me and him. He's got a giant smile and is giving the camera a thumbs up with the same hand that holds back a bunch of my hair so it doesn't fall to the toilet.

"Really, you had to document this?"

"How could I not?"

"And why are all of our clothes strewn about the room?"

"Well, that would be because you *insisted* on stripping down and dancing to Katy Perry. You would *not* get on the bed until I played "Teenage Dream" multiple times. And joined you. Dancing. *Sans* clothing. I was resisting at first until I decided it would probably be good for you to dance alcohol out of your system."

"So you danced with me to Katy Perry? That is...the sweetest thing anyone's ever done for me."

"Thanks. Not sure if you knew this, but I'm kind of a sweet guy. You need me to cut up your sausage for you?" he adds.

"I can do it myself, thank you."

"You're the boss."

I eat and chew a little bit while he leans back next to me on the bed.

"Seriously, that's really sweet of you. Thank you for holding back my hair and indulging drunk Allie. And for bringing me breakfast." Almost unconsciously, I eye him suspiciously. "Why are you being so nice?"

He laughs heartily. "You had a bad night. We all have those once in a while. Happy to be here for you."

I shake my head. "But we had it all planned out and we were going to...you know...do *it* last night. Aren't you disappointed?"

"I mean, I think we've established you're hot, and yes, I want to sleep with you — I believe the feeling is mutual — but not like that. Not like you were last night. That would have been, just, no. You wouldn't have remembered it. And neither of us would have enjoyed it."

The wind of relief pours through me as I take another bite of egg and swallow it down, then turn to him.

"Why are you being such a good guy?"

He recoils. "Not sure how to answer that question. Mind if I have some of your coffee? Thanks."

Reaching over, he grabs my little white mug and has a sip.

"It's just, I disappointed you, and you're *nicer* to me? Makes no sense."

"How did you disappoint me?" He laughs. "Honestly, even though you don't remember it, I did have a great time last night. I laughed my ass off the whole night."

"But we didn't have sex."

"Is that supposed to be disappointing?"

"I don't know. I just feel like I ruined the night."

Leaning toward me, he angles my chin to him with a

finger and kisses me on the lips. "We'll have plenty of time for that."

"Really? We only have two more days left of this trip, though."

He closes his eyes thoughtfully, and it seems like he's about to say something profound when my phone rings.

Damn. I hate when these moments get interrupted.

"Here, let me get that," he says, grabbing the phone from its spot charging on the desk. "Huh. That's weird. It's Rhonda."

I scrunch up my nose. "Why would she be calling at this time? She knows we're on vacation."

"No clue." He hands me the phone and I answer it.

"Oh. My. Gosh! Congratulations, you fool!"

I squint, confused, and Jocko whispers to me to put her on speaker, which I do.

"Um, congratulations?" I ask. "For what?"

"You and Jocko! How on *Earth* did you two keep that under wraps? You are the craftiest couple I know!"

Jocko and I shoot each other an '*oh shit*' look, and Jocko puts the phone on *mute.*

"Jesus. How did Rhonda find out?" Jocko shoots over to me. "I've *only* told my mother."

"I have no clue," I whisper urgently. "I haven't told a soul. Not even my own mom!"

"This was supposed to stay contained. Between us, my mother, and the people of this party!" Jocko booms.

"Don't have to tell me that!" I bite back.

Rhonda taps the microphone receiver. "Um, hello? Allie?"

I take the phone off *mute.* "I'm here! Yes, you found out! We were, you know, keeping it under wraps. How did you find out anyhow? Social media?"

"Nope! Jocko's mom called the office to leave him a congratulations voice message on his work phone, you know, to surprise him. Her call got routed to me, and when she said she was Jocko's mother, we couldn't help but get to talking. I told her all about you, and Jocko's budding relationship and how you've been playing cat-and-mouse for the past four months."

"We have?"

Jocko and I exchange a look of shock.

"Oh, let's be real, Allie. You've had it bad for Jocko since, well even before you broke up with Mark."

I shake my head vigorously. "Uh, not true," I try to correct. Did I though?

"Whatever. I just wanted to call and give you my congratulations."

"Well, thanks," I say sheepishly.

"You don't sound too pumped. Everything okay in paradise?"

"Of course, it's okay."

"Wonderful. Oh, and check out this throwback photo I found of you and Jocko. I just posted online, and tagged all of your parents and siblings I could find. So happy for you two!"

A wave of throbbing hits my head and I suddenly regret eating the breakfast that Jocko so nicely served me.

"By the way, have you declared this relationship to H.R.? I hope so. If not, you could end up in some hot water. They're looking for someone to make an example out of. I don't think it will be you, but just make sure you do that when you get back on Monday."

Jocko and I gaze at each other in horror.

"I'm sure we'll be fine, though, right?" I say. "I mean,

they're not going to fire *Jocko*. He brings in like five percent of our company's revenue."

"Sure, but since we're on the smaller side as a company, all it would take is one badly handled PR scandal to ruin us. And technically, you should have already declared your relationship since you're engaged. You know all this, though. Enjoy your trip! Jocko's manager Ron says hi to both of you."

"Tell Ron hi from me and Jocko."

I hang up, and Jocko is leaning his elbows on his knees, holding his head.

"Fuck," he mutters. "Well, I guess the cat's out of the bag, then."

"I guess so."

His eyes narrow. "We're smart people, right, Allie?"

"I think so. Sometimes I have my doubts, though."

He chuckles. "How did we ever think it would be a good idea to come up with such an extravagant lie?"

"No idea." I gulp, as a message comes in from my mother. She must have seen the post that Rhonda made. It is a very passive-aggressive congratulatory message:

Mom: Hey, Allie, thanks for letting me know about the engagement! ☹ But seriously, congratulations! Can't wait to meet the guy ☺

I take a deep breath. "What are we gonna do, Jocko? We've dug quite the hole. I mean, I do like you but we're not engaged, obviously. Is that right what Rhonda said about the whole getting in trouble with HR thing."

"I'm not exactly well versed in HR policy for relationships. Seeing as I was never planning on one with another EdTechX employee."

"And then what happened?"

He comes closer to me, smiling as he peels off my towel. Waves of his intoxicating spell spark my core. I'm hungover. I should only be interested in lying face down at the pool and coming up with a plan to combat HR.

"And then I discovered Allie-face's dark side. And I knew I needed to make her mine. Make you mine. If only for five days. Because five short days is better than nothing."

Chills graft my skin as he kisses me lightly on the neck.

My hands drift through his tousled hair. "Let's just finish out the trip and deal with the consequences come Monday morning," I whisper. "But until then, anything goes."

He lifts his lips off of me, then finishes undoing my towel, revealing my total nakedness. He gets up and takes the tray off from the bed.

"Jocko...I can't. Not now."

"You don't want to?" he says as he drops his pants, and I'm reminded why I once heard a college teammate of his call him cocky jocky.

"I do. But I need to rest up. I haven't had sex in many months, and let's just say yesterday's action has me a little... overactive." I glance at the time on my phone. "Plus, I'm supposed to head down to the spa and get a facial with the girls at eleven."

"I understand," he says, and I admit I'm a little sad when he walks over and puts his swim trunks on. But it's true. "I'm going to head down to the beach for a bit. I want to catch some rays."

"Wait," I say with a smirk. "I've got time for something else before my spa facial."

"What do you mean?"

"Oh, come on," I giggle. "Like you've never given a girl a facial before?"

His eyes widen. "You want to..."

"Lie down, Jay. I'm feeling better now."

He stares at me as he lies down on the bed, getting naked.

I let my towel fall, slide toward him on all fours, then take his cock in my hand and gently lick the sides.

"This time," I say, "We're going to do this my way. Nice and slow."

I run my free hand over his washboard abs, and he's soon hard, as I take his flesh in my mouth.

"Jesus, Allie, what are you doing to me?"

BY THE TIME I get to the spa, the entire world seems to have found out about mine and Jocko's "engagement."

Thanks to Rhonda's post, and then another share by my mother, the word is whipping around my family, from my brothers and sisters to my cousins, aunts, and uncles. My phone is blowing up.

Even some clients whom Jocko and I both work with at EdTechX somehow now know.

To make matters worse, the quick hangover relief I was feeling post-breakfast has all but disappeared, and now a worse, second wave of the hangover sets in as Naomi and I head into the facial room.

I take a deep breath as I set my glasses and phone off on the side table and lie down on the bed next to Naomi.

"So," she giggles as we wait for our facial attendants to come in. "How was the rest of your night?"

"Let's just say things get a little hazy after, I think, the fourth tequila shot. I'm pretty sure I had a good time, though. How about you?"

"Sooo fun," she squeals, then turns to me with dead

serious eyes. "Gill and I had drunk sex for a couple of hours. He was the perfect drunk last night — couldn't quite come, but super hard. You know what I mean?"

I clench up. Ever since I've known her, from our earliest days back in college, Naomi has a penchant for talking frankly about sex.

"Oh, yeah, totally," I nod. "Hot."

"So what about you and Jocko? Did he take care of you last night? If you know what I mean." She winks mischievously as our two facial specialists come inside the darkened room.

"For sure," I lie. "We did it all night long."

"Is it awkward being next to Mark and Barb with your new man?"

Lupe puts the soothing lotion on my face, and I instantly feel better.

"We don't see them a ton. Although..."

I chuckle, mentioning our run-in with them yesterday on our Juliet balconies.

"You let him see you topless again? Oh my gosh, I would never. Well, maybe I would," she lets out a low, throaty chuckle. Naomi has always been the slightly naughtier one of our friend group. A buxom brunette, she's just one of those girls who was always able to attract male attention.

We settle into the facial because moving our mouths feels like it'll mess up the facial gel. Closing my eyes feels wonderful, and I let the hurt of the hangover just come, because I need to get it out of my system.

And a part of me starts doubting everything and wondering what else I need to get out of my system.

17

JOCKO

I've seen exactly one picture of my parents' wedding. They got married in a small town in a Moose Banquet social club hall after they knew each other for four months because my mother was pregnant. In the picture, my mom has a faint smile and my dad has a stoic expression. Over the years, I've tried to pry a little bit more and find out about how they got together, but they didn't seem to want to open up. My dad especially.

My mother was always the strong one, the one who brought all the love to the family. My father was the ever-serious one who did his duty, put all of his ego into his work and brought home a sufficient amount of money. When I was growing up he was quiet, liked to watch TV, and came to my basketball games on the weekends when he wasn't working. He did his duty as a husband, and I suppose that's all you can ask for in a way.

Although, yes, there was that year he philandered off for a while. Being honest, I don't know if I'll ever fully forgive him for that. It just seems like a shitty thing to do.

But it's also part of the reason I don't want to settle down.

I'd rather be honest and up front with the women in my life, than make promises I can't keep. Marriage has always seemed like a good idea for 'other people', but not for me.

As I wait for Allie to get ready, I watch with intrigue from the balcony of our hotel room out over the resort, able to see in the distance where chairs are being set up on the beach. Workers also put up the white archway that Peyton and Maddy will stand underneath when they say their vows.

The whole scene reminds me of a question girls love to ask me whenever they can get it in:

Do guys picture their weddings, too?

I think women are especially intrigued to hear my answer since I make it clear I am a self-declared eternal bachelor.

My answer would be this: I don't picture the specifics of the wedding. Maybe I have a block on those details because of my parents. They always pictured it, I don't care where it is. Beach, drab church, outside, inside, or even a courthouse. The location doesn't matter.

But I *do* picture the girl.

At least, I try to. In my mind, she's a hazy, faceless figure, with hair that oscillates between red, black, brown, and blond.

And I picture — if that's the right word, maybe feel is more appropriate — the love that will radiate in my heart for the girl as she walks down the aisle. I don't see why the location matters, when everything else will be a blur besides her.

Checking my watch for the third time, I turn my head slightly, but not enough to see her getting dressed. She wanted to make it a surprise.

"Can I turn around yet?" I prod.

"No, stay out there on the balcony. Two more minutes."

"You got it."

I'm wearing white pants, a seafoam green button down, Ray-Ban sunglasses, and shoes so bright white they justify the sunglasses in and of themselves because they could blind someone from how the sunlight reflects off of them. This getup took me all of sixteen minutes to put on, shower included. I respect women for the extra time they put into looking foxy. But this is also one of those times I love being a guy. We get extra time to think while our ladies get ready.

I return to watching them set up the chairs and get the carpet for everyone to walk down the aisle.

One of the benefits of a destination wedding is that it's four or five days of partying and memories for everyone who makes it. Peyton and Maddy did it right.

Shit, I know Allie and I are never going to forget this week.

For a lot of reasons.

I don't know what's going to happen after these five days are up. Yes, we've got some consequences to deal with when it comes to our jobs and HR. I'm the type who can talk my way out of anything. So I'm not too worried about that. Maybe I should be a little concerned, though, based on the flurry of texts and bylaws Rhonda has been sending me today. But it's Friday, I'm on vacation, Peyton and Maddy are getting married, and I refuse to worry about the real world.

I've decided that no matter what happens after this week, I'll never regret the stupid fucking decision to put a ring on Allie's finger and tell a few people we're engaged. When we get back, it's going to be painful to tell my mother that, *sorry, Allie and I "broke up."*

Oh yeah, and there's the fact that thanks to my Mom's sweet heart and wanting to leave a message on my work voicemail, now the dam has broken and the whole world thinks we're engaged.

But despite these real-world consequences, I can't wipe the smile off my face this week, no matter how hard I try. And yes, I *have tried,* because it seems totally silly. I'm a logical guy, and to think that a girl whom I could feel this joyful with has been staring me in the face for three straight years, getting on conference calls with me every day, is making me question everything.

I've loved every minute with her. Even when she needed a breather from me yesterday when I wondered aloud how much of her winter workout obsession had to do with Mark. And even last night, when I had to (attempt to) pull her down after the speech she made about Maddy and Peyton while standing on the bar, then fireman carry her into the elevator.

I even found it hilarious that she wiggled free from me and sprinted into the front lobby to nab a 'rare Hawaiian wooden turtle sculpture' and bring it to our room to 'keep her company for the night because I love turtles and they love me.'

A smile crosses my face just thinking about that. I can't explain the feelings that are bubbling up inside me because I've never felt anything like this before.

"Okay. Ready," she says.

I turn around, and my jaw drops.

"Stunning," I say, searching for the right words, but I stumble over them.

She wears a mustard-colored dress that rocks her curves so well, I have to ball my hands into fists because I think I might just rip the thing right off her if I let my hands roam free. And I definitely don't want to ruin all of her preparation for tonight.

"How you went from the worst hangover ever to this... blows my mind times a thousand."

Her hands run over my white tie. "You blow my mind times a million," she giggles.

I move closer and touch her with my torso, wrapping my arms with balled fists around her.

She eyes my hands suspiciously.

"You planning on getting in a fight tonight?"

I laugh. "Nah. Definitely not."

"So...what's with your hands?"

I clear my throat and unclench my fists. As I suspected, my fingers now insist on running themselves over every square inch of Allie's skintight dress that clings to her curves. Her breath catches as I walk her into the nearest wall, then pull one of her heeled legs up to wrap around my hips.

"Jocko," she whispers, eyes flitting between my eyes and my lips. "We need to get down to the wedding. We're all supposed to meet in five minutes."

"Yeah, but the wedding isn't for another half hour."

"You're bad."

"Very bad."

I run my hand slowly down her back, hip, ass, until it lands on the back of her thigh.

Her knees quiver but she's not going to fall with me pushing into her like this. The flesh of her thigh feels silky smooth. My fingers brush between her legs and she moans softly as I push the patch of her thong to the side.

"You recovered yet?"

She nods. "I went in the cold ice pool today after my facial. I think it was really good for me. Ohhh...don't start that."

"You don't want me to touch you like this?" I say, fingering her clit delicately.

Her lips curve upward in a hazy smile. "You know I can't stop once we start this."

"You're right." I nuzzle in toward her neck and give her a kiss on the side of her jaw, close to her ear. "So let's go."

I pull away from her, and she lets out a gasp.

"Oh my God. You're an asshole," she grins.

I wink. "Maybe. But at least I'm *your* asshole."

THE RAIN HOLDS off and Peyton and Maddy say their vows underneath the white awning. A fresh salt-breeze rolls off the ocean and the sun sets in the distance. It's a picture book ceremony and, hearing what Peyton said yesterday, I couldn't be happier for the two of them.

I've been to weddings where I get a weird vibe and I wonder, secretly, how long the couple will last. I can't necessarily articulate the feeling fully, but maybe it's the difference between two people who either vibe like they're pumped about the party and the ring and 'getting it over with', or two people who, with a very high degree of certainty, are excited to grow together in partnership for all the years to come.

I can see it in their eyes that Maddy and Peyton are definitely in the latter category. As they walk down the aisle after the ceremony for the first time as husband and wife, their song is "Magpie to the Morning" by Neko Case, which I have to Shazam to figure out. A beautiful song, but not a typical wedding song, and I wonder what hidden meaning might lie behind it. I heard Peyton call Maddy 'Magpie' once. Maybe that's got something to do with it. I think about how they have inside jokes that I don't get as a relative outsider to the wedding. But it's not my wedding and I don't have to get why they choose this song. And in truth, the fact that Maddy and Peyton have such inside jokes between each other makes the positive vibe even stronger in my mind.

They kiss each other again after they make it to the end of the aisle, and it's obvious they can't get enough of each other.

They'll be together forever. Sometimes, you can just tell.

THE *COLLEGE FRIENDS of Peyton* sit at a separate table and the four-course meal begins. The wedding party is now seated, back from their photos looking refreshed and ready to party. Even though Peyton's parents aren't here, he seems very okay with that. From what he indicated earlier, his upbringing was a little tough and it was his grandmother who got him on the straight and narrow...and Allie, she definitely helped him back then. It's more than obvious he's ecstatic to marry Maddy — not only for her, because he's head over heels in love, but for her family, as well.

The dude's been through a lot, and part of me is surprised he's done so well for himself. But then, sometimes challenges in life are what fans the flames of your being, lights your fire, so to speak, and makes you get it together. And a strict grandma never hurts either.

Dinner goes swiftly, not too much dinging on glasses forcing the bride and groom to kiss. A few goofy speeches — the best man does a great job of roasting Peyton, wishing the couple well, and before you know it, the dancing begins. And more drinks. Lots of drinks.

Allie is sitting on my lap when Naomi and Gill catch their breath between songs, too.

"Heyyy!" Naomi says, clearly having had a few. She's adorable. "You guys mind if we sit here?"

"Course not," I say. "Pull up chairs."

"So," she says, doing a little neck craning thing. "How are the wedding plans going?"

I feel Allie flinch as she sits on my lap.

"We're, uh, not quite at that phase yet," she smiles, then takes a big sip of her drink. I've been getting her drinks and instructed the bartender to slow the alcohol pour, don't want my girl all hungover again because I've got plans that include a balcony tonight.

"Really? Have you thought what you might want? Would you ever do a destination wedding?"

Allie looks to me with a raised eyebrow. "I don't think we're too picky. Maybe just a small ceremony. Again, we haven't really finalized those plans. How about you?"

Naomi ignores Allie's question and turns to me. "What about you, Jocko? Have you thought about it?"

I smirk. "Was just thinking about it earlier. I mean, how can you not think about your own wedding when you're at a wedding with such great vibes?"

Allie's eyes widen. "Oh. Have you now?"

I nod. "I'm thinking, something tropical, but maybe with more of a laid-back island vibe, not at a resort but a small town."

"Interesting." She's actually looking at me like she's contemplating the idea.

Naomi turns to her fiancé. "See? Destination weddings are so much fun!"

Gill's jaw hardens. "Babe, of course, they're fun. But we

already put the deposit down on the club in Dallas and everything."

"I know," Naomi says in a sing-song tone. "But maybe... we could get the deposit back?"

She rubs his forearm, and Allie adjusts herself on my lap, making my cock twitch, then gives me a little wink.

Girl knows she's torturing me.

Deciding to let Naomi and her beau wrestle through that discussion, Allie and I get back on the dance floor for the final few songs. I have to admit, we're having a great time. Allie and I are so comfortable together in a way I never anticipated. When everyone heads over to a nearby bar to continue dancing, drinking, and making merry, we follow, too. Peyton and Maddy disappear a little earlier than I'd expect — consummating their marriage, perhaps. Pssh, that's been done a bunch I'm sure, but maybe it's different after you actually say the 'I do's'.

As Daddy Yankee sings about "La Gasolina," Allie presses her body into me.

We're both buzzed. But it's not like last night, where she was gonzo. She's got her wits about her and so do I. Thanks to Raphael cutting her drinks as requested; what she doesn't know won't hurt her.

Her body radiates heat against mine as she grinds her ass into me. I spin her around, take her and kiss her in between the bodies, like sardines on the dance floor. The smell of heat and sweat and booze and the excitement of love all mix in the air creating a euphoric mixture.

When the next song comes on, "Drop it Low Latin Remix," she spins back around and does just that.

When she pops her face back up to my eye level, I can't take any more.

"Allie," I whisper, gripping her hip roughly with one

hand and her chin delicately with the other. "Let's go up to the room."

"I've been waiting all night for you to say that."

I take her hand and we leave, but not before glancing back over my shoulder on the way out where I see Mark, Barb, and several others watching us as we head to the elevators.

18

ALLIE

Every woman has their *thing*, or in my case, *things* that push them over the edge when it comes to a gorgeous man.

I'm talking about turn-ons. There's the standard, gentlemanly stuff that's sort of an entry-level requirement for me. Holding doors open. Being snuggly when cuddling.

And then there is a next level, a secret, top floor where everything gets even more intense.

A level of desire that I now am familiarizing myself with, thanks to Jocko.

This bonus level shoots me from the *turned-on* level onto *too horny to think about normal conversation or anything else besides him being inside me.*

Crass, I know. But it's the truth.

Sometimes it's just that *look,* like he wants to devour you, or the feel of his washboard abs. Maybe it's the way he looks uber sexy in a suit, or the wave of his hair and how it curls around his neck. Lately, it's when he can make me die laughing with a joke, or grab my hand dusting it with a light kiss. His hot muscled body that grinds against me during a

Latin dance beat, then touches the right places on my body with his nice, big...

Hands.

Yes, *hands*.

There may be something else, as well.

So as the elevator doors close, Jocko turns and picks me up by the hips to press me against the elevator wall. I'm the one assaulting him with kisses, wrapping my arms around his neck.

I love the feel of his muscular weight as he presses into me while I seek more of his skin, accidentally breaking the two top buttons on his shirt.

"Oops," I grin when they pop off. My lips sink into his neck, and I accidentally use a little teeth. He growls, gripping my neck softly.

"Well, hello there. Didn't know you had that in you," he teases.

My hand rubs the outside of his pants, tracing the outline of his cock.

"I've got a lot in me that you don't know about," I whisper, nibbling his ear. "And hopefully you, too."

"Come again?" he says as the elevator dings for our floor.

"I *said* hopefully you'll be *in me* soon, too."

"Jesus, Allie-face. You're going to make me explode before we even make it to the room."

He hoists me up and carries me to our suite, kissing me all the while. Somehow, without letting me down, he opens the door, then brings me into the room and sets me on the bed. I quickly remove my jewelry and glasses, anxious for what we're about to do.

"I want you right now," he growls. "All of you."

We're a frantic mess of grabbing and kisses and pinning each other down impatiently. I get his pants off. He gets my dress off, and we wrestle on top of the covers. I'm in just my bra and thong and he's in just boxers, and we're all wrapped up in each other.

He tries to pin me down and I giggle, wriggling out of his grasp.

"You're going to have to try a little harder than that," I tease.

His eyes darken, and I swear their brown hue changes to a dark color, almost black.

"Oh, you don't want to play this game with me," he chuckles.

I squirm underneath him as he holds my palms down and pins me with his knees.

"Yeah?" I mewl. "And what if I do? What are you going to do about it?" I dare. Pulling my arm free, I grab hold of his neck and pull my face to his. I can feel his beating heart. Hear his breath. Smell his masculine scent.

He bites his lip. "I'm going to pin you down," he says. "And do the things I've been dreaming about doing since the first moment you walked into the office three years ago."

My body melts underneath him, and I lick my lips. "Please enlighten me."

He deftly undoes my bra, then rips my panties off. *Rips them.*

Well, not like I needed to wear those again, necessarily. It's hard to think a coherent thought as he slides his tongue onto my clit.

I lean back and enjoy everything about this moment. My stomach rises and falls with deep, pleasure-filled breaths. He moans into me, ravenous. I've never had a man so desperate to taste me, and his enthusiasm spurs me on even more. My hands take hold of his tousled hair and I grind into his face unabashedly, not a trace of shame within me. He's so feral with his growls, and the way he manhandles my ass and my hips. I'm totally ready and call out to him.

"Jay," I mewl. "Please. Inside me. Now."

He doesn't stop for a few moments, though. Instead, he lifts my hips up so my back is arched. My chest hitches and I grab the headboard to keep my balance, overwhelmed with pleasure as I gyrate my hips in tune with his tongue.

"Inside? Like this?"

He teases me, putting one finger in. Jocko's fingers are long and thick, but it's a far cry from the girth I know is dangling between his legs.

Literally. Because he has nothing on right now. I can see it. Like a wild animal.

"You asshole," I whimper. "You know what I want."

He moves the one finger slowly inside me, making a come-hither motion. I'm on the brink of coming already. *Fuck*, the man can play my body like a fiddle.

"You just said *inside*," he says. "You didn't say *what* you wanted inside you."

Jocko's free hand holds my ass up, and I steal a glance at him before my eyes roll up in the back of my head. My knees tremble as electric jolts continuously throb through me.

"Jocko, come on," I mutter desperately.

"Use your words, Sexy."

"I'm not good at dirty talk," I say, impressed with myself for stringing one full — albeit brief — sentence together.

"Fine. Then I'll talk," Jocko says, and he slides his hand slowly out of me, then eases my butt down onto the mattress.

Euphoria warms me when he kneels between my legs and grabs the base of his cock. I'm not normally a visually stimulated girl — but the sight of him warms the deep, dark corners of my body.

Leaning forward, he kneels over me like he did that first time, but stays out of reach of my mouth.

"Spit on it."

Gathering up what saliva I can from my mouth, I do as he says. When I move in to try to give him a suck, he backs up.

"Nah-ah-ah," he says. "I said I was going to talk."

"What's there to talk about?"

"I need to get some things off my chest before we do this," he says, and he's back kneeling between my legs. His big hand strokes his cock back and forth as he gazes down on my body, his eyes flickering with fire and smoke.

I blink, and wonder why he's pausing right now, but I think I know. I think he might be feeling the same tumble in his stomach that I am right now. That this isn't a normal one-night stand, or hell, even a five-night stand. That this was a long time coming, and he wants to live out this moment for as long as possible.

I certainly do.

I hold the headboard as I take deep breaths, and my arms extend out which flattens my breasts and accentuates my hard pink nipples sticking straight up.

Jocko tightens his jaw as he strokes himself, his face serious but with the hint of a smirk.

His body, like mine, is slick with sweat. His chest tattoo looks bright, even though the main light into the room is the moonlight seeping in through the open balcony doors.

Glistening muscles and abs and the sound of him stroking his cock back and forth, slick with my saliva.

I pulsate with pleasure, my body warming everywhere.

"What do you need to get off your chest?" I finally ask, and he chuckles.

His jaw twitches. "I fantasized about this. Even when you were with Mark."

My stomach flutters. "I never considered it. I never looked at you as an option."

"I know. But I *am* an option now."

"You are."

"Once we do this...fuck, Allie. There's no going back."

"Maybe not," I admit. "But we were great friends before, and we'll still be great friends after, right?"

He nods, licks his lips, then finally lets the tip of his cock touch me, letting me feel its weight.

"Ohhh, Jay," I moan.

"You love calling me that," he mutters. "Why?"

"Jay, right now, really?" Is he serious?

He smirks. "I mean, you've *got* to give me answers now."

I curse the stars for giving this man the all-time most self-control of any man, apparently.

"Because," I mutter. "No one else calls you that. The name Jocko never did you justice, for me. And I wanted something that was all mine."

"Even before we were together you called me that."

"Yes," I whisper as he runs his hard tip along my clit, sending dull pleasure through me. I lean forward and grab his jaw. "Now, if you don't fuck me like I know you can with that perfect cock of yours, *Jay*, I'm going to lose it."

I curl my legs around his ass and *fucking finally*, he eases into me.

"Ohhh, Jocko," I moan as I clench my inner muscles around him. He stares into me, his eyes flickering with the most intensity I've ever seen from the man.

"Christ, you're tight, Allie. Why didn't you warn me?"

I muster a slight giggle, but movement of my stomach cavity is impeded by what's inside me.

A series of moans escape me as he thrusts back and forth, and I'm surprised by the man's sexual finesse. I was expecting him to be more of a *jackhammer right away* type of guy who thinks real life is a porno.

"Jesus, Jocko. You're big."

"I'm so hard right now," he growls. "You feel so damn good bare. You have no idea."

Lurching forward, I grab hold of a tuft of his hair and kiss him. "You feel amazing inside me."

He starts to thrust a little bit faster. He's strong but still tender, threading his hand through my hair and responding to my every movement.

I flinch when he touches a spot deep inside me, and his reaction is instantaneous.

"Allie. You okay?"

The real concern written over his face explodes a fuzzy warmth inside me with my legs spread to the side. A lightbulb moment hits me that maybe I shouldn't make assumptions about men based on their reputations. Even a man with a ripped body, huge cock, and the name *Jocko*.

I lean my forehead into his. "Yeah. Fine. Thanks for starting easy." I swallow. "I just haven't had sex in so long."

"Here," he says. "I have an idea. You get on top."

Without letting go, he rolls over onto his back so I'm straddling his torso. I lean my body down a little, using his hands to anchor myself.

"There," he says, then closes his eyes quickly. "Fuck, Allie. You're going to make me come like that. Stop for a second."

He closes his eyes, frozen for a moment, then reaches up and pulls me into him for a kiss on the lips. I stay in position on top of him, not moving up or down. I just enjoy the feel of him inside me, filling me up with the warmth of his hard flesh.

His kisses roll down my neck, my chest, and he takes my breast in his hand and flicks his tongue on my nipple, causing me to throw my head back at the jolt of pleasure. I gently begin to roll my hips on him again, and I'm in control of his depth inside me. He lets his hands fall, and I lean back, gliding up and down on him, adjusted now to his size and soaking wet.

Jocko's hand on my clit, combined with me grinding against him crescendos me to my first orgasm. But that only makes my need for him rachet up. He grabs hold of my hips and helps me move up and down on him.

Now he's fucking me hard. He growls and thrusts hard into me, and the *slap slap slap* of skin on sweaty skin fills the room with noise.

The world fades away. He takes hold of both my hands with just one of his and holds them behind my back, strong and dominant even while I'm on top.

This is the Jocko I'd always imagined. Fantasized about. With his free hand he presses into my clit — he is indeed the man of dexterous hands — and I come again, my orgasm crashing through me.

I think I hear thunder clapping outside, but I can't even be sure any more.

Now he pulls out and wrestles me over on my back again, into missionary position. I can see the recklessness in his hooded eyes. He feels like I feel, warm and fuzzy and high with endorphins of pleasure.

When he plunges into me this time, I'm ready for him and he knows it.

He fucks me deep and hard and tells me to grab the bars

of the headboard. I grab them tightly, because if I don't he's going to launch my body straight into it.

He licks his lips and I think I feel him twitching inside me as I come a third time, the position too overwhelming for me not to release. Euphoria rolls through me, and I hear him making animal noises, growling in my ear and I know he's close.

His cheek presses into my cheek, and I wrap my legs around him.

"Come inside me, Jay," I whisper, pulling him into me, and he can only let out a gravelly *uhh* in response.

He squeezes my ass as he releases, his orgasm rippling through him. His hands land on my shoulders when he's finished and he kisses me as we're both gasping for air.

He pulls out slowly, gets up to grab a towel for both of us to clean up, then lies down on the bed next to me.

"We can cuddle in a few," I say. "I need to cool down after that."

"Good night, Allie-face," Jocko finally says when we're cooled down, cuddling, and under the sheets.

"'Night," I say.

We don't exchange any more words until we fall asleep.

I should say something, but I think what I'm feeling is silly.

Because I'm pretty sure the earth just moved.

And I'm also pretty sure you're not supposed to fall this hard for a man after having sex with him just *one time*.

I extend my arm out in front of me as I drift off to sleep. I can see my ring glittering in the moonlight.

One more day and I'll have to give it back, and for some reason that makes me really sad.

DAY 4: THE LAST FULL DAY AT THE RESORT

19

JOCKO

I'll be honest: I'm not a cuddler. Don't like to cuddle. Never liked it.

When I sleep, I like to spread out and take up the full bed. I'm a big guy with long limbs and I like my sleep, especially. Which is why it was a big deal to get a suite with a double king: so Allie and I wouldn't have to touch while sleeping.

But when I stir this morning, I pull Allie closer into me. I can't get close enough to her. I pull her naked body into me, and she wiggles her ass just the slightest bit, so I'm unable to tell if she's awake or just stirring.

And it hits me: Allie Jenkins has turned me into a cuddler.

I laugh, because many girls would be pissed at this scene right now.

I wonder why. Why do I feel so comfortable doing this with *her*?

Her breath is light and sweet and patterned. My hand rests between her breasts, and that's why I can feel her heart beat. I can also feel it through my own chest, pressed up against her back.

A light-sounding moan escapes her throat. I wonder if she could be having a bad dream. I try to pull her tighter into me, but that's not possible. So I fall back into a light slumber to the rhythm of her heart.

WHEN I COME to consciousness again, she's moving her ass back and forth against my hips. My cock is already hard, which explains the sex dream I wake up from. What a glorious day when the same girl you're having sex dreams about is actually in your bed. From the way she's breathing and moving I know she's awake.

My hand rolls gently down her side, and she emits a couple of loud breaths from her nostrils. My fingertips reach her clit and I feel she's already almost as wet as she was last night...

Almost.

"Morning, you," she whispers, nuzzling her head back into me.

"Morning," I echo, and trace soft kisses down her neck. She giggles and takes hold of my hand which is on her clit.

"Follow me," she whispers. "I promised you something, and I think it's early enough for this still, without either of us being seen."

My curiosity is piqued. She leads me by the hand toward the door, opens it, and I follow her to the corner of the Juliet balcony.

As if I wasn't already hard enough, watching her naked ass sway in front of me, the slender curves of her neck that seem to illuminate the sunrise — and not the other way around — the way her blond hair blows gently in the wind, turns me into an iron rod. It's almost awkward to walk with this thing.

"What did you promise me?" I ask, because it's maybe not even six a.m., my brain is fried, and all I can think about is how badly I want her.

She puts both of her hands on the railing, but doesn't turn to face me. I lean my chin down to her shoulder. "I told you I wanted to fuck on the balcony. Don't you remember?"

My chest flutters with heat, and I swallow. Holy shit. How could I forget about that? "That's right! But, holy shit, we're right next to..." I glance in the direction of our neighbor's balcony. "What if Mark..." As soon as I say his name, I regret it. It just came out though, and it's too late to take it back.

She rolls her eyes and spins her head back to meet mine for an awkward angle kiss. My hands are all over her, running down the front of her body, feeling her silky-smooth flesh.

"They were out all night, probably. They won't see us. Plus, you're supposed to be making me forget all about Mark on this trip. Remember?"

"Forget about who?" I say with a smirk, ready to play her game now.

"Exactly," she grins.

I have to admit the tabooness about this hookup makes it even hotter than it would be. On the other hand, I think that every time I get to be with Allie is the hottest time of my life.

But as she grabs onto the railing and juts her ass out just a little bit for me to take, I pause for a split second to drill this moment into my mind forever.

The sun barely breaks the horizon from the east, just

peaking out from above the ocean. The few clouds it illuminates make a purple-orange-red shade, a unique mix of sky that will never happen again. Below a few people move about, probably mostly hotel workers at this point because who wakes up this early when you're at a resort where drinks are included?

But the charmed jewel of the whole view is *her*. Not just because her ass and legs are boner-inducing hot, although they are. No sense denying that. It's knowing how timid of a girl she usually seems to be. It's seeing her blossom out of her shell. It's the fact that it's *her* and *I'm* the one she is blossoming for.

She looks over her shoulder, biting her lip. "Well? What are you waiting for?" she grits out, her tone a combination of desperation and anger.

I move closer to her, and she's got to get on her tippy toes and I've got to bend my knees a little for this to work because of our height difference. Her hair splays down her back, and she moans as I slide inside her from behind.

"Ohhhh, Jocko," she mutters, and I note that I still don't understand why she sometimes calls me by my full name.

I hold inside her for a moment, and whisper in her ear. "I just wanted to admire you for a moment. I want to remember this. You really are a dirty girl, aren't you?"

Her lips turn up in a siren's smile. "For you, I am."

I kiss the side of her neck and she turns back to look out on the world. It feels like our kingdom, and we're the prince and princess in a fairy tale.

Except this fairy tale is X-rated, and we're a lot more sexually liberated.

She crumbles into the railing as I thrust in and out of her. She clenches tightly around me at this angle, and I'm worried I might be too deep inside her. But one *harder* whisper from her dispels that idea, and I let go.

I'm reckless, and judging by her moans, she loves it. And I love her.

Not her. Her pussy.

Fuck.

Sex thoughts are never clear thoughts, I remind myself.

But you might, a voice whispers inside me.

I growl and wrap her hair up to distract me from myself, and also because the back of her neck is looking damn kissable right now but it's out of range. I suck and kiss and almost bite her shoulder and she pushes my face away and leans down more, seeking her perfect angle. Her ass jiggles into my hips, and she lets out a series of high-pitched moans. The noise, combined with her clenching, tells me she's coming.

I've only been hooking up with Allie for three days and I already know her pussy like the back of my own hand.

Her legs shake and I spank her. Knowing I'm about to come, I pull out and go down on her for a while, allowing myself to cool down.

When I push back inside of her, we find our perfect rhythm quickly.

My spine tingles and I know I'm going to come, but I want this moment to last forever. Or at least another minute. I suck in everything about it. Allie's scent. Her soft moans that are getting louder by the moment.

And then, in my peripheral vision, I spot something to my right. I don't want to look. I shouldn't look.

But I clench my jaw and I look.

It's fucking Mark, standing on his balcony next to us, cup of coffee in his hand.

His jaw drops, and he fiddles with his hand, almost

dropping his white porcelain coffee cup and spilling a little on his white shirt.

His eyes flutter, and I would wonder what's going through his mind except that I'm on the brink of coming, so my mental capacity is not all there.

Allie doesn't see him at all. She's still got her hands on the railing as I, well, *rail* her.

As if she knows something is up, Barb comes out onto the balcony, too, and her face is equally stunned.

I want to tell them to go away, to *mind their own fucking business*.

Instead? I give them a nod, and a thumbs up, because fuck them if they need to stare.

Allie reaches her hand back and runs it along my abs, and that's the final touch I need. I come like hell, a thousand tiny feathers tickling everywhere inside me.

When we're done, she leans her head on the railing, gets down off her tippy toes, and catches her breath.

"Oh my God," she groans. "I don't understand how I come multiple times when I'm with you."

"Must have something to do with my big, hard..."

"Voice," she fills in the blank, grinning.

"Yes. That's what I was thinking, too."

When we move back into the room, Mark and Barb are gone from the balcony.

Allie doesn't have a clue they were even there, and that little tidbit makes me smile. It's probably for the better.

We order room service and lounge in our room as the sun comes up slowly over the horizon. I try not to think about how it's day four of our little adventure already. I wish I had the power to slow down time.

20

ALLIE

Jocko falls back asleep in the room, and I go for a walk around the resort to clear my head. I grab a cold vanilla latte from the coffee counter, and it still blows my mind that every last thing here is included.

Beautiful people lounge on lawn chairs, outside tanning and drinking, even though it's not even noon.

I find an empty chair and sit back with my coffee, thinking to myself.

My thoughts ruminate.

What am I doing? being the prevailing message I'm getting right now.

God Almighty, I haven't had as much real pleasure as this week, maybe *ever*. Never came like that with someone. Never enjoyed sex so much or enjoyed someone so much.

Is there something in the air, or the water, in Cancún that leads to mind-blowing orgasms?

And then there's the surprisingly protective, dare I say nurturing side of Jocko I'm now fully aware of. The side that laughed and pulled my hair back despite my drunken meltdown which I thought for sure would have annoyed him.

I lean back on the chair and flip through my work emails — yes, it's a bad habit and I need to quit it.

I see that my boss Matt has sent me an email requesting my assistance with a PowerPoint, and my stomach drops.

Really? On vacation you have to send me one of your stupid PowerPoint requests?

I can hear his voice in my ear. "But you're just so good at them, Allie. I can't make them pretty like you can."

My blood boils a little bit, my mind returning to the almost non-existent raise he signed off on. As my mood drops remembering my work situation, I send Rhonda a message to see if she's around to chat.

Two minutes later, I get a call on my WhatsApp. You know, gotta use those free international calls over wifi because I'm not a baller with a raise.

Yet.

"Heyy!" she says. "Sorry it took so long. I had to jump out of the restaurant where we're doing champagne Saturdays. It's randomly above sixty degrees in Detroit today, so the patios are open. How are you?"

"That's good to hear. I'm...you know. Doing okay. Feeling a little off right now, to be honest."

"Off? What's the matter?"

"I made the mistake of checking my work email. Matt sent me another PowerPoint request. It's like does he *not* even notice I'm on vacation?"

"Ugh. Maybe it's the champagne talking, but Matt's a total dick. I tried to talk to him about your raise and he totally brushed me off. I think it's because his department gets a total budget, so basically, if he doesn't give you a decent raise, it goes straight to his pocket."

"Um...what? He told me something about going public!"

"Oh, shit. I *definitely* wasn't supposed to say that," Rhonda chastises herself.

"No, it's okay. I won't tell anyone."

"No, like, I'm *legally* not supposed to tell you what I just told you. Ugh, but Matt is such a dick!"

I hear some guy walking by on the sidewalk say, *'Hey, my name's Matt.'*

"Not you! I swear, some people," she says. "Sorry. So work is making you stressed. I can see that. We actually had a meeting with the CEO a few weeks back. I was in on it with Jocko and two of the other top sales people. Damn, I'd never seen Jocko that angry."

A smile comes over me. "Jocko was angry?" I've never seen Jocko in a sour mood over the last three years, let alone visibly angry. He's just not the type who gets flustered, or enraged. He's always totally under control.

"Yeah. He pounded on the table when they laughed about how your position doesn't 'provide any actual, measurable value.' They were thinking about eliminating it. I thought he was going to throw the CEO's laptop on the ground. Jocko got fiery. I've never seen him that mad."

I tingle. "Jocko was defending my position to the CEO? Wouldn't that get him in trouble?"

"Well, Jocko brings in more money to the company than any other single person. So when he talks, they listen. Not only did he defend your position, he said you should be making triple what you're making."

My eyes widen. "Triple? Come again?"

"Yep. One-hundred-and-twenty thousand. *At least*, Jocko said."

I feel lightheaded all of a sudden. "I don't even know what I would do if I made *half* that."

"Yeah, and they laughed in his face and he stormed out, all pissed. He told them some expletives that made their jaws drop. I think they tried to make him apologize later and he refused. I guess now that I know you're together it makes more sense. He was sticking up for you as his girlfriend."

She pauses for a beat, and my cheeks flush red as I consider that Jocko wasn't sticking up for me because we were dating *at all.*

Wow. It's a subtle distinction, but it means so much to me. My chest is unbelievably heavy all of a sudden with a mix of emotions I'm having difficulty interpreting. After believing I've been toiling away for three years at EdTechX without a soul who appreciates my work, I'm actually getting choked up right now picturing Jocko going to bat for me for no reason other than he sees and values the work I do.

"How's that going, by the way?" Rhonda asks.

She catches me off guard by the quick topic switch, I have to ask again, "How's *what* going?"

"You know, the whole *being at a destination wedding with Jocko* thing? Still trying to picture you two as engaged."

I clear my throat. "Oh. *That* thing. You know. It's been, uh, fun."

"You really kept that on the downlow, by the way. I can't believe you didn't tell me, at least!"

"Look, Rhonda, I'm going to tell you something and you have to be sworn to secrecy."

"You know I wouldn't tell anyone something you tell me in confidence."

I take a deep breath. "So, the whole engagement thing... is staged. It's fake."

A beat passes, and I hear Rhonda let out a loud breath.

"Oh. My God."

"Yes. It was Jocko's idea. His mom has been on him to get married, so he figured we could stage a few photos where we were engaged while we're here — make sure they're with other people and in a variety of settings so they're believable — and then at the end of the five days we'll break up. We were kind of trying to keep this fake engagement confined to the five days in Cancún. And we definitely hoped the office wouldn't find out."

Rhonda is speechless. After a long, dramatic pause, she finally says something.

"I just...wow. Oh my gosh, I feel so bad, though. I'm the one who blabbed about this to the whole office! Wait a second. So if the engagement is fake...have you two, you know. Have you kissed at all?"

My tongue ties itself in a knot. My silence tells her more than any words could.

"Oh my God! You made out with Jocko, didn't you!"

"Keep it down!"

"Please. I will not keep it down about this. Allie, that's awesome! Seriously. You need a rebound kiss."

"Well. We did a lot more than kiss."

Rhonda's end of the phone goes silent again.

"Uh, Rhonda?"

She clicks back on. "I'm sorry. I just had to put you on mute so I could swear loudly. Give me all the details!"

"Aren't you standing outside of a restaurant?"

"Oh, I've got time for this, Allie. I've always got time. You better not spare me the good stuff."

I hear the noise of the restaurant patio fading more into the distance and the sound of her heels clicking on concrete as she walks.

"Well, he was giving me a rub-down because I got a

crappy massage at the resort. And one thing led to another and..."

She screeches, and I stammer.

"Anyway, the whole masseuse-with-benefits story just seems to dumb down what we have to something purely physical. We really have a great connection, off the charts chemistry, and it's been amazing, honestly."

"What's going to happen when you come back from Cancún?" she asks.

"I really wish I knew."

"Well. Enjoy it while it lasts. And call me if you need anything. Okay?"

"Will do. I feel better already."

"Good. Where are you right now?"

"This instant? I'm poolside."

"Is he there?"

"No, he's sleeping in the room."

She giggles. "You should surprise him."

"What do you mean, *surprise him*?"

"Oh, I think you know what I mean."

We say goodbye and not only is my mood lifted, but I'm also thinking dirty thoughts now.

Rhonda has inspired my inner-naughty girl.

WHEN I GET BACK to the room, Jocko is in a towel post-shower. His muscles glisten as he brushes his teeth. I step behind him and run a hand down his chest and abdomen.

"Well, hello there," he says, then rinses his toothbrush and turns around. "Where have you been?"

"Just went out to go for a walk, get some coffee and stretch my legs."

Jocko's about to kiss me when I stop him, putting my hand on his chin.

"Hey, I need to ask you something," I say.

"Uh-oh," he says, raising an eyebrow.

"Nothing bad," I giggle. "But I just heard something from Rhonda off the record..."

Our eyes lock together, and my stomach tumbles. "Did you yell at our CEO on my behalf in a meeting a few weeks ago?"

I can see him tonguing the inside of his cheek.

"Fuck. Rhonda told you about that? That was supposed to be a totally confidential meeting."

"So I heard," I say. "But I just needed to know. Is it true what she said? You demanded they triple my salary?"

He nods. "Rhonda told me about that bullshit raise you got. One and three quarters percent? For everything you do? It's bullshit, Allie. And you know it."

Butterflies swarm in my chest, and I feel so corny for feeling the way I do. But the truth is, having a boss who doesn't value me has been taking its toll on me this year. Our romance aside, Jocko is one of the most respected employees at our company. The fact that he believes I deserve three times as much as I'm making definitely makes me feel valued.

"But you were joking, right? About the three times my salary part?"

He shakes his head, and tips my chin back toward him. "I wasn't. Allie, you're so smart, but you're too humble sometimes. You've got to be an advocate for yourself. You brought in millions to the company because of what you do. You've got to demand the money, because no one else is going to demand it for you." Stepping closer to me, he runs a hand through my hair.

"But you did," I say, a smile tugging at my lips.

"Yeah. And he's lucky I didn't come after him when he didn't give it to you. We've been bringing in so much extra business since you started working with the IT directors. It's like they're fucking blind to it. I told them they better watch it. I mean, Matt's been getting those emails from Google and sending those to you. They're asking for you to set up some programs for them. I'm sure you'll continue to get offers like that, and it's only the beginning. Educational tech consulting is a burgeoning industry, and word's out on the street as to what an asset you are."

Something coils inside me. "Um, Google?"

"Yeah. Matt told me about the emails Google for Education has been sending him, asking if you could give those workshops. I'm surprised you haven't taken them up on those yet. It would be a good opportunity to earn a little extra cash and get some valuable experience."

My blood boils as I process what must be happening. "I had no idea about any emails. Matt hasn't been sending anything to me — he must be blocking them from me. God, he's such an asshole."

"Jesus," Jocko mutters. "They're holding you back. I fucking *knew* it. Jocko's hands slide down my sides. Why can't they see what you do? Damn clueless fuckers."

I run my hand over my forehead. Images come crashing past me, the realization hitting me that my boss has been a deceptive bastard, and not only *not* giving me a raise, but actively working to limit my other opportunities.

"He doesn't value you. It's bullshit, Allie."

I well up with emotion. "I just can't believe this has been going on right before my eyes," I whisper.

"I'm sorry. I should have told you sooner," he says. "I wanted to. But they kept the contents of that meeting sealed.

Rhonda definitely wasn't supposed to talk to you about it. If anyone finds out she mentioned it to you, it could be her job."

"I'm glad I know now and I would never mention or do anything that would hurt her. Rhonda is a true friend."

"They might not value you. But you know who values you?"

"Who?"

His hands find their way under my floral dress, and he pulls it up around my waist.

"Me," he growls as he kisses me.

My core heats and melts into him as he tries to run a hand between my legs. I stop him.

"No, Jocko," I whisper. "Your turn this time. I had this already planned out but wanted to ask that question before I started on my plan."

Undoing his towel, I let it slide to the ground and kneel down in front of him.

Never before have I felt this strange combination of gratitude and attraction swirling inside me. And need. As I take his hard flesh in my mouth, I'm surprised how turned on I am.

But then, it's not the act that turns me on.

It's *him.*

I love that he gets me, but even more, I love the way I can feel the vibrations of his deep voice as I make him moan with my mouth.

21

JOCKO

At midday, Allie and I head down to the pool for some rays and some margaritas. Yes, margaritas. Fuck keto. They're too delicious.

Plus, Allie has me in the mood to take a load off, for once. I'm admittedly a workaholic, and after this morning, let's just say I'm feeling quite relaxed.

We see a big group of football players and their partners lounging in an area that is conveniently right next to both the hot tub and the bar. Yes, please.

Allie falls asleep in her bikini with a book on top of her head. I take it off her because what kind of a boyfriend lets his girlfriend get an accidental uneven tan?

I swallow a pit of anxiety as I set the book under her lawn chair.

It's the word *boyfriend* that vexes me.

After our *noche de orgasmos*, I have no idea what word to use to refer to Allie anymore, even in my head. Boyfriend, fiancé, friend, coworker? I'm at a loss.

Fiancé? In public, yes, but in reality, obviously not, since this is a clear ruse.

Friend? Hell no. With what kind of *friend* do you do the things we've been doing the past few days?

Maybe *friend with benefits*, but that one doesn't seem to quite do us justice, either.

We're more than coworkers but are we boyfriend and girlfriend?

It's the most logical setup, though we haven't had any talks about that. We skirted around the issue during our conversation this morning, instead preferring to talk about favorite continents and where we would travel if we had a million dollars.

She wants to go to Scotland, Bolivia, South Africa, and India, by the way. Me, I'm all about Iceland, Australia, and New Zealand.

Lovers might be the most appropriate word for us. If nothing else.

I'm antsy and I'm done with my drink, and I need a walk. I peek at Allie to make sure she's sleeping, then head to the bar on the opposite end, past the pool and up the stairs to the tiki lounge area. There's not a soul in the area, just the bartender Paco whom I recognize from the other night.

"Hey, man, you guys open?" I ask.

"Sí, sí," he nods with a smile. I can't tell if he understood me and that's his response, or if that's just what he says to everyone.

"Alright, man, well, I'm gonna saddle up then." I take a seat on one of the bar stools.

"I'll take a Cuba Libre."

He stares at me for a moment, squinting as if he doesn't understand.

"Uh, un rum con coca y lima," I say. "Doble." Because I'm stressing and I need a double right now.

"Ah, sí, sí," he nods, and pours me my drink.

I take a sip and let the cold, sweet taste of the rum and Coke roll down my throat. I've always thought it's funny that a Cuba Libre — such a fancy sounding name for a cocktail — is really just rum, Coke, and lime.

The little buzz it gives me is just enough to get the cobwebs off my brain so I can think clearly, aggressively.

"Paco, what do you know about romance?" I ask. He's cleaning down this bar, which usually doesn't get busy until later in the day.

"Sí," he nods, as if he understands me. I breathe a sigh of relief, and it hits me that Paco is the *perfect* guy for me to talk out my issues with. He doesn't understand a lick of English, so I can go ahead and speak freely.

"You ever been in love, Paco?" I ask. "You seem like a romantic guy."

"Sí, sí," he nods as he kneels down and refills a mini-fridge full of Coronas.

"Actually, I should probably back up to tell this story. You ever get so far in a hole, you don't know if you can dig yourself out?"

He shrugs and continues cleaning.

"That's where I'm at, man. Never fake your mom out. That was my first mistake. I was getting tired of her comments about my bachelorhood whenever I talked to her and wanted to drum up some sympathy. Now, though, I've got to have this girl break up with me. HR is involved. All because I had this silly, hair-brained idea about being fiancés for the week."

I take another pull of my drink.

"And you know what the crazy thing is, Paco? I think I actually might be in love with this girl. Even though the more I find out about her, she might actually be a little fucking crazy. The things she says. The dirty, sexy, way she fucks. But you know what? I'm a little crazy, too. That's right. Big Papa Jocko's got some pretty messed-up thoughts bouncing around up here." I tap my head, as if Paco understands. "And then there's the work version of her. The conference call, all-business, intelligent-as-fuck version of her. And I dig that part of her, too. The more I find out about her, the more I dig her. Is that love?"

Paco's not even paying attention to me at this point, but it feels good to speak out loud, so I go on, the rum lubricating my thoughts.

"You know what I'm thinking about this afternoon while I'm trying to read some silly book about sales? I'm wondering what our *babies* would look like. Would they have my thin lips? Or her thick ones? How tall would they be? I'm a tall guy, she's medium height, so would that put them at five foot ten? Or would the guys be taller? And they'd have her smarts, so that's good. Plus, she's got that organized, seriously nurturing side to her. She used to be a teacher. But still, she lights me up like I've never been lit up. I was so into her this morning, when we were hooking up on the balcony, her ex looked at me and all I could think was to give him a *thumbs up*. A fucking *thumbs up?* Who *does* that? She's got me in some totally crazy, new headspace. I'm losing my goddamn mind."

I shake my head and look over in her general direction, across two pools. "She's a real firecracker under all that good girl, Paco. And this week I realized that's what I need. That's why I've never thought about ending my bachelorhood phase — shit, this is the first time I'm calling it a phase: because I've never found a girl who made me want to be her forever. And for some reason, the thought of being with Allie for a long while doesn't send me running for the hills. It makes me happy."

"Sí, sí," Paco nods. He's wipes down the bar and organizes the glassware.

"How do you know when you're in love? The first time the possibility crossed my mind, I was *inside* her. Now riddle me this, Paco: how do I know it's not just desire that I'm feeling? How do I *know* I love her?"

He mutters something I don't understand.

I slap my palm on the bar and he jumps.

"I'll tell you how. Because I've wanted her for three *years*, Paco. Three whole years. Only problem is what am I to *her?* What if I'm just *her* rebound? She was with her ex for five whole years, man. *Five*. And now, what? She's going to be with the next guy she sleeps with forever? Okay, well, she said she kissed some guy over New Year's. But the first relationship-y thing she has, she's going to get married to him? And how the *fuck* am I actually thinking about marriage? I'm Jocko Brewer, king of the bachelors. What am I *doing,* Paco?"

I make a loud, frustrated noise, blowing air across my lips.

"So what the fuck am I supposed to do here? We're leaving tomorrow, and this whole five day dream is coming to an end. No one gets to stay on vacation forever. And Allie and I don't get to stay 'engaged' forever. On Monday, we're done. She gives the ring back to me and breaks up with me. That was the plan all along." I look over at her again, and even just seeing her pink bikini in the distance makes my chest flutter. "So what would you do, Paco? Christ, I'm lost here. I'll take another."

Paco refills my glass, a single this time, and slides it in front of me.

"I dig talking to you, man, I gotta say. I needed this. You're a terrific conversationalist."

I turn halfway around with my drink, about to head back to Allie when I hear a strange voice, clear English with a hint of a Mexican accent.

"It's easy. Just tell her you love her. Right now."

I spin back around, eyes wide. "You speak English?"

Paco laughs. "Ninety percent of the guests of this resort speak English. So yeah, of course I speak English. It's a requirement to work here."

"But you...you just listened to everything I said and didn't say anything."

"Yes, I did. It seemed like you just needed a good listening ear. So I decided not to interrupt you too much and just said *yes*."

"I thought you were just saying *yes* because you had no idea what I was saying!"

Paco smirks. "Looks like you made an assumption about me not speaking English. Thanks for sharing all that, though. Interesting love situation you have going on here. Does everyone else in your party know you're faking it with her? Well, the fiancée thing, at least. She wasn't faking those screams when you were behind the bar the other night." He winks.

I lean forward on the bar, menacingly. "Hey, that was between me and her."

"I'm head bartender here. I just *heard* you, not like I was gawking or anything. It was hard not to hear. I could have kicked you out of here for that, you know. Not appropriate behavior. And giving a customer a beer?"

I take a deep breath. "Sorry about that. Just thought it

was courtesy. And wait, why am I sorry? Isn't this place all-inclusive anyway? The beer is free."

"Back to your romantic situation," Paco continues. "You're in quite a pickle, my friend. Why don't you just tell her you love her?"

I shrug. "That's totally insane. We've had sex *twice*. That's not how love works."

"Maybe you should worry less about how you think love works, and just go with your gut. You said it yourself you've known her for three years."

For some reason, I reject his idea even though I can feel a lot of truth in it. "What are you, the love oracle now? You can't fall in love after two love-making sessions."

"Lots of people fall in love here. That's why we call it Temptation Isle."

"Which is weird, by the way, because it's not an island."

"An isle is not an island. Also, it's sort of an island, since most people never leave the resort once they check in. Kind of like Hotel California." He winks.

"What are you, a poet?"

He smiles. "No, of course not."

"Anyway, I need to go." I tense up for a moment. "Hey, you're not going tell the wedding party about anything I said here, are you? That was a lot of personal stuff that needs to stay secret."

He purses his lips. "Actually, that depends."

"On what?"

"I'm not a poet, but I do make wood sculptures of animals." He points to a table next to the bar. *Hand-crafted woodcarvings for sale.* "It's been a low week for sales. How about you help me out. In exchange for my silence."

I'm angry inside, but I have to hand it to him.

Son of a bitch knows how to close a deal. I could learn a thing or two from him.

"How many do you want me to buy?"

"How about all of them?" he smiles.

I clench my fists. "Get me another drink," I say.

22

ALLIE

When Maddy and Peyton finally make it down to the pool at the "early" hour of two p.m., they receive a round of applause from the wedding party. It's the first time they've been seen or heard from all day.

Peyton soaks up the post-marriage spotlight, holding Maddy's hand and taking a bow with her.

"Thank you, thank you," he announces, to the crowd who is all tanning beach side. "And you'll all be happy to know that the marriage *was* consummated, so the paperwork is official now. I got a lot of worried texts this morning, so I thought I'd put your worries to rest. We consummated it several times just to be on the safe side, as a matter of fact."

Maddy rolls her eyes playfully. After Peyton's heartfelt display the other night, he's back to being, well, *Peyton*. The cocky, joking jock who stole Maddy's heart in the first place. She pretends she's annoyed, but she's really not. How could she be when there's no doubt in anyone's mind how hard Peyton loves her?

I look around for Jocko, but he's been over at the bar in the far corner for a while. I weirdly miss his presence. I could feel him gone even when I was napping and tanning.

Maddy and Peyton find a couple of reclining lawn chairs to sit on a few down from us.

Mark and Barb then appear with a couple of flat boxes in front of everyone.

"Who wants pizza?" They sing, and cheers erupt from the crowd. Nothing makes a group of hungover, hungry people happier than pizza.

"I'm soo hungry," I belt out, agreeing with the crowd.

They walk by with paper plates and the boxes and hand one personally to everyone. When he gets to me, Mark seems to make a point of slowing down.

"Pizza with olives, pepperoni, and sausage. Your favorite."

I puke a little in my mouth, but force it back down.

See, the thing is that I *hate* olives and Mark knows this.

Once, when I was nine, I was over at the older boy across the street's house and I wanted to impress him. We had an olive-eating contest. Let's just say I won, and Barry *was* somewhat impressed. Except for the fact that after I ate the full jar, I ran straight outside to his backyard and puked my brains out.

Needless to say, I *never* ate olives again. I can't even smell one without gagging. And why is Mark being such a dick right now?

"Eh, I'm not really in the mood for pepperoni. Do you have just cheese, by chance?"

He shakes his head. "No. This is all we've got left."

Peyton looks over at me. "What's a matter, Al? Thought you said you were starving."

"My bad," Mark adds. "Jocko said he got this pizza for you when he proposed because it's your favorite. Was that... not true?"

I smile and take a piece. "Thanks," I mutter, and finally he passes on.

Taking a bite of the pizza, I try to chew it, but once I taste the olive it happens again. There's no stopping it.

I get up and shuffle walk as fast as I can toward the bathroom. Except I don't make it to the bathroom, and I end up puking in a nearby garbage can.

"I knew it." Mark's voice is right behind me.

I turn around, furious. "What. The fuck. Is your problem?"

"My problem is that you're making a scene. You're making an ass out of yourself, Allie." He steps closer to me and grabs hold of my hand, showing my ring. "This is a ruse and we all know it now. You're not engaged."

Anxiety rips through me. How would he know? He couldn't.

"Yes, I am," I spit back. "And even if I wasn't, it's none of your goddamn business."

Peyton appears behind him and I'm about to run, but his presence makes me falter.

"Al," Peyton says, stepping in front of Mark. "What you're doing this week, it isn't right."

"Oh, well, screw both of you, then!" I grit out. And where the hell is Jocko?

"Look, I heard you on the plane," Mark says.

I freeze up, adrenaline washing through me. "Heard *what* on the plane?"

"You didn't see us, but Barb and I were two seats behind you. I didn't want to believe it. I really tried not to believe it this week because I didn't want to think you'd be so shallow. But you've been taking this breakup horribly—and I feel bad for that. That doesn't mean you can just roll around here with this guy just to make me jealous. And, did you really have to go as far as to say you were *fiancés?* The guy doesn't even know your favorite pizza, Allison."

He says it as if favorite pizza is the most important thing you can know about a person.

"You do *not* get to talk to me like that," I seethe.

Peyton takes a step back, as if realizing that even the king can be in over his head. I really don't want to make a scene the day after the wedding, but I've had it up to here.

"I don't know what you think you're doing with this guy," Mark shrugs. "But it's not working if you're trying to make me jealous. I mean, having him give me a thumbs up while he's fucking you on the balcony this morning? Really? You've really gone off the deep end, haven't you?"

"You don't have the right to..." I stop as I process his words. "Did you just say Jocko gave you a *thumbs up* while we were doing it this morning?"

Peyton's eyes widen to saucers now, and he flings his hands up. "Okay, I'm in over my head now, guys. I don't know what the fuck is going on."

As if sensing the most awkward moment he could possibly enter the scene, Jocko appears with a drink in his hand.

"Hey, bae. What's happening?"

"I'll tell you what's happening, you little twerp," Mark says. "We know what's going on between you two."

Jocko calmly raises an eyebrow. "You do?"

He nods.

"Well, by all means, enlighten us. Because I'd love to hear it."

I walk over to Jocko. "Did you really give him a thumbs *up* this morning while we were sunrise fucking on the balcony?"

Jocko looks as nervous as I've ever seen him in my life. "Uh, well, yeah. Sort of."

"Sort of?"

"I did, okay. I don't know why. I couldn't think straight."

"See? I'm not crazy," Mark interjects. "The pizza, the olive thing, the thumbs up, the conversation we heard about them staging this engagement, it's all true! As in, it's all fake! Jocko's just using you for sex, and bragging about it, obviously!" He looks to Peyton for his approval.

"Is this really what's going on, Al? You're faking this engagement?" Peyton asks me this, and the disappointment on his face is worse than if he were my father.

I gulp. "It's...complicated," I say, but anger bubbles up at the surface for the first time at Jocko...a real, true anger. *He gave him a thumbs up?* Someone who cares about someone, someone who's not trying to prove a point or one up someone does *not* do that!

"I needed a date and I asked Jocko to be my date. That's true. The fiancé thing, well, we may have taken it too far."

"Definitely took it too far," Jocko adds. "That's my fault, though."

Oh my God! Thanks for the support. I don't even get what's going on right now.

"So why didn't you just come clean once you realized that?" Peyton asks.

I look down, feeling utterly silly. "We didn't want to ruin your wedding and make a scene."

"Well, it's a little late for that," Mark says, acid lacing his voice. Funny how right now I'm so glad we broke up. Just thinking of dealing with his condescending attitude makes me want to kick him.

I think I can now finally say I'm over Mark the fucker. Finally.

"Dude, shut the fuck up," Jocko bites out. "Why are you invested in what Allie's doing at this point, anyway?"

"Because I care about her, still," Mark says. "As a friend."

Jocko hands me his drink. "If you were such a good *friend* to her, you two would have gotten married long ago. *I'm* her friend now. So why don't you go worry about your own fucking fiancée."

Mark shudders, and right now I'm enjoying seeing it.

I've never seen Jocko's jaw so twitchy, and his neck vein popping out so much.

If there's a fight, it's clear who would win. And I have a bad feeling Mark would end up in the hospital.

If he's lucky, a voice inside me says.

"*Now*, we're making a scene," Peyton says, stepping between them.

"Hey, fuck you, too," Jocko growls at Peyton, and I freeze. So does Peyton.

"Watch it," I say, and now I'm standing in front of Jocko. I honestly don't want a fight to ensue. I'm thrilled Jocko is supporting me, standing up for me, but I don't want to cause more of a scene.

Besides, Jocko on Mark was an easy win for Jocko. But now two on one? This would be very bad.

"No, I'm serious," Jocko grits out. "Who cares what Allie and I are doing? Fiancé, no fiancé, date or fucking on the balcony and giving thumbs up or whatever. We're having an amazing week. Best week of my life, as a matter of fact. And that's no lie. That is one-hundred percent truth."

"He's right," I say. "I can take care of myself. I- I like Jocko a lot. That's all that matters. Sorry, Peyton. Sorry for making a scene. Now, please, can we just disengage this...whatever this is? You guys aren't *really* going to fight, are you? I mean, come on. We're all friends here."

I've never felt Jocko's body so tense.

"Not so sure about that," Jocko belts out, which only antagonizes Peyton more. Mark looks as though he's ready to dig a hole and disappear, and I wish he would.

"Come on," I say, taking Jocko's forearm and guiding him away from the pool.

"Where are we going? I'm not done here, Al — they're the ones who started it and owe you, *us* an apology." Oh boy, not as easy as I'd hoped.

As we walk a few feet away, I try to calm him, "They are sorry, I know my friends. Let's just change clothes and go for a hike or something and enjoy our last day here," I feel him relax a bit, but I know how he hates to lose a negotiation, so I know backing away from an unsolved argument is not normal for him.

"A hike, seriously? After what they just said to you?" he asks as we head toward an elevator that opens right as we get to it. We wait a few seconds as other guests come out of it.

"Yes," I say. "There's actually this ruin of a pyramid near here that I've always wanted to see." I put my hand on his chest. "Let's just get out of here for a few. So you can simmer down. I've never seen you like this."

Jocko's tense, and I admit it turns me on a little that his state was in the name of defending me.

I also have a flash of insight that this was how fired up he might have been with the CEO when it came to defending my position.

Although I hope he didn't threaten to fight him.

"Come on," I say. "It'll be fun. We've been cooped up in this resort for too long."

I kiss him gently, and he finally relents.

"Alright. Let's get out of here for a little bit."

"After all," I remind him. "We've only got one more day to be engaged."

23

ALLIE

It's a forty-five-minute bus ride to the pyramid ruins. I take the window seat and nuzzle into Jocko as the landscape rolls by. Palm trees, shop signs all in Spanish, a few stray dogs.

His hand rests on my thigh and a sense of déjà vu comes over me from four days ago when we got off the plane, and he touched my leg the same way.

Only now, it feels different. So much has happened in a few days. His touch feels familiar. Not that it ever felt 'strange', so to speak. Over three years at work, we developed such a strong bond as friends, so now that we've extended our friendship to the physical, my walls have crumbled rapidly.

I wonder how much of my enthusiasm for what we have is the newness of being with someone else after having only been with Mark for five years and how much is just my pure connection, and attraction, to Jocko.

I'm deep in thought when Jocko nudges me. "Hey. We're here."

I come out of my trance and notice the bus has come to a stop.

"Coming."

Outside, the afternoon sun beats down on us. We follow the other tourists to the roped-off entrance and pay the fee to enter.

Jocko slips his hand into mine. "Hey. Sorry about that. I flipped my shit in front of your friends. That was totally inappropriate, and I rarely lose my cool like that. My apologies."

He removes his sunglasses to wipe the sweat from his brow with his forearm, and his eyes look navy. Darker than normal.

I nod, lightly. "I appreciate that."

"Plus," he goes on, "this whole blowup is my fault anyway. I'm the crazy one who insisted on this elaborate dance of us being fake fiancés instead of just having a regular five-day vacation like normal friends."

"I can't let you shoulder all the blame for the whole fiancé thing," I say. "The truth is, I've enjoyed our role playing, strange as it has been. I could have turned you down. But real talk, I've enjoyed touting this ring around in front of everyone. This week is just what I needed to truly get over Mark. I needed you, Jay. It might sound crazy, but after your blowup back there, I'm actually less anxious about the past, *and* the future. That relationship just wasn't meant to be, and ultimately it's a blessing it didn't work out."

Jocko grins stoically. "Well, that makes me happy. I was worried about you for a while at the beginning of this trip. And let me say this, Allie. I didn't expect any of this to happen. I really did have zero expectations going into this week. Am I completely shocked? No. I've tried to pretend my feelings for you didn't exist because you had a boyfriend. But that didn't stop me from wanting you."

I swallow and run my hand up his forearm. "I think we both know something much beyond a normal friendship has been bubbling up for some time."

Jocko smiles faintly. "I can't deny that. We've never been 'normal' in most facets of our life, have we?"

"Speak for yourself," I joke.

"You're probably right. I'm a total nutjob," he grins.

We stop at the foot of the pyramid and look up the stairs.

"Shall we?" I ask.

"We're not going to be sacrificed once we get to the top, are we?" Jocko says, deadpan.

"I think we might."

He shrugs. "Well. Better to die a brave death than a cowardly one. Let's go."

My recent Jocko bootcamp workout sessions did not include as much cardio as I would have liked, so by the time we make it to the top of the ruin, I am huffing and puffing pretty hard. Luckily, it's late afternoon and the sun is farther down the horizon, so it's not as blazingly hot as it would be at high noon.

At the top of the pyramid, we turn and look at the lush landscape down around us. Even Jocko is winded.

"Can you imagine the poor saps who had to build this thing? They were probably toiling all day in the sun," Jocko comments.

"Yikes. And setting up those booby traps so that no one could get into the pyramids and steal the treasure must have been hell. There's no way some of them didn't die."

Jocko brings his shirt up to wipe his sweating brow, and I steal a glance of his abs. I've been looking at them all week at the pool and in the hot tub; so why does my body warm right now? Maybe it's seeing them out of the confines of the resort. And it's not lost on me that a couple of women to my left are checking him out, too.

"How do you think they got the idea to build pyramids both in Egypt *and* Mexico?" Jocko surmises. "I mean, this was thousands of years ago. You're telling me those civilizations had zero contact with each other, but they still came up with the idea for the exact same structure?"

I run a video in my head of men all over the world hauling rocks up. Yeah, checking out Jocko makes me think of the chiseled men who look like the movie *300* toiling in the hot sun.

After thinking for a moment, I say, "Well, both structures are pointing straight up in the air, toward the sky. And during that time, huge buildings with four walls were difficult to build because of the lack of technology. Maybe it was just an easy-ish shape for them to build? And they wanted to give thanks to some god in the sky, hence pointing it straight up."

Jocko wiggles his eyebrows. "Or it could have been aliens."

I giggle, and he wraps his arm around my shoulder. "Let's take a selfie," he says.

I turn my face so I can kiss him easily, we snap a photo with the pyramid in the background.

He pulls the photo up so we can look at it. "We almost look like a real happy couple in this one."

"Yeah. Almost."

Jocko takes off his sunglasses, looks off into the distance, and squints. After a few moments, he turns back to me.

"So where are you at with Mark and Barb? This might sound like a weird question, but are you fully moved on from him yet?"

I pause. "I think I was avoiding the breakup on some level for a while. I guess I just thought we would always get married — you know, like that was how relationships naturally evolved. I've been reflecting on some things while we've been up here."

"Like what?"

"After you told me about your parents' relationship, I got to thinking. My parents met in college and got married, and they've always been super happy together, and deeply in love. Mark and I met in college and I assumed we would follow a similar pattern. You actually helped me come to this conclusion when you got a little irate about me only wanting to get in shape for my 'revenge body'. I realized that our parents' models of happiness — or discord — greatly affect our own ideas of how we want to live our lives. And I also know I should work out to show love to myself, not to impress some guy who might never have loved me the way I deserve."

He arches an eyebrow. "Yes. And true. I've always had a lump in my stomach about long-term relationships, in general. Even though they made it work, my parents weren't the happiest together. To me they didn't seem that way, at least." Jocko pauses then mumbles, "Hmm. Interesting."

"What?"

"I wonder if that's a big part of the reason I'm so hesitant to settle down."

"That's a big realization," I say. "I don't know if this helps, but I realized that what was good for our parents doesn't necessarily make it good for us."

"And vice versa. If my parents didn't have the happiest relationship, that doesn't mean I *won't*. It just means that every couple is different."

"Yes. And by the way, thanks for helping me come to the

realization I did. You've truly helped me get over Mark, in a real way. You're such a good friend. Now I know there *will be* something — or someone — else out there at some point."

Jocko's face twitches. "Right. Well, whatever I can do, Allie. You know I care about you and it's been rough to see you all out of sorts for such a long time."

"Thanks."

I twist my face up and touch the big-ass ring on my finger.

"As much as I hate to do this, I have to. The time has come."

I slip the ring off my finger and hold it for a moment.

"It's been a fun run together. But we're going back to Detroit tomorrow and back to work. So we may as well rip the Band-Aid off," I say.

With an even expression, he accepts the ring back.

"Your great grandmother was a lucky woman," I add.

Jocko fingers the ring, "That she was."

Then, with a sideways grin on his face, he kneels down again.

My eyes widen, and I slap a hand over my mouth.

Dear God. Not again!

"Jocko, what are you doing?" I breathe.

A few people stare at us around the standing area at the top of the pyramid. He's drawing attention.

He smirks up at me. "I'm reverse proposing to you."

"Reverse...proposing?"

"Yes. Allie Jenkins, will you make me the happiest man in the world and go back to being friends with me? Real friends. Not like our fake engagement."

I laugh. "Of course, I will. Now will you stand up. People are staring."

"Come here. Let's seal this with a friendly hug."

Jocko stands, wraps me up in his arms, and his cheek brushes against mine as he hugs me.

A jolt of electric heat coils through me as he squeezes me, a little harder than "just friends" squeeze each other.

And the heat inside me is *not* friend heat. But both of us know that this is how it has to be as we head down the pyramid and make our way back to reality.

It truly does feel like I'm starting to come down from a high. And I have a bad feeling about the fall.

24

JOCKO

Allie Jenkins, will you go back to being just friends with me?

I had to force the words out of my mouth.

I didn't like saying them, but what else could I say? Especially after she expressed that I was a "great friend" and she would "meet someone else great *at some point.*"

I've dated enough women to know when someone is into me and not into me, and clearly, this is not that point. Allie's pushing me back in the friend zone, and I've got to respect that.

She probably wants to have a few single years to see what's out there, and I sure can't blame her. After all the dating around I've done the past decade, I'd be a hypocrite to critique her strategy.

But damned if it doesn't sting. I thought, for however brief window of time that Allie and I might be something really special.

And we are special — and I have to accept what that is... very good friends.

Allie and I get back from the pyramids in the evening.

Since it's the day after the wedding, everyone makes their own dinner reservations. Turns out everyone got pretty hammerslammed at the pool day-drinking after we left.

No one has heard from Maddy and Peyton, who apparently disappeared into their Deluxe Suite after they spent the afternoon at the pool.

I can't imagine what a newlywed couple would be doing alone in their room in Cancún. *Snort.*

It's a chill night, to put it lightly. Tomorrow is Sunday, day five of this adventure, and we have to take the four-hour flight back to Detroit, back to reality and what we were before this five-day jaunt, and I have a hard time accepting that realization.

Everyone knows that we're play acting now. Well, everyone in the wedding party, at least.

Neither Allie nor I can believe we messed up that early in the trip — to blab about our fake setup when Barb and Mark were literally right behind us on the plane.

They knew all along. That's why they were acting so weird.

There's no sense in denying what we've got to face up to. It's been a week of highs, but we've got a low coming Monday, and we both know it.

I hope my 'reverse proposal', corny as it might be, broke the ice so we can go back to being what we've been forever at the office: terrific work friends. I've valued our work relationship from the moment she stepped in the office, and I'm going to do my best to make sure things aren't awkward when we get back to Detroit.

Allie and I end up making dinner reservations with her friend Naomi and her fiancé, who is a pretty cool guy and makes good company for guy talk.

We finish dinner, say our goodbyes to Naomi and Gill,

then go for a walk barefoot along the beach. Stars are out, a warm breeze blows gently, and calm night waves wash up to our ankles.

We walk in silence. Both of us know the jig is going to be up when we get back to Detroit tomorrow.

Allie holds my hand, but it feels weird now, for some reason. I think about mine and Paco's conversation as we walk. A pang of regret pops into my head from this afternoon for playing the 'let's go back to being just friends' card just a little too soon.

The thing is, if I told her what was really on my mind, I would have freaked her out good and hard. But the voice is back, not letting the advice Paco gave me die:

Just tell her, man. Tell her you love her.

As many times as I run that program in my head, the outcome never goes well.

So, uh, Allie. This might be weird, and I know you only recruited me for like a five-day thing here, but I love you.

I can see Allie's face now.

Um, excuse me?

Yes. I love you.

This is so awkward. The reason I asked you is you are a known bachelor who doesn't get attached to girls...right? I was looking for a rebound screw, that's all.

Oh yeah, for sure, just kidding! Ha...let's go tell H.R. we're broken up now.

Yeah, it never goes well no matter how I spin it.

"What are you thinking about?" Allie asks, probably sensing my silence.

"Just thinking, it's been a fun week. No matter what happens, I'll always remember this week."

She giggles. "I think all of Peyton and Maddy's friends will remember you, too."

"Everyone remembers me," I wink, and she rolls her eyes.

"I've been thinking about these five days, too. Well, four so far. Tomorrow, since we fly out at two, that's hardly a day."

"Right."

She stops walking and turns to me, wrapping her hands around my shoulder. "This is the most fun I've had. Possibly ever."

My heart warms. "I'm happy I could be of service to you."

"I'm happy you could, too. It's a shame we have to go back to the real world. And leave this behind as just a fantasy week."

Just a fantasy week.

Those words echo in my head. And it's confirmed: I'm reading the signals correctly.

She lets go and we continue walking along the beach, not holding hands this time.

"And I am fully, officially, moving on from Mark. Single Allie is finally here!" she says loudly, opening her arms up now, twirling about.

I smile faintly, enjoying her gleefulness, but the meaning of her shouting those words isn't lost on me.

Yes, sir, I'm the rebound.

Inhaling a deep breath of salt-sprayed air, I see the smile on her face, though, and I just don't care. A few days as Allie's lover — yes, *lover* is the word I settled on for myself — are better than no days. She's a true prize and I envy the man who will be with her some day.

"We can deal with the consequences of reality on Monday," I say. "But we've still got one more night here."

"I know." I wrap my arms around her from behind, and she leans back into me.

"Thanks, by the way," she says. "Thanks for coming with me here and everything. I know how much you hate getting away from work."

I rest my head on top of hers, because that's how our height difference works. I let her statement sink in for a moment, and it drums up some loose thoughts I've been having all week. "You know, actually, this whole trip has made me realize how much of a workaholic I've been since I started working there, right out of college."

"You said that before, how is that even possible that you don't take vacation?"

I shrug. "I just don't take it. I give it back to the company. Great for sales. Bad for mental health."

"So you're thinking about taking vacations now?"

I shrug. "A vacation. Or maybe..." I clear my throat. "Maybe I'll look for another company."

Her body shivers when I say that. "No. Why would you do that?"

"I was going through Rhonda's messages yesterday. She showed genuine concern, so I looked up the bylaws myself and read through them. I'll be honest, this is not going to look good on me. The whole situation where everyone thinks we're engaged and have been carrying on a relationship behind the scenes is the one that crosses some company lines. And they've been cracking down on stuff like this in the current climate."

"But we haven't been doing that until now — we just started things this week."

"I know that. But it's bad optics. Customers already know. You know how gossipy our IT directors are."

I feel bad for bringing this up because Allie is looking so devastated. Maybe the probability of us not working together anymore is worrying her. "They are indeed dying for some good gossip," she says.

"But that's not even the full reason. I think I need to take a break from the sales cubicle grind. Maybe travel the world. Not like I don't have enough money to do that." In truth, I had been thinking about this before when talking with Travis. Life is short, and while I'm single and have no other pending responsibilities, now's the time to consider it. If not now, when?

"You've thought about traveling the world? I've always seen you as the straight-edged sales guy who stays put." She frowns a bit in thought.

I smirk, and take advantage that we're still in lover mode to let my hand slide down her side and land it on her hip.

"And I thought you were the goody-two-shoes Educational Technologist who liked missionary style sex only, in the dark."

"Oh, please. There's a lot you don't know about me." Good, I wiped that frown from her beautiful moonlit face.

"Besides the fact that you don't like olives? Which I now know."

She nods. "True, but there's so much more."

"Like what? Give me a fun fact."

Turning around, she lifts her eyes up shyly, running her hand along my chest. "Here's a fun fact. I'm attracted to you when you're angry. And I don't like that about myself. But it's true."

My *friend-vs-more-than friends* barometer spikes. Maybe there's still a chance?

"That's nothing to be ashamed of. I don't get mad easily. Almost never, actually."

"I know. I've never seen you lose your cool at work. I think that's why you took me by surprise so much today."

"I'm attracted to you in so many ways, Allie-face."

She giggles. "It's kind of weird when you call me that, you know."

"Well, I feel like Peyton has a monopoly on 'Al'." I hear a song playing in the distance on the dance floor outside. "How about I just call you 'my girl'."

"I suppose you can do that," she says. "For one more day."

I reach down and give her a kiss on the cheek. Yes, there's still hope. Our magical carriage won't turn back into a pumpkin until our plane takes off tomorrow. "One more day, huh?"

"One more," she smiles, though it doesn't reach her eyes.

"C'mon, *my girl*," I say. "Let's go dance."

We grab our flip flops at the edge of the beach and head back to the dance floor where everyone is.

My heart dies and thrives at once.

We've only got one more day.

But at the same time, we've got a whole day.

And I plan to enjoy it.

SHE WALKS up the stairs from the beach to the path where the music is coming from. I watch her. And I don't want to face the fact that this is all over tomorrow.

"Jay. You coming?" She turns around to check on me.

I nod. "Coming," I say.

"Good," she says. "Let's get one more dance in."

I bound up the stairs and take her hand, leading her to the corner of the dance floor where we're less conspicuous, even though there's hardly anyone around.

After an hour or so of dancing, my body is hot. So much for 'one more' dance.

She faces me as we dance. I lay my hands on her hips, pulling her body closer. Even our eyes dance, looking at each other, looking away, and coming back.

Both of us wondering what the other is thinking.

Now that we've gone back to being 'just friends', it gives the whole interaction an added element of heat. We might have made that declaration out loud, but that can't stop an attraction as visceral as ours.

Allie's got on a cute little romper that, I'll be honest, barely covers her ass. We stare at each other, both sweaty, lips parted. Her skin is rosy from four days of sun and heat.

She's too tempting, and I can't take it anymore.

I nudge her hips to indicate I want her to turn her back toward me and dance, and she does. I hold her hands and she grinds into me, swiveling her hips in a slow, sexy pattern, her ass pressing into my front. Everything, everyone else, fades away. Most of the crowd are strangers, and all I see and feel is her. Like there's a spotlight on us.

My heart pounds as she subtly guides my hands to the front of her thighs, and I press my fingers into her flesh. All of my senses are heightened. She reaches a hand back and rubs it against my abs over my shirt.

I bring one hand just above her chest, then slide a finger onto her cheek. Turning her face gently, I lower my face to reach hers. Our eyes smolder, and finally we cross the threshold and we kiss.

It's not the first kiss.

But it's the first kiss after our seemingly mutual 'just friends' declaration.

Maybe it's the way her back is turned to me, and she

doesn't miss a beat dancing. Maybe it's how my hand rests on her throat. Maybe it's the heat and the music.

Whatever the case, this kiss is hot as fuck.

Something about this new tabooness, about trying (and failing) to follow a rule we've set, spurs both of us on. We make out ravenously and she moans into my mouth.

My right hand creeps up her thigh, higher, higher, until I'm reaching under her romper. She lets out a whimper as I find her clit with my hand and gently finger her opening. At the same time, I kiss her neck and I can feel the goosebumps rising on her skin.

I look around, and no one is even looking at us. The few who are left at this hour are off in their own little world.

We're an upward spiral of heat and pleasure. My dick is hard now as she continues grinding into me. I undo a belt loop for her, and she's able to reach inside my shorts and grab my dick.

The angles for both of us are awkward, but we make eye contact and there's fire in both of our eyes glazed over with pleasure.

I bring my head down to meet her lips again, and after our kiss she moans, "You ever done anything in public like this?"

"No. Have you?"

"No. But I like doing it with you."

Her eyes flutter closed as I touch her wet opening.

I let out a low, throaty growl and she pulls me down for another greedy kiss.

"You ready to go up to the room and finish this properly?" I say.

She nods. "God, yes."

DAY 5

25

ALLIE

Jocko sleeps like a log after sex. An unmovable, unawakenable log.

I thought I was ready to sleep, but I'm wired now.

I didn't want to cuddle because I'm sweaty from dancing and everything else. So I pushed him away and told him good night.

Now it's four a.m. and I still haven't slept a wink.

All night, there's been a tension rising between us and our time between the sheets did nothing to relieve it. For me, at least.

I put on sweats, a t-shirt, and flip flops, grab my glasses, and keycard and head downstairs and outside. There's some lawn chairs close to the beach where I can watch the stars. I lean back and look.

You can see the stars here a lot better than in Detroit, at least. But not better than when I used to visit my grandmother's cabin two hours outside of Kansas City.

So I lean back and look at the stars. When I'm feeling anxious, looking at the sky has a way of making me feel at peace with the universe. No matter how big my problems might seem, what's life but the blink of an eye in the bigger scheme?

A cool breeze brushes my arms and I wish I'd brought a sweatshirt to keep me warm. Or Jocko.

I smile thinking of him. And then I remind myself we leave for the airport at two.

This week has been the most surprising of my life. I chose him to be my date because I knew he'd be a ton of fun, which he has been, and more. Yeah, things did go beyond what I thought they would've, but I'm glad they did for many reasons. I discovered Jocko's got a sweet side to him, too. And *that* I definitely didn't see coming.

We embarrassed ourselves beyond belief yesterday. Thank God it was the day *after* the wedding because I never would have forgiven myself had it happened any earlier, or the day of. *Cringe.* And it was important to hear that our actions didn't affect Maddy and Peyton's moods, as Naomi conveyed to me. I've been good friends for a long time with everyone who attended the wedding. We've all seen each other's shortcomings and moved on. We're supportive that way, unconditionally, and that's the most important.

Jocko's got all of the qualities in a man that I've dreamed of. Tall. Smart. Handsome. A big family. Even the whole fake fiancé plan was concocted to sort of assuage his mother's worries, which was sweet in a messed-up way. And although it backfired spectacularly now that H.R. has found us out, well, the funny thing is I don't regret a single day here. With him.

I've had such a blast. I've done things that I never imagined myself doing.

You know, like balcony sex, Spiderman BJs, and *finally*

confronting Mark. Thinking about Mark now, I really question what the heck I saw in him in the first place.

By the end of the day today, it's all over. We'll go back to Detroit, and the Monday morning vacation hangover will probably be the worst of our lives. And I have a feeling our H.R. meeting Monday — yes, I checked my calendar while on vacation, some bad habits are harder to break — will have no small part in that. Jocko is right. They really are cracking down.

Deep down, though, I feel transformed after this week. It's been the longest winter of my life, one with lots of nights filled with bottles of wine, countless tissues, and inviting Rhonda over.

Spring is here, summer is on the horizon, and for the first time in a long time, I feel a new era dawning.

I know I would have gotten here by myself eventually. But I think I made it here faster with Jocko by my side.

I snort. Mr. self-proclaimed 'ultimate bachelor'. It's too bad, because deep down, I get the feeling that he and I could make something great together.

Instead, I'll just enjoy the rest of this day with him. Our friends with benefits relationship, if you could call it that, will be over once we get on that plane.

The very first signs of dawn appear on the horizon. I head back upstairs and snuggle into his warm body to catch a few winks of sleep before the sun officially comes up.

Sunday morning we go to brunch with the group, and everyone's in high spirits. Well, high yet dulled over from five straight days of drinking. There is no drama, just laughs and recounting the highs of the trip, and the lows.

Peyton and Jocko are somehow buds again already, laughing over some old college drinking stories. Apparently, they've made up since yesterday's tense run-in, though I'm unsure of when.

I head to the bathroom, and when I come back to join the group Mark is waiting in the hallway.

"Oh, hell no," I say to him before brushing past. What a fucker.

He scurries after me. "I just wanted to say I'm sorry. You're right."

Stopping in my tracks, I feel a chill go down my spine. I turn and arch an eyebrow toward him.

He continues. "I'm done. You seem...happier now. Without me, I mean. And deep down, I knew that's what would happen. I knew I wasn't the one for you. This guy... whatever, he makes you happy. I can see that. I don't have to know if you're serious or not. It *is* none of my business what you're doing now. Sorry if I ruined your trip."

"Thanks," I say, barely audible. But it's all I can say because I'm over him now? Sooo over him.

He nods, looks at the ground, and passes me to get back to the brunch table where everyone is eating omelets and drinking fruit juice.

My heart warms and I wonder *what's this feeling?*

I'm feeling, I don't know, virtuous after this last encounter? I think because it is the last, I sure as shit am not going to be in contact with him anytime soon. Is that what closure is? When you just know, when you finally accept that what you've been mourning this entire time is really over? Praise God, I think I'm experiencing closure.

A rush of emotion washes over me as I walk to the table. Jocko's hearty laugh reverberates through the room, and he eyes me the instant I walk in, then licks his lips exaggeratedly.

I giggle from the heart, and my chest suddenly feels light.

I realize why: I have a flashback to the very first week I met Jocko. I was sitting next to his desk as he was showing me the ropes of his job, which I needed to understand for my new position. He kept cracking low-key jokes while I was trying to be all work-serious since it was my first week. But he informed me he was joking around, or, as he liked to say, *"I'm just jocking with you, Allie-face."*

I died laughing at the pun, so much so that our boss came by to see what the commotion was.

In that moment, I couldn't help but wonder what would happen if this goofy, sexy man and I kept *whatever we have* going when we get back to Detroit. Could every day feel as good as this week?

But then I remember the poster he's got hanging up in his cubicle.

Bachelor 4 Lyfe

With a picture of Frank Sinatra, one of the biggest bachelors of all time.

To think he's ever going to settle down would simply be foolish.

I realize I'm lingering and creepily staring, while Jocko is giving me a *what are you thinking* squinty-eyed look. And then I realize we're on the level where we can communicate words non-verbally. How did we get this far so quickly?

When I sit down next to him, he brushes a couple of loose hairs behind my ear (because my hair is up), and kisses my cheek, sending my stomach fluttering.

Then, he says, in a whisper, "Even with your hair up, I

do declare you'd give bacon a run for its money in a 'who's sexier' contest."

I die laughing, and when someone at the table asks me what's so funny, I just shrug and say that it's a long story.

And indeed, Jocko and I are a very long story.

THE REST of the afternoon happens in a flash — we pack, say our goodbyes to the wedding party, and Uber to the airport for our afternoon flight home. The flight is uneventful as we're both quiet and sleep most of the way. Customs lines move swiftly, too, since neither of us bought anything substantial to declare. Grabbing our luggage off the baggage claim, we both have to take our sweatshirts out of our bags because we forgot to check the weather in Detroit. I guess I was just hoping it would be seventy or eighty and sunny like Cancún. I think we're both in a little bit of denial. About both the weather and the end of our little adventure as more than friends.

Jocko suggests we go back to his place to plan out what we're going to say to H.R. tomorrow, and I agree. Post-vacation depression begins to seep in.

His place is a three-story house; he rents out the bottom two floors and lives on the top. It's a tasteful brownstone, not overly luxurious, and just so *Jocko*. Inside there are minimal decorations, but a bar and a killer sound system are the bachelor-like highlights.

I have a seat on the couch, worn out from the day spent traveling.

"Drink?" he asks, raising an eyebrow.

"But we have work tomorrow."

"*Tomorrow,*" he repeats. "As far as I'm concerned, we're still on vacation. C'mon Allie. One more."

"You've sold me," I say, because to be honest, I wanted one even though I protested.

He brings me a tequila mojito, which I've never had before, and it is delicious.

"Well, Allie, cheers. To a great fucking week," he says. "Thank you for bringing me along, and I really mean that. You got me out of my comfort zone."

"Thank you for coming," I say as I take a drink. "I mean, *to* Cancún. Dammit. Why can't I think of a simple word like *come* the same anymore?"

Jocko throws his head back in laughter. "I get what you're saying. The travel *and* the orgasms were my pleasure."

I clear my throat. "So did you go through with the plan? Tell your mom that you're not engaged?"

"Gotta do it," he says, flipping his phone around in his hand, and grimacing. "I thought this would be an easy way to get Mom off my back. Turns out, I actually do have feelings."

My eyes widen. "Really? Your blood isn't made of steel?"

He sighs, and swigs down a healthy amount of his drink. "I wish. Alright. Doing it."

His thumbs pound out a text to his mom. "Hey, Mom," he reads. "So some bad-ish news. I'm no longer engaged. It was sort of a whirlwind thing, and you know what? It was a quick decision and we're not engaged any more. Sorry to get you all excited."

I nod somberly.

He throws his phone across the room and it lands on a beanbag chair. I follow his example, because talking to Jocko is more fun than phones.

"We're a crazy pair, you and me," Jocko says. "I'm sorry this stuff got so out of the bag."

"What do you want to do about H.R.?" I ask, and I realize we're both sitting on the couch, but it feels like an awkward first date where we don't know if we should hook up, but we both kind of want to. I inch my body ever so slightly toward him. His arm is laid across the back of the couch, so close to my neck I can feel its heat.

He blows out a deep, thinking breath. "Well. We should just tell them the deal."

"Which is...?"

"That we were together for five days, but we're not any more. And since we technically never did anything at work, we were out of their jurisdiction."

I swallow a lump in my throat. "Will that...work?"

"I flipped through the employee handbook on the plane ride home, and I think we'll be good."

"So I guess that's that."

"That *is* that," Jocko echoes.

I take another swig of my drink, almost finishing it.

"Jay, I want to say som-"

"Allie, I want to say something," he bursts out, then pauses. "Oh, sorry. Go ahead."

"No, you."

"I insist."

"Alright. I just wanted to say..." he starts and then trails off, his eyes wandering around the room as if he's deep in thought.

I wonder what he's thinking about. I mean he's the world's biggest bachelor. He might as well have that tattooed on his forehead. And maybe it's wrong of me, but I can't help that my veins are hot with desire in his presence.

Even in grey sweats and a white T, he's hot.

And maybe it's because I know him intimately now that being in his presence heats my body.

I want to put my drink down, move closer to him.

I want to straddle him on the couch, and tell him.

We're still fake fiancés until midnight, right?

Want to do this one more time, please?

But some voice nips in my ear that we're back in Detroit now, and that would be truly crossing the line. The magic is gone.

Jocko clears his throat and finally finishes his thought. "I was going to say that I enjoyed the time with you. No matter what happens with H.R. And I've got your back, obviously."

"Thanks. And same."

"What were you going to say?"

"The same thing, pretty much."

Silence creates a chasm between us. I barely felt awkward this entire week in Cancún. Now that we're back here, it's awkward just like I feared.

After another beat I finish my drink. Yep, I read this right. "Well, I should go. See you at the official meeting in H.R. tomorrow?"

He nods. "See you there."

Outside, it's raining, so he loans me an umbrella. He brings my luggage down the stairs and loads it into the Uber for me, and smiles as I get inside.

He goes in for a hug, and I'm a little bit spacey, but since we're back to being just friends, I turn my head so he can just kiss me on the cheek, which he does. No more lip stuff, unfortunately.

I catch a glimpse of him in the rearview mirror as my car pulls away. He just stands there in the rain, staring.

I'm not sure what feels more surreal: the fact that we spent the past five days in the throes of a whirlwind romance, or the fact that our romance is now officially over. Either way, I'm not sure I'll ever be the same again.

At home, I pick my outfit for tomorrow, a classy blue power suit, button-up blazer and killer heels. I have a glass of wine to calm my nerves.

I miss Jocko already. I wish he was here. I wish I could feel his warm body pressed up against mine every night.

I flip my phone around in my hand, thinking about texting him.

But I'm exhausted from the night of barely any sleep, and it's not too long before I crash hard in my bed.

Thinking of him.

26

JOCKO

So I guess this is goodbye.

I heave a heavy sigh as Allie leaves, and a light rain begins to fall. Not moving from my spot on the street a few feet from the curb, I stare at her Uber as it fades into the distance.

My stomach is a brick. Something about this feels eerily final. It was the cheek turn. She fucking *turned her cheek* on me.

After the incredible week we had?

My stomach churns as the Uber turns a few blocks down and heads out of sight. I've never had a breakup with someone I cared about. Maybe this is what that feels like. I just feel miserable from the inside.

"Hey, buddy, trying to park here," a man shouts to me through his rolled-down car window as I stand in the street. His voice sounds far away and I'm in a trance. I move a few steps to the grass beyond the curb so he can park.

Look, I'm no stranger to failure. The key to being a top salesman is being okay with failure. No, actually, *thriving* on failure. I lose more deals than I win. My *cojones* are steel-plated at this point from all the deals I've lost at EdTechX.

Yet, as the rain comes down harder, I feel as if in a daze. My mind clouds, and this doesn't feel like some lost deal.

Shaking off the feeling, I head inside.

Probably just nerves, and the come-down from being with fun people and drinking for five days straight.

Fun *people.*

Please. Those people were fun, sure, but they weren't your friends. Allie was the reason this week was so much fun.

I sit down on the couch and throw on the Jaguars baseball game, trying to take my mind off things. Jake Napleton's on the mound for ESPN's night game tonight. The man is a beast and fun to watch.

But then I realize Detroit is playing Chicago today in the NBA, so I click channels over to that. As a former college basketball player, watching Carter Flynn and Chandler Spiros play together is like watching Picasso paint on the basketball court...or something like that.

Art analogies are hard to make when it comes to sports, or anything for that matter.

I have another beer, but the anxious feeling in my gut doesn't go away. This is a completely new feeling to me. I just don't get like this when thinking about a woman.

I'm watching TV but spacing out. The past five days run through my head like a cheesy Hallmark movie.

Hell, more than five days run through my mind's eye. I think about the two months we spent in the gym preparing for the trip. How enthusiastically she took to my workouts. My accusations that she was trying to make her ex jealous. Silly me.

I bite my lip and think about the mental journey I went on in Cancún. Seeing Peyton and Maddy so in love, and feeling like maybe — just maybe — that could be me some day.

That feeling was a huge step up for me.

Because for the first time in my life, I could actually *picture* a wedding with someone specific.

And now, we're all broken up. The plan is set in motion, the wheels are turning, and there's no stopping what's about to happen. We *need* to do it, anyway. Or else H.R. is going to have our heads on a spike.

I PICK up my phone and face my evils head on by following up that text to my mom with a call and telling her that yes, the whole fiancée thing is off now.

She's surprisingly not disappointed. Not at all the reaction I was expecting.

"Well, that's okay. This one came on so quickly. You've got to take your time, honey."

"Take my time? You ask me every time we talk when your grandchildren are getting here?"

She laughs. "Oh, Jocko, honey. You didn't think I was serious, did you? I figure if you have them, it'll be in your forties. You'll be one of those older dads."

My chest tightens. "So you don't care...that I'm not ready to settle down?"

I can hear her rocking in her classic rocking chair. She's probably on the porch right now. "I would never want you to rush through something to please me. I'm your mother, and of course I want grandkids. But you've got to do things at your own pace, too. I understand that. Never sacrifice your own happiness for me."

All of a sudden, I feel hot. Like nerves-hot. Not like the hot Allie makes me.

Well, my entire plan has just backfired gloriously.

Leave it to me to overthink every last thing. And not just tell my mother.

I chuckle, thinking how I'm unafraid of confrontation in every facet of life...except when it comes to the women I love.

Just then, my skin turns electric and a lightbulb goes off.

The *women I love,* I repeat in my head.

It's more than one woman, now.

I stand up.

"Hey, Mom, thanks for that. Say, what's dad up to right now?"

"Oh, he's in the main room watching TV and drinking a beer."

"What's he been up to today?"

"Just that."

"Okay."

"Why do you ask?"

"Just curious."

It's hard to explain to my mom what I'm thinking right now as a major realization dawns on me.

My therapist — I went to one in my mid-twenties — had tried to unpack something she called 'unconsciously learned relationship dynamics.'

Random bits of our conversations flit through my mind, pieces she tried to dig into about my parental role models and how that affected me. My mother and father were so non-confrontational, she said, that I sought out confrontation in sports and in my work life. It's part of what makes me the ultimate salesperson — I literally *thrive* on conflict in some areas of life. But she also informed me that when it comes to my mother and also my romantic life, I'm not that way.

The phrase *conflict avoidant* flashes through my mind.

"Jocky? You there?"

"I'm here, Mom. Thanks for that. Tell Dad I said hi. I've got to go."

"Love you, honey."

"Love you, too."

As soon as I hang up, my phone rings again. I don't usually answer numbers I don't know, but for some reason I get a funny feeling and decide to pick up this time.

"Yeah?"

"Jocko," comes a low, gravelly sounding voice. "It's Peyton."

My skin tingles. I stood up to him, yes, but something about the man has an intimidating presence.

"Well, this is a surprise."

"Yeah. I wanted to talk with you."

My body throbs, a little nervously. I recall what he said about being able to find a hit man. Not that he'd do it, but he did have those crazy eyes that worried me.

"I just wanted to say, sorry about the way shit went down, my man. Me and Maddy and Paco got drunk this afternoon after everyone else went home and we were talking about you."

"Wait, what do you mean, Paco?" Alarm bells go off inside my head.

"Oh, come on, man. Don't play dumb. That bartender you spilled your guts to because you thought he couldn't speak English? When he got off his shift this afternoon, we got to talking about his art — that you bought a bunch of it — and he started laughing, telling us all about you."

"I swore him to secrecy. That dick!" Cost me a fortune to

ship that stuff home — I'll return it, damn him.

Peyton laughs. "Yeah, well, I think he knew the right time to talk. So you're in love with Allie, eh, Big Boy? Is that true?"

I clear my throat.

I've not allowed myself to think about the L word today. Being the last day of our five-day extravaganza, letting that word enter into my liminal space just seemed to be adding to my own demise. But he's right.

"I might have said something along those lines."

"Well, did you or didn't you say that? Shit, man. I thought you were a straight shooter."

"I did, I did say that," I admit. "But she's gone home. We've got to go back to work tomorrow and tell H.R. how we're no longer a couple just to save our jobs."

"You said that to Paco, having no idea he'd tell a soul. Why would you lie to a guy if you didn't even think he spoke English? So I gotta ask, did you mean what you said?"

I rub my temple with my thumb and forefinger. I've never admitted this out loud to anyone. Well, except Paco. That double crossing S.O.B.

"I did mean it."

"Did you tell Allie?"

"No. Of course not."

"Why not?"

"It was five days, man! What kind of guy falls in love after less than a week! That's not how love happens!"

Peyton chuckles. "I didn't know there was a formula for love. Where is she?"

"I told you, she's gone home. Didn't even let me kiss her goodbye on the lips."

I hear Maddy's voice. "Well, of course, she didn't let you! She thinks you were just each other's playthings for a week.

And you're a bachelor for life, Jocko. She's protecting her own feelings."

"Am I on speaker?!"

"Yeah, bro," Peyton says. "You're on with me and Maddy."

"Paco is here, too!" The traitor chimes in.

"Paco! How dare you tell them those things. That was part of the bartender-customer confidentiality agreement!"

"Chill out, *hombre*," Peyton says. "We're trying to help you. And I'm not one to meddle in another guy's business, but after all the stuff Paco told us about, you've got to just tell the girl what you're feeling. That's what you've got to do, sometimes. Hell, worked out for me. Ain't that right, baby?"

I hear him smooch Maddy in the background. Hey, they're newlyweds. So bully for them.

I stand up and walk to the window. It's pouring cats and dogs now.

"That's sissy stuff, man. A guy can't confess his love first. That's the woman's job."

"I saw the way she looks at you," Maddy says. "I don't know if it's love. But it's damn close."

I nod, seeing my own reflection in the window.

"Fuck it," I whisper. "Thanks, guys. Talk again soon. Have a great honeymoon."

I don't wait for their goodbye.

Suddenly, a sense of urgency hits me like a bolt of thunder. I dial Allie's number frantically.

It goes to voicemail after one ring. I call again. Same thing.

Thunder claps outside. Life is short. And if I'm feeling this right now I've got to let Allie know. Somehow I feel like if I tell her today, there's still a chance the magic will be there but if I wait until tomorrow, it'll be all over.

"Fuck it," I say out loud.

I call an Uber to come take me to Allie's.

ALLIE LIVES in the second story of a three-story building in Midtown.

When I pull up, I ring the buzzer a few times but it seems to be broken.

I'm soaking wet. It's really pouring now, and I've got no umbrella. I try to stand close to the door, under the tiny awning, but the wind is blowing the rain right into my back.

After an hour or so, the guy from the first floor is coming out of his place, and I smile and say I'm heading up to Allie's. He reluctantly lets me inside the common area of the apartment, which I appreciate as I am wet and getting wetter.

Once inside, though, I have another conundrum: there is a small common space porch, not quite a lobby, and I do not have the key to go up the stairs. So I'm stuck in this small, eight-by-eight space with just a welcome rug.

I call her again and it goes right to voicemail. Again.

I bang on the door. Nothing.

I sit down on the floor and check the time. Getting late. Almost midnight.

The clock passes twelve, and although I'm not a pumpkin, hope leaves me. I'm chilly and wet and Allie and I will never be a thing. She's ignoring my calls.

I blew my chance, and that's that.

With tired eyes, I fall asleep on the welcome rug in that first-floor common area. I don't feel very welcome.

I dream of Cancún and weddings and balconies, but it seems worlds away now.

27

ALLIE

My hangover is surprisingly not so bad when I wake up the next morning, even before my alarm.

Though there's an ache in my chest that won't go away, I can't quite tell what it is.

I pick my phone up and think about taking it out of airplane mode, but set it down instead. I have a habit of checking Instagram first thing in the morning that I'm trying to break. And I have a feeling that seeing more pictures from the wedding — which is what my friends will surely be posting — will just send me into a precarious *fomo* emotional state that I have no interest in being in right now.

Getting back into the swing of work after a vacation is never any fun. Plus, with our stressful H.R. meeting coming up — I'm going to need that double shot of espresso this morning.

I put on my power outfit that makes me feel the best. Well, and look the best, too.

After my makeup is on, I head to my armoire where I keep a lovely selection of my favorite glasses, I think a pair of Hillary Duff's will suffice. I then straighten myself up in the full-length mirror, satisfied with what I see. I definitely caught Jocko checking out my butt a couple of times in this outfit.

A giggle escapes me, but then it turns quickly to sadness. There won't be any more of that. If anything, we might be awkward today. And I made a decision, if anyone has to be let go today, I'm going to be the one. Yes, it was Jocko's idea to concoct that ridiculous engagement, but I was the one who invited him to the whole destination wedding anyway.

And to be honest, I'm not sure I can work as closely with him as I have in the past after all we've been through — because I truly care for him, *I love him*.

Yes, I've said it before. But after realizing Mark is not what love is; Jocko's caring way about him, his fun-loving, easy-going style, his *GQ* looks and the way he notices *me* and looks out for *me*... how could I not love him. I. Love. Jocko.

It's dreary outside today, grey and cloudy. Cancún is a world away. It never happened.

Jocko's words from when we were just arriving to Mexico play themselves over in my head.

What happens in Cancún stays in Cancún.

He's never said a truer thing. Though, it still doesn't feel good, because I'll never forget the week or him.

I lock the door behind me and head downstairs. It feels like a funeral march — I'm in a brain fog and barely watching where I'm going.

When I go to open the door to the common area, however, something's blocking it. I get the door open a few inches and I can see through the crack, it's a person.

A ball of anxiety whirls around my gut. We've had problems with homeless people stealing their way inside this area before. Probably a drunk who needed refuge from last night's rainstorm. However, I can't get out until this heavy guy moves. I poke him with the door, opening it a few times.

"Excuse me!" I sing. "I need to get out, please!"

Groaning, the body rolls over a little bit, and I gain enough of an opening to just about fit through. I attempt to slide through, by my ass catches between the door and the frame.

I sigh. Hashtag bubblebutt problems.

"Sir," I say again, and turn my head down to look at him.

And that's when all of the blood rushes out of my face.

Jocko.

Jocko is the homeless man blocking the door.

His eyes flutter open. "Ah. Hey, Allie-face," he mutters. "Morning."

My pulse races. "What are you doing here?! Did you sleep here?"

He rubs his eyes and props himself up on his elbows. "Sleep here? Of course not. What do you think I am, some kind of heathen?"

He moves just enough so I'm able to sneak the rest of me through the door and step into the lobby with him.

"Uh, well, then, why does your bedhead match the wall just as you were sleeping right now?"

He clears his throat and comes to his feet. "Coincidence."

He's wearing jeans and the same white polo he had on when I left his place yesterday.

"Allie. I need to come clean about something."

"You do?"

My heart panics. Eyes widen. I race through the possibilities of what he could be referring to.

He regrets what happened in Cancún. It was fun, but it never should have happened.

Maybe I'm just doomed to be single forever.

"Allie." Goosebumps roll over my skin when he says my name again. He takes a step toward me and puts his arms around my waist and I heat up.

"Yes?" I whisper.

"I don't want this to end. I don't know what this is. I don't think either of us can be sure yet. But we can't just call off this thing because our five days are up. We don't have to get engaged. I mean, obviously. But I'd like to ask you..."

He stumbles for a moment, his eyes running around the room before they finally land on me. "To be my girlfriend."

I freeze up. This was certainly not the wakeup I was expecting today.

I giggle. "You're not forty yet, though."

He laughs. "True. And you haven't dated around yet. So, there's reasons for you to say no. But I couldn't go another day without asking you."

"Seriously, I thought you don't go steady. What with the whole bachelor-for-life thing?"

Jocko steadies his gaze on me, his eyes dead serious. "You're right. I have said that for a long time. Turns out, that attitude works for everyone else but you. I can't let you go, Allie. Not when I feel the way I do."

There's no hesitation when he says those words. A chill rolls down my spine, and my eyes well with emotion.

"Just for me?"

"Allie, I don't throw the L word around lightly."

My eyes glaze over and my whole body heats like crazy. My eyes are as wide as an alien who sees Earth for the first time. I'm dumbstruck.

Does Jocko mean *the* "L" word? I'm almost scared to ask.

But the truth is, I've had very intense feelings for him

this week, too. I was terrified to go down that road, thinking my own feelings wouldn't be reciprocated.

Definitely not the wakeup I was expecting.

He continues: "What I feel for you is more than I've felt for a woman. In my life. You're much more than a five-day phase for me. I want you to be a really long phase."

"Oh, yeah?" I whisper, moving in closer to him. "How long?"

He smirks. "Not sure yet. How long do you plan on living?"

My knees go weak and my body melts into him. "I can't believe what I'm hearing. You're not fucking with me, are you?"

"I've known you three years. I think we both know this thing started long before Cancún."

I grin. "Just needed the booze to get it out of you, eh? I thought you were the man with the steel *cojones*. That's what you always told me."

We kiss, and a warm euphoria bleeds into me from his warm body. His hand mischievously explores around my lower hips, touching me over the front of my skirt.

"Fuck, Allie. I need you now."

"Jocko, not sure if you know this about me. But you should. I am a woman with a high sex drive. And I'm not about to pass up a chance at make-up sex with you. However," I glance at my watch. "I'm also responsible. And if we don't leave, *right now*, we're going to be late. We're barely going to make it to work as it is."

Jocko kisses me on the lips once more and then bares his teeth.

"Alright. Fine. But this isn't over."

I bite my lower lip. "It's never over between us, is it?"

"Not a chance."

"Seriously, though, what are we going to do about this H.R. meeting? We have to tell them something," I say to Jocko in the Uber on the way to work. "And we can't make it up."

"By the way, can you even wear that to work? Not like it's a casual Friday or something. The boss is going to ream you out." He's still just wearing his white polo and jeans.

"Quite honestly, I couldn't care less what the boss thinks of me at this point. Oh. And as for our H.R. meeting." Jocko gets this devilish smirk, then leans in and whispers in my ear.

"No!" I shout back. "Really? But we can't do that!"

He shrugs. "Why not? I'd do it with you."

"You're...serious."

"You don't want to?"

"I feel like we should have a larger discussion about this!"

He wraps his arm around me and pulls me into him. "Come on. YOLO, Allie-face. We already know we want to do it."

"I'm probably crazy. But alright."

Janet from H.R. pushes her glasses up and purses her lips, staring at us from behind her long desk with papers stacked on either side of it. I was hoping they would have had Rhonda here with us, since this involved her area, and let's face it, I needed a friend in my corner.

Jocko and I sit a few feet from her.

"So," she says. "I was made privy to your unauthorized relationship on Friday afternoon, as a result of the social media sharing that was going on. Luckily, snooping on social media is my middle name. And I didn't have much going on this weekend, so I was able to put a file together on you two. And this morning, I got a few statements from your coworkers."

My stomach rattles around a little. "Why would you need statements from them?" I ask.

"To see how early this relationship started. It looks as though you were spotted canoodling at a work event at Pizza Palace? That's what a few of your coworkers said."

"Canoodling?" Jocko echoes. "What does that even mean? Is that a technical term?"

"Mr. Brewer, please, let me finish."

I give Jocko the nod, and he reciprocates. It's time to put our plan into action. "Janet, with all due respect, this isn't really necessary."

"Oh? And why's that?"

"We're breaking up," I say.

Janet's eyes widen. "Oh? Well, even so, ah, the courtship for the engagement must have taken place in the office..."

"And I don't mean with each other," I glance at Jocko, then add, "We're breaking up with EdTechX. Jocko and I are both putting in our two weeks."

She jerks her head back in surprise. "Excuse me?"

Jocko clears his throat and puts his hand on top of mine. "That's right. We'll be telling our boss right after this conversation. It's our understanding that we have to report first to H.R.?"

"Uh, well, if this is about the relationship filing and you being worried about getting in trouble, we can certainly see what we can do to soften the blow." The change in her demeanor would be funny if we hadn't already made up our minds.

Still, my posture stiffens. "Isn't that what you're here to do, though? Bring the hammer down?"

"I'm not the bad guy here, Allie. Really. We can sort this out. There's no reason this should be anything more than a blemish on your records."

I shake my head, feeling Jocko squeeze my hand. I look at him and nod.

He then fills her in on our entire plan. "We're leaving the company and traveling the world. Look, Janet, it's not you, it's us. We've been here a while, and it's time to get out and explore. Sorry."

"Oh," Janet mutters, touching her throat. "Well, then. You're sure?"

Jocko and I nod in unison. "Yes. We're sure," I say.

My skin tingles. As we leave the office, I get a fluttery feeling in the stomach. It's something that so many people dream about: quitting their day job for a little while and traveling the world.

Turns out, I just needed a strong enough partner to help me realize that dream.

28

ALLIE

The very last day of work. It's kind of a 'parting is such sweet sorrow' moment and it's also not. They still marked our employment records with fraternization, so if we ever came back for rehire we'd have that to deal with. I don't think Matt gave a rat's ass that I was leaving, but he's been crying in his soup over Jocko.

"I'm going to miss you a ton. God, I really am," Rhonda says as she sits down in an empty chair next to me in the cubicle and we sip our iced lattes. The very last time we do, our ritual is bittersweet.

"We'll still hang out." I say.

"After you finish taking your around-the-world trip," she reminds me, shaking her head. "You and Jocko. If you would have told me even last year this would be happening, I would have laughed in your face."

I shrug. "I know. Life is crazy sometimes."

"I don't think Matt believes you're really leaving. Like he's actually in denial."

I throw my head back in laughter. "I don't know. He's really more concerned about losing Jocko, I think."

"I don't know, girl, he's been asking me all these questions about PowerPoint lately," Rhonda shakes her head. "I refuse to be his PowerPoint bitch now that you're gone."

"Indeed, I was his PowerPoint bitch, wasn't I. No longer — I'm free!"

We hear Jocko's voice behind the cubicle wall, his deep laugh echoing throughout the floor. It makes me smile.

Rhonda opens her mouth to say something, then closes it.

"What?" I ask.

"It's silly. But I can't ever remember you being so happy as you've been these past two weeks. Is it because of Jocko or leaving the job?"

"Both," I beam. "I've needed a change for some time now."

She sighs. "Well, I'll be following your couple's vacay-insta. I hear bossman coming, so I better get back to work."

As the day goes on I continue finishing up project after pending project. I'm helping train two employees, Rhonda, too, as they'll take over my responsibilities when I'm gone. Ha! Takes three people to do my job, like my one-point-seven-five-percent raise would have spread that thin — sometimes it's good to get away and get another perspective on things.

And Jocko...we've been peas in a pod. Sleepovers every night, and although our sex life is shaking, it's less manic, more relaxed and natural now, I guess. We're obviously feeling more comfortable with one another, and happy knowing we have more than a five day limit on our relationship.

My phone dings and I see it's a text from my boyfriend. (*Boyfriend!* Gah! Love it.)

J: Babe, let's get lunch, I'm starved.

I send him a smiley emoji with the three hearts around it (he says it's his favorite emoji I send him), put my computer on sleep mode, then walk around the cube to go get my man.

~

LATER THAT DAY, I knock on the door of Matt's office.

"Oh, uh, hey there. What are you doing? Did you get that email I sent about that one last PowerPoint?"

I push the door open and head in, ignoring him and following the plan Jocko and I came up with this week. Ignoring his question, I say, "I just wanted to say bye. Thanks for everything. I hope we're leaving on good terms."

Never burn any bridges. One of Jocko's iron rules of sales.

Although some rules are made to be broken. As Matt's about to find out.

He purses his lips together. "I wish you weren't leaving."

"Well, I don't *have* to leave. I can stay."

He furrows his brow. "You can?"

"Yes," I say, plopping down in the more comfortable chair on the side of his office, not the uncomfortable one he had me sit in during salary negotiations two months ago. "Let's talk salary. I'm thinking one-fifty?"

His eyes widen. "So you'd stay on for an extra hundred-fifty dollars per month? That's tough, but doable. If you're serious right now. Are you serious?"

I smirk, get up, and then lean on his desk. It might be mean of me, but seeing how desperate he is gives me a strange sense of satisfaction.

"No- no, I don't mean one-hundred-fifty per month. I mean one-hundred-fifty thousand, annually. If you can pay me that, I'll stay for another year. I talked it over with Jocko."

He swallows. "Oh?"

I nod. "Yes. We ran *the numbers*," I pause for emphasis since those seemed so important to him last time, "and one-hundred-fifty thousand is approximately *ten percent* of the extra revenue I've brought into the company, personally, through my unique relationships with technology directors, teachers, and superintendents. So it's not even that big of an ask."

His jaw hits his desk. Matt is trembling. "Allie, one-fifty is more than I make. And...if that's true, how am I going to hit our goal! The stockholders are going to be pissed."

"Yes, they will. By the way, how many deals have you brought in for the company?"

He stammers. "Uh, that's not what I do. I'm in an admin role."

Just then, Jocko's deep voice reverberates at the door. "I'm not interrupting anything, am I?"

"Oh, boy," Matt says. And even though he's much older than Jocko is, it's evident who is intimidated by whom the way Matt's body languages shrinks down.

"Matty boy," Jocko says as he strolls in wearing a suit, and it's all I can do not to crack up.

"She tell you the raise request?"

"She did, and frankly, it's a little ridiculous what you both are doing right now. It's very unbecoming."

Jocko sits next to me, a devilish grin on his face.

"Matty, I've been here for almost ten years. I know talent when I see it. Since our CEO will no longer meet with me — he says I'm dead to him since I'm leaving — you tell him this." Jocko leans in and whispers in Matt's ear.

"When you get A-talent, you better pay and not skimp next time."

His hand grazes my knee, and a shot of warmth rolls through my body.

Matt notices, what a pig.

"Also," Jocko adds. "I know about the bonus structure. No one knows more about this company than me. You've basically been stealing from Allie. And that's fucked up. I wonder how a guy like you sleeps at night."

He gives me the nod. My heart hammers hard. I've struggled with whether or not to go through with saying what I'm about to say, but Jocko assures me this is a clear-cut instance where I've been getting royally screwed over.

"Fuck you, Matt," I say. "I wouldn't stay here for a million dollars."

"Neither would I," Jocko says. "And we'll be starting our own company. A competitor. Just so you know."

"You can't do that," Matt protests. "You signed away your contacts, plus a non-compete disclosure. You can't talk to them. It's a serious breach of contract. We'll sue the shit out of you both."

"For a year, my man, only for a year," Jocko says.

"Excuse me?" Matt answers.

"We can't talk to customers for one year. And then we can."

Matt is silent, because Jocko is right.

"Hey, Allie, how long did we decide to travel around the world for?"

"One year," I grin, and the expression on Matt's face is priceless.

~

Despite our run-in with Matt today, Jocko and I do like a lot of things about working for our company, not least of which is the amazing people we get to work with who are changing the lives of young people by their amazing work with technology in schools.

So later that day, Jocko and I sit in a conference room on a call with our favorite client of all time, Lisa. She's the IT director for a small school in Ohio, and was one of the very first clients Jocko and I worked with together.

Jocko gets up to grab the door when someone knocks. It's Rhonda.

"What are you guys doing? Aren't you heading down to Mason's Bar?" she asks. "I mean, it's your *own* going away party. Figures you workaholics would even miss your own party."

"We're wrapping up with our last client and we'll be down in ten," Jocko says.

"Maybe even five," I add. "Just about done."

"I'm going to miss you two! See you in a little. Drinks on the team budget!" Rhonda smiles, and goes to close the door, but I hear her mutter something under her breath before it's completely shut. "*Always knew those two had the hots for each other.*"

"Sorry about that interruption, Lisa," I say, taking our phone off mute. "We're back."

"So she always knew you two had the hots for each other?" Lisa says. "Who was that talking in the background?"

Jocko purses his lips. "Lisa wasn't on mute. She heard everything."

I look down, and it seems I'd just pressed the *volume* button and not the *mute* button.

"Whoops. My bad," I say.

"Oh, come on! I'm your best friend client anyway. I better meet up with you all on this trip of yours. Remember, Lancaster, Ohio, is always open for your trip whenever you want to come by."

Jocko belly laughs. "Lisa, if we're ever close to Lancaster, we'll let you know. Absolutely."

He creeps his body closer to mine as I lean forward into the phone on the table, standing up.

His tall, broad frame looks extra sexy today in a grey, three-piece suit he wore as a celebration of the last day of work.

Me? I wore my second favorite blue pencil skirt.

It's a little worn and faded, but it's the one I wore to my interview here, and the first thing Jocko ever saw me in.

I also did not wear panties today. Hair up in a bun. All per Jay's request.

Yeah...he makes me a little naughty. Well, more than a little.

Lisa sighs. "So my new account rep is Josh Maloney? Well, he better not be a bunch of baloney."

We both crack up. Lisa's got this corny sense of humor that we've both come to know and love.

"He's pretty good," Jocko says. "I mean, not as good as Allie and I. Obviously."

His hand runs up my thigh, causing goosebumps to roll across my skin.

"Lisa, it's been a great pleasure getting to know you these last three years," Jocko says. "We have your cell. And your Facebook. We'll talk soon."

"Bye!" I echo. "Love you!"

"Aww. Love you guys, too."

Jocko pushes his finger into the red button to hang up

the phone. His other hand is running up my inner thigh. Heat pools between my legs.

"What are you doing?" I mutter breathlessly, as I turn my head around. My ass presses into his suit pants.

"Oh, Allie," he growls into my ear. "You should know what I'm up to by now."

"But we can't do this here," I protest. "It's not even that late. What if someone finds us?"

I've been worked up all day with Jocko mulling around here in that suit of his. I figured he told me not to wear panties because he wanted to rip my skirt off the moment we got home. But still, something about *really* doing it here gives me pause.

He chuckles as his finger finds my already-soaked clit.

"What are they gonna do? Fire us?"

My skin tingles, my heart races and pleasure pulses through me.

"Fine," I moan. "Make it quick."

"Fat chance of that." He kisses my neck. "I've been dreaming about fucking you in this office for three years. I think I'll take my time."

The sound of his zipper coming undone ripples pleasure through me.

His eyes hood over, and I lean in so he can feel my breath. "No panties," he says as he touches me, sounding surprised.

I laugh. "You told me not to."

"I know," he growls. "Can we just pretend this is your first day, you're the young, naïve intern, and I'm the experienced sales guy who can't keep his hands off you?"

"That *is* a very hot scenario. But how about we just pretend we're coworkers who have been in love for longer than they care to admit...and are fucking each other's brains out on their last day at the company?"

"I can get on board with that." He smirks. "What if H.R. walks in here, though?"

I laugh. "Really? Still worried about them?"

"Nahhh," he growls, and spins my body around so my hands are on the wall. "Just playing. Fuck H.R."

"No," I giggle, hopping on the desk and spreading my legs. "Fuck me."

"You really are my naughty girl, Allie," he says as his hand creeps down the inside of my thigh. "And I love you for it. And everything else."

"Wait," I mewl as our clothes come down around our ankles. "Did you really just say that?"

"I wanted to wait. But you're right. Three years we've been brewing. I'm done holding back."

"You were...holding back this past week?"

"A little."

"So what's it feel like when you're not holding back?"

"It feels...like this."

A loud moan escapes me when he enters me, plunging into my warm center.

"Oh, Jay," I mutter. "God, you're hard."

"God, you're wet."

"Yes, Jay. For you."

I'm so hot and worked up, I come in record time as I clench around him. With every thrust of his warm flesh inside me, another wave of pleasure rolls through me, and I feel him twitch and moan as he unleashes inside me. Deep, feral moans of pleasure escape him and turn me on even more.

And the surrealness that I felt coming back from

Cancún has converted into something wonderful: the fact that those five days will go on for much, much longer.

This is real.

This is the furthest thing from fake.

Being with Jocko is the realest I've ever felt with a man.

And I know it's going to last a long time.

EPILOGUE - JOCKO

F*our Months Later*

BOLIVIA, South Africa, India.

Iceland, Australia, and New Zealand, Scotland.

We hit all of our dream travel spots. In some, we go all out and stay in luxury hotels with five-star views.

In others, we're weary travelers dependent on the hospitality of the people around us.

Like the time our bus broke down in a small town in Bolivia and the locals put us up for the night. They refused any money, and it was still our favorite part about the trip.

Needless to say, we've had some adventures.

After Allie and I have backpacked around all summer, and as August ebbs into September, we land in Scotland, which she's been talking about nonstop.

For a week, we visit seaports in Aberdeen, find the house

where Allie's grandmother was born in the north of Scotland, and we may have caught a glimpse of the Loch Ness monster.

It's still undetermined.

Tonight we head out in downtown Glasgow to a pub called *Nancy Whiskey*. The last wisps of summer are in the air, and a band is playing some tunes on the patio. We're at the bar finishing our fish and chips.

"Personally, I think the people who put the Loch Ness monster there are the same ones who created those pyramids in Mexico *and* Egypt," I say.

She throws her head back in laughter. "Maybe it's the fact that this is my second ale of the night, but you know what, Jay? I think you may be onto something there."

I grin broadly, finish my food and push it toward the bartender. "I think you're onto something by seamlessly inserting 'ale' into a sentence."

She runs her hand over my shoulder and down my forearm. "Maybe we should change our technology company idea into a brewery?"

I smirk. One of the fun games we've been playing on this trip is to decide what would be our best life once we get back to Michigan.

If we even end up back there. I sold my shares of EdTechX when we left, and since I started when the company was in its early phase, I made even more than I thought I would, into the eight figures.

Funny enough, as soon as Allie and I left, the company's stock took a substantial hit. Could be coincidence, or it could be that we were actually propping up that much of the EdTechX's clientele. I suppose we'll never know.

When Rhonda informed us that Matt got fired for

underperforming, we had to laugh. That's what happens when you undervalue your best personnel.

Anyway, life is amazing and we've got eight more months to decide what we'll be doing with the rest of our lives.

Yes, at least eight. We've decided to wait until winter is over before we go back to Detroit and gather our things from the storage unit. Can you blame us?

Allie smiles nonchalantly, watching the band and sipping her ale. After all the crazy adventures we've had together, this is one of my favorite things to do with her. Sit, eat, listen to music...and this, of course.

Catching her off guard, I brush her cheek with the back of my knuckle and guide her lips to mine for a kiss. She lets out the tiniest of moans, and my dick does the tiniest of twitches in response. I'll never be able to get enough of this girl.

"Well, hello there, good sir." She bites her lower lip. I used to be the guy who hated couples who did this, but you know what? Fuck it. Not like we know anyone here. We kiss again, and I slide my hand down her bare shoulder — she's got a sleeveless dress on — to her hand and run it over her ring.

I love feeling her in any way, and since I proposed at the beginning of this week when we arrived in Scotland, I can't get enough of feeling the ring on her finger to remind me that she's mine, *for real* this time.

When we snapped a few selfies of her with the ring and sent them to my mom, she littered my messages with happy emojis like only mom's can. Then she wrote a heartfelt message. 'I'm truly happy for you, Jocko. This isn't a prank, right?'

We chuckled, called her and reassured her that this was very much for real this time. I think she could sense a change in me, and how my love for Allie has grown during these past few months. I suppose it was a fast engagement considering we've only been romantically involved since the spring. But the reality is we've been sowing the seed of a friendship that's been alive and thriving for more than three years.

When Allie and I pry our lips apart, I notice a few of the guys checking us out. Whatever. *Fuck 'em.*

Plus, our love signs tell us we were lovers in a past life. Maybe that's why it feels so natural with her.

I love Allie and I'm going to show it.

"Be right back, I'm going to hit the water closet, as they say here."

In the bathroom, I'm washing my hands when I overhear a couple of guys talking next to me. American accents, unlike most of the people here.

"You notice the girl in the red dress?" one in a hat says.

"Shit, yeah, I did. She's hot as hell. You think he's sleeping with her? You think I have a shot if I ask to buy her a drink?" says the other.

I clear my throat and wink. "Not a chance," I say, and then wink at them.

"Why do you say that?" says the one in the hat.

"Because she's with me," I say, evenly. Not angrily. But yeah, a little territorially.

"Wow," the other one says. "Nicely done."

I'm about to leave when the other runs close to me and asks me a question, startling me.

"Hey, man, how'd you get a girl like her? She's beautiful. How'd you get her to sleep with you?"

I squint. "How did I get her to sleep with me? She's my fiancée."

"Ahhh," says the guy in the hat. "You played the long game."

I slap him on the back nice and firmly. "With some girls, son, the long game is the only game."

He looks at me wide-eyed, like I've just imparted some dramatic lesson on him. I shrug and head back out to the bar.

The band is done playing, and Allie's got her hand on her neck as someone chats her up. I recognize him as the lead singer from the band who just finished playing.

A feeling like jealousy flairs inside me. She doesn't see me yet, and I pause to watch.

Not because I don't want to interrupt them, but because something dawns on me which I need to process.

I used to *be* those guys.

The ones in the bathroom.

The guy hitting on the girl at the bar.

Shit, never the first, never the last was my *motto* for a good long while.

Allie nods awkwardly at whatever the man next to her is saying, clearly signaling disinterest.

I smile. There was no secret thing I said to her, no magic pickup line or something like these guys are looking for.

It was just years of love, pure love. It started in the form of friendly love and now, well, it's ravenous, romantic love.

Looking back now, all those years of being single seem like purgatory. Because this, what Allie and I have now, is the real thing.

A hot feeling wracks through my chest. I feel as high as if I were on drugs. Walking toward the man, who keeps hitting on Allie, I tap him on the shoulder.

"Excuse me," I say. "This seat's taken."

"Uh, oh, sorry, man! I didn't mean anything," he says, backtracking quickly.

I chuckle because I didn't mean to insinuate we would have a problem here. But the guy still seems scared.

After he walks off, clearly sweating bullets, I kiss Allie and ask her, "Am I that scary?"

"You forget how intimidating you are sometimes. And, well, that guy was a total wuss. I'm surprised he didn't notice this."

She holds her ring up to the light. "Were you worried he was going to move in on your territory?" she jokes.

I squeeze her thigh. "Not for a second."

"Good." She sighs. "It's just been so weird to see you turn from 'Jocko who hits on everyone at office parties' into 'Jocko who is a little territorial about his fiancée'."

"You seem worried."

"Sometimes I wonder what I've gotten myself into, falling for the guy who had a poster of Frank Sinatra with the words *Bachelor 4 Lyfe* written on it."

I let out a gravelly chuckle. "Do you know why Frank became a bachelor, though?"

"Wasn't he always one?"

I shake my head. "Nope. He fell hard for a woman named Ava Gardner. They were incredibly in love for a time. But then she left him, and it broke his heart. He was never the same again."

"I had no idea. Makes Frank into much more of a softy."

"Yes it does."

"Well...I've got an idea," she says. "Let's make a deal. I won't break your heart. And you don't break mine."

"I've got no plans to break yours."

"Why?"

"Because I love you, Allie."

"I love you, too."

I lean in and give her another kiss on the lips, sealing our little deal.

"Wow. We're really good at that," she comments.

"With the kisses? Well, we already had a practice run."

She smiles wryly, takes a sip of her ale and orders another. "By the way, are you ready for the next phase?"

I wrinkle my forehead in confusion. "Which phase would that be?"

Nibbling at my ear, she whispers, "How about France, next week?"

"Sounds good. Oh, and one more thing, Allie."

"What?"

"I love you."

"You said that already," she rolls her eyes, laughing.

"I know. I just wanted to emphasize it again." I squeeze her thigh and lean toward her so my lips brush her ear. She thinks I'm joking around, so I add, "I'm saying it again because I really love you, Allie. More than you'll ever know."

She sniffles and wipes away a tear, then looks at me, glossy eyed.

"I think I have some idea. Because I really love you too, Jocko."

THE END

YOUR NEXT STEAMY READ:

CAN an NFL superstar fall for the girl next door?

Find out in this #1 Sports Romance!
Read ***The Substitute*** FREE in Kindle Unlimited!

Click here to read THE SUBSTITUTE

Available in Kindle Unlimited, and also in Audio form with Sebastian York and CJ Bloom!

SPECIAL PREVIEW OF THE SUBSTITUTE - CHAPTER 1

Maddy

I THOUGHT I was seeing a mirage.

I rubbed my eyes as I pulled the car onto the driveway pavement, my head drawn toward him like it was on a swivel that hot summer evening.

My neighbor, Peyton O'Rourke, was mowing the lawn shirtless in front of his house.

It was his Grandmother's house to be exact. Peyton left my town on the lake after high school, and hadn't been back since.

Idling in the driveway, I watched him from behind as he walked away from me, wearing only athletic shorts and sneakers.

When he turned the mower around and came toward me again, I felt my stomach twist and churn, my pulse racing as he locked his eyes on me. From a distance, his irises looked almost black, though I'd seen their true grey color up close.

I squinted in disbelief, wondering what on earth he was doing back in Pentwater in August.

He played professional football. Well, 'played' was an understatement.

Last year he was the league's MVP and Super Bowl champion.

I wasn't a big-time fan, but I knew by now he should be deep into the exhibition season. I'd seen him playing on TV just last Sunday night.

The cranking of the mower became louder as he walked toward me, a slight smirk on his face as he looked in my direction. I couldn't keep my gaze off him, in spite of the fact that he clearly saw me staring at him. His sweat-glazed torso was perfect, with shredded abs women everywhere dreamed about licking. His shoulders were broad and muscular. Yet he still retained this salt-of-the-earth grittiness about him, like he'd just woken up.

I swallowed hard as he came closer to me, feeling my adrenaline rush like crazy.

An object sparkled off one of his fingers, and almost blinded me.

Was that . . . a wedding ring?

Was Peyton O'Rourke—who barely kept girls around long enough to learn their last names—actually wifed up?

Or 'husbanded' up, to be exact. Isn't that what they'd call it?

Shoot. 'Husbanded' wasn't a word. I was getting riled up in my elated state.

My heart pounded. Wouldn't I have seen this on *Entertainment Weekly*, if it had happened?

Not that I still followed him on Instagram or anything.

Okay, I did follow him. And he hadn't posted anything about a marriage.

I felt frozen, trying to make out the giant ring on his finger, and I realized the lawn mower had shut off.

Peyton was saying something to me that I couldn't quite make out from inside my car.

I flinched and cleared my throat, turning off the car and pulling the keys out of the ignition like I hadn't just been caught staring at him for almost a full minute.

When I turned to grab my bag from the passenger's seat, I jumped so high my head almost hit the ceiling when I heard the *rap rap rap* of his ring on the glass.

Without looking him in the eye, I opened the door.

Peyton smiled. "Just so you know, the windows of your Honda Civic aren't tinted or anything. I can see you staring at me."

I blushed. As I stepped out of the car, I cast my gaze downward.

"Not sure what you mean," I said, clearing my throat. "Also, hello. It's been a while."

Mustering my nerve, I brought my face up to look him in the eye. Their deep grey color sent a chill reverberating through me in spite of the hot day.

"Aw. It's alright, Magpie," he continued. His voice sounded rough and grizzly and with the very slightest hint of a country twang. "Looks are free. It only costs if you want to touch," he winked, apparently picking up right where he left off—which was poking fun at me throughout our teenage years.

"Glad to see you've matured so much since high school," I gritted out. "At least you got married though," I said, my eyes flitting to his left hand. Up close, I noticed it seemed a lot bigger than a wedding ring.

"Married?"

"Your ring." I pointed.

He looked me in the eye for a few moments before he busted out in laughter.

"Oh Magpie, you kill me. Goddamn my sides are gonna split. Allow me to explain my thoughts on marriage." He brought his eyes back to my face after he'd given my body an up-and-down. "It's only for guys who can't get laid without commitment."

I felt my heart squeeze every time his lips said the nickname only he called me.

"Oh," I said. "That's not a wedding ring. From far away it looked like one."

He lifted his giant left hand to my eye level so I could see.

"This is my Super Bowl ring from last year. Although, you're right, in a way. I *am* married to the game."

"Right," I said, feeling like I asked a stupid question. He kept the huge golden thing on his left ring finger though, and from a distance it gleamed like a wedding ring. "What are you doing back here, anyway? Isn't this football season?"

He shrugged. "You don't watch Sportscenter, do you?"

"No."

"Well, there was a strike this week. Big labor dispute. First one since the eighties. The players union decided on a walkout until we get better contracts and insurance for players whose careers are destroyed by injuries and concussions."

"I see," I said. I'd been deep into planning for the new school year this week, and football gossip wasn't exactly something to which I paid attention. I wanted to steer the conversation over the one thing I couldn't quite figure out.

"So you came back to Pentwater? Why didn't you stay in Dallas?"

"How'd you know I was playing for Dallas?" he asked, and it seemed like a silly question to me.

"Uh, because I watched the Super Bowl last year and I don't live under a rock."

He nodded with a smirk, and ran a hand through his hair. "Good to know you're keeping tabs on me."

There it was. He wanted me to acknowledge I was keeping track of him just so he could emphasize that fact once I admitted it. "I'm not 'keeping tabs' on you, but it's impossible not to know what you're up to when you're all over the internet."

"It's okay. I won't make you admit you're stalking me," he said with a smirk, and as I rolled my eyes I pushed out my hand instinctively toward him, meaning to push him away. Instead, I just let it linger on his upper abs for a moment, not really realizing what I was doing.

His gaze followed my hand, and I tried not to react to the fact that I accidentally copped a feel.

"Hands off the merchandise," he said in a low voice, and truthfully I couldn't even tell if he was joking like we used to in the old days, or if this was some new man in front of me.

"Uh," I stammered. "My bad. I just wasn't expecting to see you again, here."

The corners of his lips quirked up in a smirk that sent shivers to my core.

"I mean, I *get* that it's kind of hard not to watch me, though." He took a step closer to me and brushed my hair behind my ear, before he whispered, "If you want to watch me, we can work out a price. How's that sound?"

"Screw you! That's disgusting," I eeked out, though I felt

suddenly like I let him win, since I bit the bait. "I don't want to 'watch' you."

My comeback fell very flat, not fazing him at all. Maybe because we both knew I'd been staring at him from my car just five minutes ago.

Note to self: buy new car with tinted windows.

"So where are you living now? Somewhere around here?" he asked, innocently enough.

I leaned one hip into the side of my car, and I realized he didn't know if I was visiting my parents. I wished the truth weren't the truth, but there was no avoiding it.

"I'm back here living at good old 602 Bass Lake Lane," I admitted.

"Back with your parents? Really."

"Really."

His expression changed gradually from an even look to an evil smirk.

"So. I guess that means our windows get to face each other again, eh?"

"I guess so," I answered.

He clenched his jaw. "By the way, you have something here." He looked down and pointed at the space just below my neck.

"I don't think I have any—" When I looked down, he brought his finger up and tapped me on the nose.

"Boop," he said, biting his lower lip.

I blinked several times, then stared at him disbelieving. "Did you seriously just *boop* me?"

"Yes. You just fell for the oldest trick in the book. Come on, haven't those third graders you teach taught you anything?"

I crossed my arms, swearing I could feel my body

temperature rising. "Glad to see you've matured so much since high school."

He shrugged. "What can I say? I'm young at heart."

As I fantasized about how I could get him back for this, Peyton bit his lip again, and his eyes drifted to something behind me. I turned my head to see him staring at my dad, who was watching us with his arms crossed from my porch.

"Hello Mr. Cooper," Peyton called out, offering a wave.

"Peyton," my dad said in a stern, unfriendly tone, giving a token nod.

"I think your dad wants you to stop talking to me," Peyton said, stating the obvious.

As I turned and headed up the stairs to my porch, I could feel Peyton's stare on me. I hoped my father wouldn't notice how red my cheeks were.

"Hi honey," my dad said, kissing me on the cheek. "How's my teacher of the year?"

"Fine," I said as the screen door slammed shut. "Got my class all set up today. I'm ahead of the game this year."

Just then, something dawned on me.

How did Peyton know I was teaching third grade?

I didn't think he knew I existed, much less cared what I was up to. Yet he dropped it into casual conversation like it was nothing.

After all these years, he could still make my body respond in a way I'd never felt with any man.

I heard the lawn mower start up again in Peyton's yard, and my chest flushed with heat. It was frustrating to know he could turn me on without even touching me.

-

END OF PREVIEW

Keep Reading The Substitute FREE in Kindle Unlimited!

THE SUBSTITUTE

Available in Kindle Unlimited, and on Audio with Sebastian York and CJ Bloom!

ABOUT MICKEY MILLER

Hi. I'm romance author Mickey Miller.

I've written fifteen books, five top 100 Amazon Bestsellers, including my Amazon Top 25 Hit ***The Substitute*** which is now available in audio featuring narrator Sebastian York.

The easiest and best way to stay in touch with me for news and new releases is to sign up for my email list here:

https://mickeymillerauthor.com

You can also find me on Instagram @mickeymillerauthor. Reach out and let me know what you think about my books! I love hearing from readers, so don't be shy!

Lots of Love,

Mickey

OTHER BOOKS BY MICKEY MILLER

Forever You Sports Romance Series

Hatemates | ***Easy Access (coming soon)***

The Brewer Brothers Series

The Lake House* | *The Hold Out* | *Five Day Fiancé

The Love Games Duet

The Lying Game* | *The End Game

The Blackwell After Dark Series

Professor with Benefits | Mechanic with Benefits

Boss with Benefits | Bartender with Benefits

Biker with Benefits

The Ballers Series

Playing Dirty | The Casanova Experience

Dirty Trick

Standalone Sports Romances

The Substitute | Black Ice | One Vegas Night

Windy City Bad Boys

Dirty CEO | Irish Kisses

Other Standalones:

Ten Night Stand |

Big Daddy SEAL

Mickey's Short & Hot Stories

Afternoon Delights | Alphas of Seduction

Thank you for reading!

Made in the USA
Middletown, DE
24 September 2022